pharo and the
clever assassin

pharo and the
clever assassin

Steve Skurka

atmosphere press

Dedicated in memory of my dear father,
Fred Skurka

ז"ל

Introduction

Buffalo, New York, September 1, 1901

The hall to the hospital room of Pharo Simmons contained six numbered suites and after opening the doors to three of them to find beds stripped of sheets and absent any visible sign of being occupied, he entered a room to be greeted by familiar chirpy laughter.

"Oh, do come in Mitchell, grab a chair and make yourself comfortable."

Pharo sat perched upright on her bed with a damp paintbrush. "I'm painting under the most dreadful conditions," she said. "Modigliani didn't have to grope about in a darkened cave." A splinter of light from the window framed the silhouette of Pharo's sallow cheeks. "I just counted six fingers on the left hand. Now who will ever trust me as a painter if I can't count to five?"

"I have to get back to court. Burford asked me to check on you. He's terribly worried. He insisted that I tell you that a letter arrived from your publisher inquiring about your next novel."

"Burford is worried? That must explain why he hasn't bothered to visit his sick wife in two days. How like my husband to relent and send his young associate in his place! I am fond of you, Mitchell. My anger is not directed at you. What heteroclite is Burford defending now?"

"It's the sad case of Woolard Kettle. The poor man's wife was stricken by tuberculosis and she died one month later. Our client was overcome with grief. He couldn't sleep in the bed he had shared with his wife or dine at their kitchen table. One afternoon, he napped on the couch while smoking a cigarette. He awoke to the curtains ablaze and plumes of grey smoke petering into the living room. He sat fixed to his chair as the fire engulfed the house. Woolard ran out at the last possible moment to save himself. Only the paved shell of the floor remained by the time the fire truck arrived."

"Where is the crime?" Pharo asked sharply, like a wasp's stinger aimed at its mark.

"Well, a policeman soon arrived and questioned our client about the fire. He blurted out that he'd deliberately set it."

"Now what possessed this foolhardy fellow to admit to a crime he didn't commit?"

"Because he was vanquished and gave up on life. Burford told the jury in his opening address that our client had a shattered soul and a wounded mind."

"It's comforting to know that my husband isn't representing a spawn of the devil on this round. Good luck with your trial, Mitchell. Please let Mr. Simmons know that the nurses are pleased with my progress. One of them is a brute, I must tell you. She complained that my tattoo is an omen of misfortune. I feign sleeping when I hear her clunky steps outside my door. She's quite an accomplished billiards player and lives rather lavishly."

"How do you know that?" Mitchell asked.

"I've been reading the Sherlock Holmes stories Burford sent me. While my nurse arranged the blanket on my bed this morning, I observed chalk on the tips of her fingers. I concluded that given the time of her play, she has a billiards table in the parlor of her home. Only a serious player would venture a game in the early hours of the day."

Mitchell stared glumly at the floor. "Don't despair," Pharo said. "The physician entrusted with my care is Harvard-trained, enjoys a picnic by the river or a splendid Wagner opera, and is confident that I'll be gone from my dungeon existence in a couple of days."

"The fainting spells have ended?"

"The truth is that I've made such a pest of myself in the hospital that they'll be delighted to be rid of me. My bold strategy is a success."

"That there is fool's talk, Mrs. Simmons." Mitchell paused. "I didn't mean to call you a fool."

"I deserved it, Mitchell." Pharo understood that a young colored man openly deriding her character might lead to dire consequences. And Mitchell's mother Bessie, who worked as the housekeeper at the Simmons home, would certainly scold him.

An orderly knocked and entered carrying a tray of food. "It's lunchtime, Miss Pharo."

The young lawyer rose. "I was just leaving. I'll share the excellent news with your husband as soon as I return to court." Mitchell spoke sincerely and without guile, unflattering qualities for a lawyer, she decided. Burford spoke of the courtroom as an actor's stage and the oratory as a virtuoso performance. He had mastered the skill of crying on cue.

"I do have one more matter to discuss," Pharo said.

"Of course."

"In the story I read last night, Sherlock Holmes lectured a Scotland Yard detective that there is nothing new under the sun and it has been done before. Do you think that's true?" Pharo didn't wait for his answer. "I certainly hope not. I always wonder what grand adventure is peeking around the corner."

Chapter One

"Martin Beliveau to meet the Prime Minister."

Martin was ushered down a winding corridor to the library. Wilfred Laurier sat reclining in his favorite Louis XV chair, a writing pad folded on his lap and a pile of books stacked on a nearby desk.

"Come, pull up a chair and sit down," he urged Martin, pointing to a chair with gilded arms. "I'm translating a Quinn's fashion catalogue into French. I've met my challenge with a London smoke felt Homburg." He moved the writing the pad to the floor. "I imagine that you're curious why I summoned you to my official residence at this late hour."

"I did wonder what pressing matter required the attention of the Minister of Railways, Prime Minister."

"Are you aware of the Pan-American Exposition in Buffalo?"

"The World's Fair with fancy rainbow lights and Jumbo the Elephant. There was a photograph in one of Jocelyn's magazines of the Temple of Music. It resembled a shimmering jewelry box."

"I want you to take a trip to Buffalo with the governor general. You'll be our country's representatives at the Canada Day festivities at the Pan-American Exposition."

Beliveau opened his palms in bafflement. "But why me?" he asked. "I won't be able to disguise my distaste for such a wasteful ceremonial function."

Laurier grinned. "Oh, nonsense, Martin. You can charm a snake to release a hare from the clenches of its teeth. Consider the brief trip an exercise in improving our sunny ways with our American neighbor. We're all citizens of the same century."

"The Exposition is merely an excuse to display American might and innovation. I'll feel like a lonely guest at their grand celebration."

Laurier pulled his lanky legs from the stool and led Martin to an ivory globe of the world mounted on a stand affixed to a great seashell, a parting gift from a Tongan king. Laurier spun it halfway to display the continent of North America. "Look at our country's southern border," he said, pointing. "It kisses the border of the United States. With our vast resources of timber and agriculture, we're perfectly positioned to be America's strongest trading partner. The Grand Trunk Railway may one day extend from the coast of the Atlantic Ocean to the Pacific. I fervently believe that the new century will be Canada's. It serves our nation's interests, Martin, to maintain a strong and emboldened alliance with the American republic. We have the bitter lesson of France's rivalry with its neighbor Germany to draw upon. It's taken the French three decades to recover from that humiliating debacle."

"And you genuinely believe that attending a World's

Fair serves Canada's interests?"

The prime minister nodded. "Without a speck of doubt," he said.

Martin shrugged, resigning himself to his leader's decision. "When do I leave, Prime Minister?"

"You'll take the train to Toronto in the morning. You'll arrive in time for William McKinley's speech at the Pan-American Exposition for President's Day."

"President McKinley will be in Buffalo?"

"Yes, and I expect that you and the governor general will be granted a private audience. Please return to your home and get some rest. And do be careful, Martin. We've all been warned. Anarchist bands may be scouring government targets for violent attacks."

*

Martin Beliveau's one drawback inhibited a flourishing career in federal politics; he was too handsome. A useful feature for artistic endeavors, though. Martin had appeared in his twenties as a clothing model for an Eaton's department store catalogue, in a newspaper ad for a harness shop, and modeled at an artists' colony in northern Quebec. The dilemma confronting Beliveau was that many of his colleagues in Parliament refused to accept him as a serious politician. No-one with a face like his, carved to perfection as if by a sculptor's tool, could possibly have a worthy thought to express. His father suggested growing a scraggly beard. Wilfred Laurier wasn't dissuaded. "I only care about what's inside that box over your neck," he said.

Laurier had been Martin's closest colleague in the Quebec provincial assembly and inspired him to join the plunge into federal politics. After Laurier rose to lead the Liberal party and become Canada's prime minister, he had invited Martin to join his cabinet in government.

His father, Pierre, had preceded him in politics as the leader of the opposition Liberal party at the time of Canada's confederation. Martin recalled being outside his home as a child on a baking hot summer day in 1867 when his father picked him up in a single swoop and hugged him, his cheeks flushed and a sparkling twinkle in his eye, declaring that *notre famille* finally resided in their own country.

*

Martin and the governor general were greeted on the grounds of the Pan-American Exposition by the governor of New York. He invited the Canadian delegation to the United States Government Building where an attendant stood on a ladder moving around model ships from the American fleet on a great map of the world. The governor explained that the fleet included hundreds of battleships, gunboats and submarines and their location in the various seas and oceans was constantly updated.

Martin and Governor General Tupper were directed to the Esplanade bandstand for President McKinley's speech. From his prime seat under a covered partition, Martin looked down on an impressive crowd of tens of thousands of milling fairgoers, bobbing parasols and tanned straw hats under a burst of autumn sunshine. A film crew wove deftly to the front of the bandstand to capture every word of the president's speech.

William McKinley entered with great fanfare and stopped to greet Martin and the governor general. "Please extend my warmest regards to your polite and kind prime minister," he said. "We met at the Washington Conference in 1896. He sent me a gracious congratulatory note on my re-election, comparing it to Abraham Lincoln's political fortunes."

Beliveau knew that Laurier, a keen admirer of the iconic Lincoln, held in common the former president's steadfast principle of good government: no cause, even the most noble, was higher than the survival of the nation.

Martin listened raptly as the president advocated for trains and ships in his speech. He described the world as being smaller than ever, with fast trains making room for trade. Canada's trains were ready for the burgeoning trade, Martin mused, as the speech ended.

As Beliveau and the governor general dismounted the steps of the podium, an earnest-looking young man approached.

"Are you with the president?" he asked Martin. "I saw you speaking with him," Exhibiting a congenial and measured disposition, the man appeared to be in his twenties, tidily dressed and pleasant, his hair neatly parted and clean shaven.

After Martin replied that he was the railways minister from Canada, the man surveyed him up and down, like a tailor fitting him for an English tweed. The startling inquiry that followed rankled Martin. "Did you see all those people bowing to the great ruler?"

Martin paused, to be certain that he'd heard the question correctly. "From my vantage point on the stage, I can assure you that I saw no-one bow. I thought that it was a splendid speech. Inspiring words from your president."

"He isn't my president."

"I'm sorry," Martin said. "I didn't intend to insult your national background. Where are you from?" He evoked no response, only a sullen glare.

"I'm from nowhere," the man finally said.

Martin detected a glint of a smirk, then turned his back in a defiant gesture, locked arms with the governor general and parted his way through the dispersing crowd at the Esplanade.

"Where did that fellow say he's from – Norway?" And what did he say about the president?" Borden Tupper asked. The governor general had a severe hearing problem and Martin shouted his answer.

"He asked if we noticed the people in the crowd cheering the president."

Martin Beliveau digested the pluses and minuses of the troubling encounter. The young man didn't resemble the profile of a wild-eyed anarchist and he hadn't reacted belligerently or with a violent gesture when the minister ignored him. The president's speech passed without the threat of harm. Yet, comparing the bountiful applause after President McKinley's neutral speech to diffidently bowing to an emperor, did raise a disturbing red flag. Martin reproached himself for not pursuing the unconventional conversation with the young man.

Chapter Two

The august committee of judges in charge of vetting the application of Solomon Knox as a judge had failed miserably at its task. Judge Knox suffered from the malady of chronic indecision, a trait ill-suited for an arbiter of liberty. Each day, the judge sat perched on his elevated bench, his hand wrapped around the creases of his forehead, mulling the decision he was required to make. He'd make copious notes of the lawyers' arguments with his quilled fountain pen, intermittently gazing at the arched ceiling, as if seeking divine intervention, and then conclude by postponing his ruling to a later date.

"I'm going to permit Mr. Simmons to ask the question of the police officer," Judge Knox pronounced. He'd adjourned the jury trial for a recess to consider the prosecutor's objection.

"Here is the question once again, Officer Pernell --- did you believe that the fire in my client's home was deliberately set by him before you started his interview?"

"I had my suspicions."

"And your suspicions were aroused because Mr. Kettle was calm and composed, not the typical reaction of a man whose entire house has just been consumed by a spreading fire."

"That's correct."

"You'd expect a victim of a fire to be roused and frantic."

"Yes."

"Do you have a university degree in the study of psychology?"

"No, I don't."

"Let me ask you this, Officer. Would you expect the winner of the Irish Sweepstakes to be jumping up and down with glee?"

"Sure, I wish I'd win it someday." The jury chortled with laughter.

"If you won the prize, you'd certainly be excited?"

"Yes."

"But what if you came home with the winning ticket and found that your Auntie May choked on her meal of sausage and beans and had to be rushed to the hospital. Do you think you'd still be joyful about having the winning Sweepstakes ticket?"

The officer's face turned somber. "No sir, I don't think I would."

"Mr. Kettle told you that he'd burned down his house. Did he ever give you a reason why?"

"I asked him in my interview at the police station, but he didn't have one."

"But it's not like he kept secrets from you. According to you he'd admitted to setting the fire."

"Yes."

Burford gazed at the jury with a puzzled expression. "And as you stand in this courtroom today, you never received a reason from Woolard Kettle for starting the fire, did you?"

"No sir, I didn't."

"Just the words of a man whose wife died from tuberculosis a few weeks earlier."

Chapter Three

"Be alert for the clever assassin."

The detective tucked his crumpled reminder, composed with the benefit of a thorough study of the bomb attack on the Russian Tsar and the gunning down of the King of Italy by an American anarchist, back into his jacket pocket.

In both those incidents, after ruthless planning the target was murdered. The detective believed those outcomes were preventable. He re-read the caution in that note at various times during the day: at bedtime; after the president invited him to meet in his private railway car; with his morning omelet; and immediately before any presidential reception with the public.

Detective John Garcy leaned against a towering clay sculpture next to a revolving globe with lettering carved into a wood base that read: A CENTURY OF PEACE AND PROSPERITY AHEAD. He ran through a mental checklist of every security precaution in place to protect President McKinley. It was his watch and his grave responsibility, as the president's worried personal secretary constantly reminded him.

George Cortelyou, a former teacher and stenographer and now the president's omnipresent and devoted guardian against the peril of anarchists, vainly attempted to be within a shadow's distance of McKinley at all times. He had attempted to limit the president's greeting reception to ten minutes. McKinley dismissed that suggestion, declaring that mingling with the public showed strength.

The reception hall had been scanned for explosives: a carriage bomb had killed the tsar. An abandoned attic, discovered in the hall, was filled in with sand on Detective Garcy's order. The hall was locked and guarded by mounted soldiers. The poison-taster (there was no less insidious description of the task) for the president's lunch would arrive promptly at noon.

The detective nibbled on a couple of roasted chestnuts and watched the strip of yellow glow from the sunrise bouncing off the globe. A couple of stray dogs tugged at his pants beckoning him to drop a few crumbs their way, and a swift kick to their hides followed. A braided golden rope blocked the entrance to the reception hall outside of the Temple of Music. It remained in place for a couple of hours. A plush red-carpet led to the rotunda where the American president would be seated beside Detective Garcy in front of the mayor of Buffalo, ambassadors, senators and the governor. A couple of seats were reserved in the corner of the second row for the Canadian delegation.

Only two months earlier, Garcy had been a hustling street detective in New York, investigating gang wars and chasing purse-snatchers down the alleys of the borough of Brooklyn. Always the first detective to arrive at the station in Greenpoint, he'd seen the sign-up sheet for volunteers to act as security for the president on a cross-country train tour set to embark the following week. Garcy printed his name and badge number, ripped the paper from the bulletin board and dropped it in the staff sergeant's mail slot. A message arrived the following day with instructions to appear at Union Station in Washington on July 20 at 7 a.m., with toiletries, clothing for a six-week journey, and his gun.

Detective Garcy moved through the square at a measured pace, watching as it filled with guests. He'd left his coat in the train car and shivered as he encountered a gust of wind, but the daily weather report called for mild temperatures and patches of brilliant blue skies. A separate line with chairs was set up for guests with invitations to the reception. The detective scoured the square for anything arousing suspicion, but it was like looking for a sullied blade in a farmer's field. He knew that anarchists didn't wear identifying badges on their sleeves.

Pushing forward to the center of the square, Garcy began the roll call of the Exposition police, detectives and Secret Service agents assigned to the president's security detail at the World's Fair: McDowell, Falowich, Veel, Wilburn, Zealander, Putter. He recited the names with authority, a performance designed to project a strong police presence. A six-member security detail under his command, standing upright, snapping to attention, like good foot soldiers. Garcy reminded them that they had been carefully chosen for their task, "the pick of the litter." A responding scowl earned one of the older detectives a harsh reprimand from Garcy.

A deep, cone-shaped umbrella in front of the chestnut

stand where they gathered, offered Garcy a shaded view of the long rows of people gathered outside the Exhibition Hall. The buzz of anticipation was discernable, but far less than he'd witnessed at the boisterous lineup at the soup kitchen by the pier on his morning walk from the train. A couple of older teenage boys with patched sweaters in gaudy patterns, likely knitted by an overzealous aunt, were complaining about the waiting time to meet President McKinley. Garcy ignored them. The noisy ones rarely portended danger.

To his men he said, "You must assume that every guest attending this reception is a danger to the president – never let your guard down for a second. The terrorist, the alien, the assassin will be analyzing our every move and will be waiting for the weakest and most vulnerable moment to strike. *Be alert for the clever assassin.*"

Garcy had delivered the same speech – word for word – at the twelve ports of call across the United States. His enthusiasm hadn't lessened by its repetition. He carried an apple, a pistol and a badge threaded on a string: the apple, his lunch, was dropped into his suit pocket, the pistol tucked into a hidden shoulder holster and the detective's identification tag hung prominently around his neck.

Garcy watched every step of the president intently as he was escorted to the covered rotunda decorated with waving flags and red, white and blue bunting set up outside the hall. The admirable McKinley worked too hard, he believed, and his health surely suffered for it. As the president passed the juice stand, he paused, nodded at Garcy and tipped his top hat at him, a sign of gratitude from McKinley for Garcy having promised to spend the next morning with his wife, Ida, in the train's parlor, so the president could snatch a couple extra hours of sleep. During their train stop in Detroit, Garcy had played several losing hands of gin rummy with the president's wife, and had enjoyed her account of the president's recent trip to Egypt. The story of President McKinley's repeated failed efforts to mount a camel near the Pyramids was especially rousing.

As the president passed on, a severe-looking woman in a shiny, green ostrich coat remarked loudly to a companion: "He's a short, stout, simple-looking man, really – you wouldn't know how ghastly he is from his photographs."

McKinley brushed the snide comment aside like fragments of dust on his white vest and kept pace with his escort.

Garcy's first thought was to rebuke the sour offender with a reminder that one of the president's critics once called him the professional beauty of his party, or to indulge in a sarcastic snipe – 'it was the reflection from your coat that you're seeing' – but he refrained, knowing that a confrontation would anger the president.

"People rush to celebrities like a moth to the light," McKinley had once told him. "But they equally delight in exposing every imagined frailty and blemish when they get a close-up. You force yourself to act presidential and rise above it." In the six weeks of Garcy's employment guarding the president, the decorous lesson had never been breached.

A young woman approached the detective with purposeful strides. He noticed her incongruous grin and engaging smile, as if she greeted a longstanding friend. Her pigtails bounded against the sides of her freckled face. She appeared to be fifteen or sixteen.

His eyes dropped to her press badge.

"The president's assistant has a press briefing scheduled for mid-afternoon."

"I have no interest in the president's business," she replied. "You're the subject of my piece for the newspaper, Detective."

The answer startled him. "Me?" Garcy checked the tag for her newspaper: *'Brooklyn Daily Eagle'*. "How old are you?" he asked warily.

"Twenty-two. I've been a reporter for three years. Journalism school, cub reporter, feature writer for the *Daily Eagle*. I support myself in a rented apartment in Flatbush. Is there anything else you need to know about my credentials?"

Garcy warmed to his Brooklyn neighbor's plucky spirit. "I can spare a few minutes after the public reception with President McKinley."

"Perfect. My name is Willow Hooper." She grabbed his hand. "I'll have a photographer with me to take a shot of you accompanying the president. We'll set up on the steps of the Temple of Music."

Garcy nodded and returned to face the president's security team.

"All right," he said with authority, "everyone knows the drill."

An elaborate training exercise accompanied by maps and floor plans had been taken at the downtown police precinct a couple of nights earlier.

"Take your positions, gentlemen." As the men scurried to their marks, Garcy called over a sleek, smartly dressed officer, a photo album tucked under her arm.

"Any problems, Picard?" he asked her.

"No match," she replied, precisely the answer that Garcy hoped for.

Officer Picard was an identification officer with the Lexington Police Force, assigned to assist Garcy on the presidential tour. It was Picard who had discovered the attic after observing that the hall roof was elevated above the ceiling. The detective relied on her photographic memory. The album she held contained pictures of the usual suspects and criminal types who might be expected to show up to brew trouble at a presidential reception. Picard had committed the catalogue of faces to memory. Her confirmation of no matching face in the crowd brought a measure of comfort to Garcy, one fraction of the security issues for the day solved.

"Let me know the count," he instructed her.

The detective then moved to the row of chairs where the president sat. A marine guarding the president saluted before allowing Garcy to replace him.

A member of the Secret Service nodded in approval at Garcy.

"Good morning, Detective. A brisk day today, even with the sunshine. I'll be glad to be indoors soon."

The president was dressed in his customary black frock coat, with a crisp white shirt and standing collar peeking through. The nickel-sized grey badge of the Loyal Legion appeared on the left lapel of the president's coat.

"Good morning, Mister President. A good day to you, sir. We'll be entering the hall in a couple of minutes. Can I fetch you a glass of water?" he asked.

"My throat is parched, but I'll have to decline your offer."

"I don't understand."

"All these people in line waiting to greet me, have been waiting for some time without food or water. I don't want to foster any resentment that their president is getting preferred treatment."

The weaving line to greet President William McKinley had started forming at six o'clock that morning and now extended to the Esplanade Fountain. Garcy nodded. "A glass of water will be ready if you need it, sir. I'll get a chair set inside the Exhibition Hall. You could be standing for more than an hour with the line as long as it is."

"I'll feel like Santa Claus offering Christmas good wishes if I'm seated."

Both men laughed. A bell rang inside the hall and the doors to the hall opened.

The detective checked the positions of the security detail spread around the crowd of people, making eye contact with each officer and agent. In turn, each waved in recognition before progressing to the hall. A tap on the forehead had been devised as the signal to be alert for trouble and to be prepared to instantly draw their pistols.

*

The detective stood a couple of feet behind President McKinley during the reception.

"How's your wife feeling today?" McKinley asked.

"She's doing much better, sir. I spoke to her on the telephone. The doctor thinks it's just a nasty bout of the flu. She's resting, on a strict diet of chicken broth and liquids."

"The miracle cure. My Ida swears by chicken soup too.

She forced me to ask Rabbi Adler at his synagogue in Georgetown what the secret ingredient is."

"Did he share the secret with you?"

"He told me to add a dose of prayer with a teaspoon of salt."

"You must be weary of all of this pomp and ceremony, Mr. President."

"These are challenging days, it's true. But overall, I find these receptions exhilarating. It's a rare opportunity for me to connect with Americans of every walk of life. Just the other day, I met a woman whose mother and sister had died of cancer. She was just diagnosed with breast cancer herself."

"I know sir, I was there with you in Cleveland."

The president had halted the line to devote five minutes chatting with the emotionally fragile woman, instilling her with hope. As a witness to the president's kindness, Garcy marked McKinley as an inherently good and decent man.

*

George Cortelyou climbed the steps to greet the governor general and Martin Beliveau in their seats on the rotunda. "Gentlemen, the president has requested that you meet him at the Temple of Music in one hour. He'll be honored to accompany you on the walk across the Esplanade and the Mall for his visit to the Canada Building."

Martin's mild reaction belied his excitement at this news. An escorted walk presented an ideal setting for a tête-a-tête with the American president about Canada's hefty investment in the march of progress. The Canadian

Commissioner had arranged for the Canada Day ceremony to be held on the expansive second-floor balcony of the Canada Building, with a freshly stained bronze dark green shingled roof and Union Jack and American flags draped prominently overhead. The decals over the entrance depicting Canada's national emblems, the beaver, and the maple leaf, were polished. A two-colored sealskin cover encased the piano. Martin beamed as he contemplated showing McKinley the display for The Canada Atlantic Railway. "We do have our own fast trains," he rehearsed boasting to the president. Martin checked for his lucky Confederation coin in his pants pocket.

Chapter Four

The conductor of the marching band held his baton firmly in the air, the cue for President McKinley's entourage to proceed to the Temple of Music. A regiment of the 48th Highlanders from Canada accompanied the band. Martin watched as the marching band began to weave through the Esplanade with the bouncing echo of a drum, two horns and a tuba clearing a breezy musical path for the president to the reception line.

Inside the hall, Picard handed Detective Garcy a scrap of paper containing the count: 567. Five hundred and sixty-seven potential suspects without a single check by the police or Secret Service. If the security check had been assigned to Garcy, there wouldn't be a line of strangers to greet President McKinley without a firm pat-down to check for weapons and a careful check of purses and bags. The ensconced system of lax monitoring seemed feckless and dangerous to Garcy. George Cortelyou shared the detective's fearful concern for McKinley's welfare.

President McKinley waved his outstretched hand to

greet the tide of people passing. Out in, out in, out in, his hand rotating steadily like a roasting pig revolving on a skewer. He reserved a firm handshake for the strong; a gentle pat on the wrist for the elderly and infirm; and a feathery stroke of the cheek or arm for the children. Standing beyond the perimeter of the reception, it appeared a vapid exercise, but William McKinley, the consummate politician, knew better. A fleeting brush with the American president would convert to a treasured memory and create political capital: a future voter for the Republican party.

A mother approached President McKinley carrying her infant, sucking its thumb, indifferent. She began to cry when the president patted the child's wrist.

"It's a good thing that she was too young to vote for my opponent," he commented, with a wink to the blushing mother.

Next, a Princeton University student wearing a sweater with his school's design appeared, followed by a soldier in uniform and a stooped, elderly couple who recounted details of their arduous journey from Maine to meet him. In the fifth year of his presidency, McKinley had logged hundreds of hours in similarly, languid receptions; he complained to his wife, Ida, that he felt like a weary battleship in need of a fresh coat of paint.

He drew now from his vast repertoire of quips and clichés. "I'm grateful for your devoted service to our great country," he said to the soldier, and to a construction worker, "America was built on the backs of laborers like you."

The president glanced down the line: a couple of dozen greeters left. He had asked Ida to relax and wait for him in the train and planned to join her for his favorite dish of tender roast beef followed by fruit cake and tea after he returned. There were government policy papers to review before a meeting with a Congressional Committee representative and an intelligence report from the Security Service about a problem brewing in Hawaii. The train was set to return to Washington the next afternoon.

He watched Martin Beliveau and Borden Tupper being escorted past the reception line.

"John," he said, pointing the Canadian officials out to Garcy. "Please apologize on my behalf to Minister Beliveau and Governor General Tupper and assure them that I'll be finished shortly."

*

Martin Beliveau surveyed the people remaining in line to greet McKinley.

A familiar-looking man with a cast on one arm, his other hand concealed in his pocket, snapped into view.

"That's the same...," Martin blurted, before catching himself.

"Is there a problem?" the governor general asked, detecting the minister's discomfort.

The young man who had approached him the day before near the Esplanade bandstand stood waiting to greet President McKinley, one arm tucked inside his jacket. Martin didn't recall the man's arm being injured during their earlier encounter. He pondered the troubled man's plausible explanation for shaking the hand of the 'great ruler'. With a surging sense of panic, he studied his face for stiffness or a nervous tic, but the calm fellow with the mellow smile didn't appear to pose any threat. Martin chose to avoid an untidy confrontation. He resolved that the chatter in Cabinet meetings and cautionary newspaper reports about the peril of anarchists made him unduly paranoid. Jocelyn had read to him in bed an article from *Harper's Weekly* about the worrisome plague of anarchists.

Martin was to replay the next couple of minutes in his mind thousands of times, attempting to explain his fateful decision at that grave moment not to intercede.

*

A stocky man with a sailor's baked face, in an oversized Belvedere camel coat, strode towards the president. He was frowning, and this drew the attention of the president's security detail.

Garcy tapped his forehead and discreetly slid his hand towards his gun belt.

"Johnson, Gus Johnson," the man announced himself.

The president responded genially. "And what do you do, Gus?"

"I build bridges," he said. "The finest bridges in America."

The president beamed. "I can't imagine a more honorable vocation than linking communities. Tell me, where do you live?"

"Binghamton, although I'm hardly there lately. I'm thinking of selling my house."

"I'm pleased that you travelled to the Pan-American Exposition to meet me."

"Mr. President." Johnson stepped a foot closer.

Garcy clamped his hand on the holster.

The man whispered, his hands in his pockets. "I just

wanted you to know that I voted for you twice --- and if you could run a third time, I'd vote for you again."

"Fortunately, my dear fellow, that decision is beyond my control," McKinley replied cheerfully, and shifted his focus to the next greeter in line.

The next man was in his mid-twenties, smartly dressed, and hair perfectly parted, moving with a relaxed gait and reposeful manner. He bore a striking resemblance to the train engineer's polite assistant. Seeing that the man's right hand was bandaged, the president thoughtfully reached for his left hand to greet him.

"What's your name, son?" the president asked. There was no answer.

Instead, the man took the revolver hidden inside his jacket, pressed the muzzle against the president's chest, and fired the gun twice.

"Am I shot?" the president asked in a controlled voice, falling backwards into the detective's arms.

Garcy rushed to unbutton the president's vest. His shirt was soaked in blood.

"Yes, I fear you are, Mr. President."

Garcy tended to the injured president while the man who shot him was swarmed by a throng of a dozen policemen and Secret Service agents. Shouts rang out through the Temple of Music that the president was shot. Chairs flipped over as people began to rush to his side, a ring of Garcy's security team struggling to keep them back. The revolver was seized still encased in a handkerchief spurting with smoke. The Secret Service agent carrying the revolver was mistaken for the president's attacker and set upon and beaten.

"Stay with us, sir," Garcy pleaded with the president,

as he silently recited a prayer. A cacophony of wailing voices filled the room, like the disquieting cry of wounded soldiers on the battlefield.

"Get me Cortelyou..." The president was eased onto a chair before addressing his personal secretary. "My wife, be careful, Cortelyou, how you tell her --- oh, be careful."

Cortelyou trembled as he leaned over him. "I will, Mister President."

The dire word spread quickly around the grounds of the Pan-American Exposition about the president's shooting. The shrill sound of the gunshots led many fairgoers strolling along the Esplanade to rush towards the Temple of Music. Hundreds of people soon congregated behind barriers of ropes as a few police officers attempted to impede their entry. The bubbling hostility of the crowd led to a forward surge and the barriers collapsed as simply as shoestring at the stampede. Fighting erupted with police officers and soldiers as chaotic efforts continued to reach the president's attacker. Chants of fury mounted to a bellowing chorus: "Lynch him. Lynch him! Hang him! Kill him!"

Leon Czolgosz, his face covered in blood with a gash over his mouth, was handcuffed and brought outside to a waiting police carriage. The rabid crowd clawed nearer, beating back the police resistance. A clamoring group of protestors lunged at the horses of the police wagon as Czolgosz climbed in. The driver lost grip of his whip and a police officer rushed to retrieve it. Soldiers lifted resisters clinging to the wheels of the wagon, desperate to prevent it leaving, but the wagon finally made a safe getaway between two sturdy lines of soldiers, with the battered prisoner inside.

Willow Hooper arrived at the entrance to the Temple of Music to a jeering and cursing crowd.

"What's happening?" she asked.

"Some crazy fellow just shot the president," the distraught lady beside her said, pointing to the departing carriage.

"Where is President McKinley?"

"He's still inside the building."

Hooper instructed the photographer from the *Brooklyn Daily Eagle* to position himself for an unobstructed picture and canvassed the area for reporters' badges. There were no other journalists present.

*

Railways Minister Beliveau watched the shooting of the president and the frenzied aftermath in a series of terrifying snapshots, each image frozen in the recesses of his mind. He had observed McKinley stare bewilderedly at the young man who shot him before collapsing. Martin quickly determined that the only truly secure spot in which to take refuge was at the president's side.

Through the bedlam that followed the two gunshots, the president sat still, with precautions taken not to trample him. Interminable moments passed until the ambulance arrived. The governor general knelt and gently held the president's hand until he was placed by the ambulance men on a stretcher.

Martin offered to assist and struggled mightily to carry a corner of the heavily weighted stretcher as it moved to the waiting ambulance. He pushed a photographer aside with his free hand on the way. The photographer tumbled to the ground, his camera held upright.

"I'll update the prime minister," Martin advised the governor general as the ambulance pulled away. He searched Borden Tupper's face to detect signs of displeasure: the governor general appeared shaken and on the verge of fainting and welcomed Martin's arms for support. "He had not recognized the president's shooter standing in line," Martin concluded, relieved.

On their solemn walk from the Esplanade to locate a cab on the closest street, Martin and his compatriot were intercepted by a reporter running towards them, a notebook in her hand.

"Willow Hooper's my name. I need to chat with you about what you gentlemen saw," the young woman said, panting. "I watched you both leave with the president. I assume that you observed the shooting."

It occurred to Martin that the police might also be keen to interview him as a witness. He was determined not to heighten law enforcement's interest with a vivid eyewitness account.

"I didn't see anything," he declared. "Everything that happened inside the building is a complete blur. Governor General Tupper assisted the president after he was shot. He's your prime candidate for an interview."

He didn't wait for approval, but passed into the steady stream of people hurrying towards the Temple of Music.

The alarming news about the attack on the president had evidently spread. A pond of sorrow-stricken people grew into a sea and filled the walks and cross street of Franklin Avenue. Many in the crowd wept openly. Martin turned back to the Canada Building, affectionately known by government staff as the Swiss Chalet.

He decided to take shelter in the smoking and writing room for men. He could prepare his notes in solitude for his grim conversation on the telephone with the prime minister to update him. The shooting of an American president would be a matter of heightened interest to Laurier. As he walked on, immersed in deep thought, he felt tinged with shame. It wasn't the American president's survival that troubled him. He trusted the excellent medical care that awaited William McKinley. He had appeared conscious and alert on the stretcher.

Martin tried but could not suppress the indelible image of the young man confronting him on President's Day, and the renewed sight of him waiting his turn to greet McKinley. Two grand opportunities to forestall President McKinley's attacker, neglectfully missed on his part. He confronted an unassailable and discomforting truth --- he could have prevented this tragic outcome.

Chapter Five

Mortimer Hanus, son of Lewis and Ottilie Hanus and grandson of Will Hanus, twice imprisoned for breaking the limbs of his adversaries, regarded himself as the luckiest man in the world. Hanus once sued the publisher of *Great Expectations* for five hundred pounds for modelling the character of Compeyson, the debonair marauding con artist, after his own exploits. The nuisance claim settled without regard to the fact that Dickens had written the novel thirty years before the launch of the lawsuit.

Yet another bout of incredibly good fortune proved the maxim to be accurate. The Italian police boat pulled up to the starboard side of the converted frigate Hanus had chartered for his latest criminal enterprise. He presented the forged seaway bill on request, documenting the load of mahogany furniture that lay below deck, ready to be delivered to the port of Istanbul.

"Where are you from?" the police captain asked officiously. Two officers stood rigidly at his side.

"Canada."

"Oh Canada, I visited New Brunswick once. The best lobster that I've eaten in my life. *Fantastico*." The captain's acerbic tone softened to the sweet lull of a church hymn.

"What an incredible coincidence," Hanus replied. Mendacity flowed for him as smoothly as the flowing intake of oxygen. "I've lived my whole life in Moncton, New Brunswick. You'll have to return one day as my guest. Let me give you my business card." He handed the officer a card with his name and company logo from his overcoat. "I know the best shops in the Canadian Maritimes to purchase fresh lobster."

"I may take you up on your generous offer one day."

"*Meglio sorridere*."

The police captain beamed. "You speak my language? I'm impressed."

Hanus had learned to translate the phrase 'better to smile' in twenty-two languages and used it in his travels to charm his audience.

With the brusque brush of a hand, the two officers stepped off the frigate's deck to the ladder reaching the anchored police boat.

"I'm sorry to have delayed you," the captain said before leaving. "Have a safe and prosperous voyage."

Hanus leaned over the deck of the frigate. Flashes of sunlight gleamed from the marine blue water of the Mediterranean Sea. He pulled a plug of chewing tobacco from a bag, rolled the savory cud around his mouth, and began spitting it over the undulating guard rail. "That was as easy as pulling grapes from a vine," he said jubilantly. The act of procuring a retired military boat had required an unparalleled degree of chicanery on his part. On learning that the French Navy had converted its naval fleet exclusively to armored cruisers and that there remained a single un-protected cruiser banished to a naval stockyard, Hanus had enlisted a counterfeiter's assistance, and with the forged credentials of a Deputy Minister with the Canadian Navy, finagled the purchase of the old frigate at a steeply discounted price.

Good fortune had smiled on Hanus yet again. A cur-sory examination by the police captain below decks and his extravagant fittings, ashen marble table and palatial parlor would have unraveled the fiction of a transport ship.

Hanus remembered his very first con job, the one that inspired him on the path to riches. He discovered that there were regular pick-up baseball games in the park at Christie Pitts. The games were umpired and fiercely com-petitive. At the end of each game, the players on the losing team anted up wads of cash to the winning side. Hanus traveled around the city assembling a baseball team of semi-professional and retired players to create his own stellar team, provided their shoddy uniforms and caps and gave the players clear instructions to dress as shabbily as possible. Their gloves were stomped on with dry dirt and returned to the bewildered team members. "I get twenty percent of our take," Hanus told them. "Leave the game arrangements to me." He brought the team to play at the ball ground at Christie Pitts and found an enterprising team ready to bet twenty-five dollars for a match. Two hours later, he deposited five dollars into his coat pocket. The baseball team journeyed around the province of On-tario garnering winnings of hundreds of dollars.

Mortimer Hanus's most striking encounter with good fortune became his closely-guarded secret. A few years earlier, he had befriended a medical doctor, Dr. H.H. Holmes, visiting Toronto from Chicago. They met in the waiting area of a pharmacy and discovered they shared a mutual interest in potent and toxic drugs. After Holmes learned of Hanus's export-import business, he peppered him with questions about methods of securing payment for merchandise. "I'm thinking of buying an apartment in Chicago," he told Hanus, "and renting rooms to visitors to the Windy City."

A few years later, Hanus received a call at his office from the visiting doctor, inviting him to dinner. "You were so helpful," the amiable Dr. Holmes told him. "I wanted to express my gratitude."

Hanus set off to the doctor's address. On the way, a searing pain in his chest forced him to halt the trip and rest on the sidewalk. After ten minutes passed, Hanus reversed his path and returned home. It turned out to be a bout of food poisoning, the result of some raw fish he'd eaten for lunch. The protracted delay and the ensuing loss of appetite left him with little choice but to forego his dinner plans. Hanus never heard back from Dr. Holmes but one day he discovered a riveting front page story in the *Globe* about the sadistic exploits of Herman Webster Mudgett.

Mudgett, using the alias of Dr. H.H. Holmes, had been involved in insurance scams, bigamy and fraudulent schemes. He earned the ghastly description in the press of being America's first known serial killer, leaving a gruesome trail of at least ten victims, many of them visitors to the Chicago World's Fair. He had reportedly murdered two of his victims in Toronto and buried their sparse remains in his basement of his rented house. The untold and chilling part of the article, Hanus grasped immediately, was that *he*, Mortimer Hanus, had been selected by the evil doctor, to be his third Canadian murder victim.

Hanus wrote a letter to Dr. Holmes in jail, congratulating him on his masterful deception, but before he mailed the letter, learned of Holmes' public hanging in Philadelphia. Oh, how he deemed himself cheated. He had been certain he could persuade the masterful killer to spare him and forge an alliance. Two partners in waiting, kindred spirits in artful deception, an inestimable coupling premised on a single enduring truth: that goodwill and charity cannot withstand the repelling force of wickedness, which always reigned victorious. Food poisoning had deprived Mortimer Hanus of a golden opportunity.

*

"Shelby wants to see you, pronto."

Willow Hooper stopped typing in mid-sentence and crossed the floor of the newspaper room to find the managing editor of the *Brooklyn Daily Eagle*. This was only the second time in two years she'd been summoned to Shelby's office. The first was a memorable disappointment: Shelby had asked her to organize the decorations for the office Christmas party.

This time, he greeted her enthusiastically, like an early arriving dinner guest. "Come on in, Hooper. Find yourself a seat."

She moved a stack of racing forms from the closest chair to the floor, sweeping away the clutter like a broom.

"Hurry up, I don't have all day," Shelby said. Gruff, impertinent, with long grey sideburns stretching to a saggy chin, Shelby stalked the floor of the newsroom barking instructions to timorous reporters. Now he said,

"Relax, I called you to my office to commend you."

Shelby thrived on his reputation for being intimidating, vacillating between growling and purring like a friendly cat. "What story are you working on?" he asked the investigative reporter.

Hooper opened her notebook. "There have been a spate of deaths involving men working on skyscrapers. Two were crushed to death, and a third slipped on a girder and fell twelve stories. So I'm investigating shoddy safety conditions for construction workers."

"Good stuff. We'll run a feature story on the front page. These tall buildings are shooting up everywhere. I called you in to talk about our Thanksgiving party."

Willow looked at Shelby with a stern frown.

He grinned, clapping his hands. "Just kidding. The story that you wrote about President McKinley's shooting in Buffalo is getting a lot of attention. I received requests this morning from newspapers in Atlanta and Des Moines to run your piece. They want the photograph of McKinley being carried out on a stretcher. Yesterday, I granted permission for a paper in Birmingham, England to run the Willow Hooper eyewitness account. You've caused quite a frenzy with your close-up reporting. A colleague at our Washington office pressed me why I had one of our reporters stationed at the Temple of Music. Frankly, I'm not sure what the correct answer is. I told him that you're a crackerjack reporter working for America's finest newspaper." Shelby chewed on a burnt-out stogie. Ashes filled his ashtray and the office reeked from stale cigars.

"I had an interview set up with the president's head of

security after the reception at the Temple of Music. I did my research and discovered that he once served as a detective in Greenpoint."

"Ah, a Brooklyn boy. Excellent idea for a story, Hooper. Pursue that interview with the detective. Get the paper an exclusive. Let's wait a few days for McKinley to recover."

"When can I get back to writing my piece?"

"Shuffle it aside for another day. Who knows? Another worker may tumble from a building in the meantime." He ignored Hooper's glare. "The boys in the editorial department decided to run a lead editorial in tomorrow's edition calling on Congress to pass a new law guaranteeing that the president's security detail be confined to Secret Service agents. And they'd like you to write it."

"Why me?"

"You'll add the personal touch. A reporter showing up at the scene moments after the president's attack is a bonus. Push aside any sympathy you have for John Garcy. Look, he's a human being. Anyone can make a mistake in their line of work. But it rarely ends up with the president of the United States being shot." Shelby brandished a newspaper. "Hey, who is this Canadian politician carrying McKinley on the stretcher? Quite a striking-looking fellow."

"That's Martin Beliveau. He refused to speak to me. The governor general told me that Beliveau rushed to help the president. The Canadian delegation was standing a few feet behind the president when he was shot."

"Bingo," Shelby said, punching his fist in the air. "I want you to take a trip to Canada's capital city."

"Ottawa", Hooper interjected."

"--- and interview this hero fellow, Martin Beliveau. I

can see the headline: *Canadian Diplomat Runs Through Bullets to Aid McKinley.*"

Chapter Six

Burford Simmons removed his eyepatch, and paused to become accustomed to the sunlight, flaring like a flashlight through the Nottingham lace curtains. He reached across to the bedroom dresser and grabbed a yellow pad of paper and pencil to jot a few notes from his dream during the night:

The eyewitness claimed to see Dax carrying a burlap bag outside the bank before driving the getaway car after the robbery. It was raining at the time and a permanent wet stain may have remained on the bag. Must inspect the bag seized from Dax by the police at his arrest.

The morning newspaper, located, as usual, lay on the corner of the dresser beside his sprawling four-poster bed. The headline of the *Buffalo Morning Express*, in bold lettering sized for a declaration of war, was obscured.

'PRESIDENT MCKINLEY IS ---' he read. The newspaper had been folded in half and steam ironed. Burford Simmons's daily ritual involved reading the front page; moving next to the daily sports report and ending with a perusal of the closing prices on the stock market. The missing part of the caption presented an opportunity to practice his detective skills, honed by devoted reading of his favorite Sherlock Holmes stories, *The Sign of Four* his latest foray.

Burford propped two feather pillows against the wooden headboard, rolled up his pajama sleeves and began the contest in earnest.

President McKinley is Dead?

A most unlikely scenario, he decided, pressing the tips of his fingers against his forehead. The president's personal physician, Dr. Maray, had vouched for his patient's robust, good health during the re-election campaign, assuaging any skeptical voters' concerns about an ailing leader by announcing, "My sincere wish as I grow older is that I can be as healthy as my president."

President McKinley is Missing?

Burford's roaming imagination struck into unventured territory here. But rumors did persist that the president enjoyed indulging in midnight strolls along the Potomac River. If true, a golden opportunity presented itself for a rogue riverboat captain and a group of armed thugs to kidnap the president. But surely an entourage of armed presidential guards would foil such an ambitious scheme.

President McKinley is Knighted?

Rousing acclaim had been directed at the American president after his private audience with Queen Victoria in London. The elderly monarch had apparently been taken with McKinley's witty repartee, and reports followed that she respected his grand, imperial vision. Burford recalled an official palace photograph of the solemn and stoic queen laughing heartily with the president. By one royal observer's count, it marked the fourth time that she had smiled during her reign as monarch. Queen Victoria had died, but the new king, Edward, might be inclined to bestow a knighthood on his mother's favored president. Upon reflection, Burford calculated, it was a century too soon for the title of Sir William McKinley to be conferred by a former enemy of the American Revolution.

President McKinley is in Buffalo?

This had the virtue of prevailing logic. "That's the one, Watson," Burford exclaimed, his thumb wagging in the air. He'd forgotten that McKinley had left Washington. The president had a public reception scheduled at the Pan-American Exposition. McKinley had chosen Buffalo as his final stop on a presidential cross-country railway trip, and a president's recognition was noteworthy for the city of Buffalo, often ignored and slighted.

Burford and his wife, Pharo, had planned a trip to the World's Fair on the upcoming weekend. They had missed McKinley's speech on President's Day as Pharo had preferred a restful day at home at her writing table.

Burford marked his calendar for the year, 1901, with a red circle around the date of September seventh. It became an integral part of Burford's daily routine, validating the fact that he was awake and able to think. He then recited a passage dedicated to the biblical warrior, Joshua: "Be strong and have courage, do not be terrified or dismayed, for the Lord your God is with you whatever path you choose." There had been moments in the past few weeks when he'd struggled mightily to adhere to that credo after a jury's disappointing verdict in a client's embezzlement trial.

Habits had evolved into the immutable rules that governed Burford Simmons' life, a stern lesson imparted to him by his father, Walter Simmons, who began each regimented day with a couple of sips of whiskey and a piece of herring followed by ten push-ups and a brisk walk around the block of their home. The name of Walter B. Simmons was renowned by the end of the nineteenth century as the inventor of the smoke alarm. Burford could slip his father's name into conversations and be rewarded by grateful customers of the fire detection device. The bank had offered a percentage less on his mortgage when he purchased his home; the butcher sent extra steaks and lamb chops with the weekly delivery; an anniversary order for a dozen roses at Molly the florist was doubled – all on account of his father's fame.

Yet in truth, Burford's father's true vocation had been a chimney sweep. Wally Simmons would gingerly wiggle into a box-shaped chimney, with the blurred visibility of a mountain tunnel, to clear the ashen debris. Wally returned home with his face and clothes smothered in smoot. "The bathtub will earn its keep today," he'd say smirking, whistling his favored Irish bar tune during his soapy bath. For the innocent stranger, a handshake was never part of Wally's introduction; only a boisterous back slap followed by a chuckle as the surprised victim tumbled to the ground. Wally Simmons' childhood dream was to be an actor, but the talent did not match the aspiration. When the town of Elmira staged a production of *Hamlet*, he garnered the role of the courtier, Guildenstern. His stilted acting and flubbed lines left his fellow actors indignant, but the audience howled its appreciation and ticket sales soared. He was a perennial practical joker. On the day his father was buried, Burford peered into the coffin to say farewell and was surprised to discover a paisley bowtie wrapped around his dad's eyes as a blindfold and a lollipop wedged into his mouth. His will read simply: "So long Sonny Boy – it's all yours – just don't blow it all at the racetrack!"

Burford's schooling became a fixture of his father's grand plan. He was sent to the best public school in Buffalo and upon graduating high school, won a boxing scholarship to attend Amherst College. In the fall of 1877, he set off to the University of Michigan school of law and paid the fifty-dollar tuition with money saved from his summer jobs as a lifeguard. Burford returned to Buffalo and secured a position as the in-house attorney for an insurance company. But the irresistible allure of courtroom battle drew him to establish a solo criminal law practice. The shingle outside the front door read: "Champagne of Justice for Sale."

By the turn of the century, in his forty-fifth year, Burford had a sprightly new bride, an elegantly furnished three-bedroom newly built bungalow on an oak treed boulevard on Johnson Park, and a partnership in one of the city's top law firms. And to honor his father's request, he assiduously avoided the racetrack.

Burford reserved the morning reading of his neatly-folded newspaper for the tight quarters of the carriage conveying a group of four men nattily adorned in suits, and top hats (two being quite stout and a third, his law partner Alex Proctor, rakishly thin) to the Buffalo waterfront. That journey was followed by a short jaunt on foot to Burford's law office; the whole trip took most of an hour, unless the carriage lost a contest with the mud on a rainy morning.

Today, not being a workday, the alarm clock had not

been set to ring. The newspaper beside his bed lay on a silver pewter tray with a plate of two poached eggs, a boiled potato, rye toast soaked in butter and a dish of tomato sauce with a teaspoon and fork.

Burford spread the paper's front page across his bed and gasped. 'PRESIDENT MCKINLEY IS SHOT.'

The *Morning Express's* detailed report described the attack at the Temple of Music, only a few miles from Burford's home. According to his attending surgeon, McKinley was expected to recover, although his condition was reportedly dire. One of the bullets couldn't be removed from the president's stomach. The assailant, with no previous known criminal ties, was a twenty-eight-year-old man, Leon Czolgosz. His sketch appeared in the paper with a menacing caption: '*The President's Foiled Assassin.*' Czolgosz had fired two rapid shots at the president's chest as he was being greeted in the receiving line. McKinley fell back into the arms of a Detective Garcy, from his security detail. The president had been rushed by ambulance to the Exposition Hospital for his emergency surgery. He was now convalescing at the nearby Milburn house under the watchful care of doctors and attendants.

In his haste to get out of bed and share the news with Pharo, the tray flipped onto his sheets with streams of egg and tomato sauce dripping to the mahogany floor and onto the corner of a note from his wife, which must also have fallen from the tray, and which he paused to read.

"*Good morning Burf and HAPPY BIRTHDAY*," it began. Pharo went on to say she would be occupied in the garden bed loosening the sod for next season's tulips and extended an invitation to join her if he could stand his pants and shoes getting a bit muddy. She reminded him the wood stored in the shed needed to be chopped for the fireplace. "*And beware*," she ended her note, "*the blade of the ax faces the wood!*" She knew his vulnerabilities well. There was no mention of President McKinley being shot, but Pharo would soon become aware.

News of the brazen attack would spread quickly across the country. Burford calculated that the mood would be somber, even for the president's most virulent opponents. Vice-President Teddy Roosevelt, who according to the *Morning Express*, had hurried to Buffalo from a banquet of outdoorsmen beside Lake Champlain, would temporarily assume the president's responsibilities. The army would be on standby. America's enemies might seize the vulnerable moment to strike. Wall Street would plunge into a steep dive. One lone, crazed madman had the ability to change the course of history.

Yesterday, the most pressing issue in his home had been his extra rest. Pharo had informed Bessie, their affable and efficient housekeeper, at dinner, of Burford's upcoming birthday and that her husband would be sleeping in. Under no circumstances should her husband be disturbed in the morning. Perhaps an exception for an assassination attempt on the president must always be appended to those orders.

The ornamental English table clock in the hallway struck ten o'clock. Burford snapped his suspenders to the buttons at his waistband and tied his striped cravat around the tabs of his sash-vest and pressed white shirt. He combed the part in his hair and brushed the tips of his moustache. An inveterate early riser, he felt drowsier with the few additional hours of sleep. *Habits, habits.*

He had set aside the afternoon to prepare for a

challenging homicide trial: a trapeze artist from Tonawanda accused of tampering with the safety net that failed to catch his partner after she slipped on the rope and fell. An audience of one hundred and forty people had borne witnesses to her fatal plunge; at least three people fainted and were rushed to the hospital. The police reported that no children had been present, a fortunate fact providing little solace to the adults who watched the horrid spectacle. His client, with the unfortunate name for a criminal defendant of Horace M. Quilty, told the police that it was a terrible accident and that he faced a similar risk in his trapeze act. The police investigation uncovered that the trapeze act had been performed by the pair hundreds of times safely, with the net holding intact. Horace Quilty's arrest on a charge of manslaughter followed a police interview with the victim's sister. She disclosed that days before the tragedy the victim, racked with guilt, had decided to meet Quilty's wife to spill the secrets of a two-year affair. The police had located a diary tucked into a slipper wherein the victim described Quilty threatening to kill her when he learned of her plan to reveal their affair.

The manslaughter case had been passed around several lawyers in the city like a boiling hot bean bag before Burford Simmons was retained. Incensed, Pharo forbade mention of the case in their home. Accepting unpopular causes and winning trials for hapless defendants had become Burford's specialty, something that his wife compared to collecting the carcasses of dead rats from the alleyways.

"That's not a reasonable comparison," he protested.

"You're right," she shot back. "I'm not being fair to the rats."

Pharo had risen to be his most formidable adversary, telling 'the saintly lawyer' when he quoted scripture that his cast of rogue clients did not fit the story of David slaying the giant, Goliath, with a slingshot. They were, she scolded in a tone seething with contempt, the goose-droppings of society. Pharo complained that she had been tossed from her bridge group and lost her golf club membership because of her husband's dastardly trials. The churchwomen's book club evicted her one week before she was set to present on The Picture of Dorian Grey. Oscar Wilde must have based Lord Henry's imperfect character on her, she wryly observed, pointing to the author's description that "he was always late on principle, his principle being that punctuality is the thief of time."

Pharo had repeatedly urged Burford to join her father's oil business. Years before, John Rockefeller and Henry Flagler, the two richest men in America, had visited her father, Mervin, at one of the oil wells outside Lexington, Kentucky and offered him a quarter of a million dollars on the spot. He sold them a fifty-one percent share for a hundred thousand dollars and continued to manage it; Mervin had issued a standing offer to Burford for the position of vice-president. But Burford openly mocked the offer. "I'd rather give away the oil to the poor to heat their homes than sell it."

He stopped to greet Bessie, leaning on the jagged balusters of the staircase as he climbed the stairs.

"Don't forget, Mr. Simmons, Mitchell will be dropping by at two o'clock this afternoon. He's quite excited that you've asked him to work on your new case." As ever, she beamed at the mention of her sole child and the newest associate of Burford Simmons' law firm.

Mitchell's hiring, the fulfillment of a promise Burford made to him as a schoolboy, had not passed without controversy at the law firm, but Burford stood firm. He'd paid Mitchell's tuition to Cornell Law School in Ithaca and had hired him the day after his graduation. Bessie's parents, Harriet and Rufus Harris, had been slaves in Virginia emerging from the blistering labor in the plantation and made their escape with Bessie in the middle of the night. The slave catchers were on their trail. Rufus had a map and instructions on a folded piece of paper outlining a route through the Underground Railroad that would take them to Niagara Falls. Burford's mother found the family huddled beside a fire pit burning in her backyard. When the slave catchers arrived, she menacingly held a rifle with a tomato red ribbon tied around the barrel, pointed at them. She warned them that she won the blue ribbon at the county fair for hitting the bullseye. After they left, Burford's mother invited the family into her house, made them a hot supper and tended to the welts and bruises on Rufus's back. "You'll stay with us," she said in a soothing voice, "until you're healthy enough to travel."

A month later, the patrolman on the beat in their area, showed up unannounced at Walter's door with the pair of slave catchers. Burford stood beside his father.

"Wally," the officer said. "These men claim that you have a family of Negroes living here."

"Don't know nothing about that," Walter replied. "They showed up here one night passing by and then scattered."

"He's lying!" one of the slave catchers shouted.

"Thank you, Wally," the officer said with a wink. "Well, gentlemen. I'm very sorry, but you'll have to return to your homes in Virginia empty-handed."

From then on, under the patrolman's watchful eye, Bessie's family lived in the cramped basement and assisted with the household chores and repairs in exchange for room and board. Bessie grew up in the home, attended a local school, and married a carpenter from Buffalo; she continued to commute to work as housekeeper and cook for Burford and Pharo Simmons after their marriage.

"Another president shot, just like that poor Mr. Lincoln. Oh, my Lord," she moaned.

"How did you learn of the shooting, Bessie?" Burford asked.

"Miss Pharo told me a few minutes ago. She's waiting for you in her writing study. She must have read your newspaper before I brought it to your bedroom." Bessie pulled a card from her pocket. "This is for you," she said handing him the brittle card. "A lawyer from your office dropped by early this morning and met with Miss Pharo. I've seen him at the house before. He gave me the card on his way out."

Burford checked the card and saw the name of Alex Proctor, the senior partner of his law firm.

"Did the gentleman tell you the reason for his visit?"

"No, sir. But he couldn't have been in the house for longer than a minute. In and out, I'd say. I'm going to say a prayer for President McKinley. He is a good man for the Negroes. He fought for the Union. Mitchell told me stories about his bravery as a soldier. Why do all the good presidents get shot?"

A third American president shot in his lifetime. Abraham Lincoln, James Garfield and now McKinley. Burford remembered his parents and grandparents hurrying to church to pray as soon as they heard the news about President Lincoln being shot at the Ford Theater. Young as he was, he never forgot the wailing of his mother piercing his bedroom wall from the front yard after she learned that her beloved president was dead. "I'd rather hear the roar of a hundred cattle facing me in a stampede," he once told Pharo, "than my mother's cries of grief."

Now it was his turn to grieve for a president. Despite the hopeful news report, Burford believed that President McKinley's wounds must be fatal. Two gaping wounds to his abdomen at close range. No-one, even with the finest medical care, could possibly recover. He wasn't a fan of the president's imperial policies and had resolved not to vote for McKinley's re-election. But he felt only genuine affection and empathy for his beleaguered president now. As he entered his study, he muttered a prayer for the president, and for his successor, Teddy Roosevelt.

Chapter Seven

The practice of re-examining a witness following a withering cross-examination is akin to climbing onto the seat of a Ferris Wheel with the latch unhinged. The tumble will be far worse than the rocky ride. There was the case of the defendant pressed in cross-examination by the prosecutor to explain the delay of reporting his alibi to the police. His attorney stood and repeated the question in re-examination, to which his wobbly client replied: "What, now *you're* bothering me?"

*

Burford tucked the *Buffalo Morning Express* under his arm. In her desk chair, Pharo sat pensive, gazing idly through the bow window at her dirt-filled garden, with an empty pot of coffee resting beside a burned-out wick candle. The bright hue of her heather yellow shirt-waist meshed with the sunlight and the golden coronet perched on top of the window. Her hair had been loosened and her flaming red curly locks drifted below the nape of her neck.

"Good morning," he said. "Did you manage to get any writing done?"

"Two hundred words. Is it proper to count participles?"

"It's just a smudging of unconnected words in a sentence without them," Burford replied respectfully. Pharo's publisher recently compared her elegant prose to Jane Austen's style of writing, a match that her husband amusingly discounted to his chagrin. Furious, Pharo refused to speak to him for two days. In his groveling apology, he conceded her supreme talent as a writer with two published novels of romantic intrigue. He'd read the impressive first chapters of her new novel about an archeologist and his assistant falling in love during an excavation in a Tanzanian gorge, but had quibbled on later learning that their families were on conflicting sides of the Boer War raging in South Africa.

"I'm aware that our president has been shot." She swung the chair to face him.

Burford could see her eyes swelling with tears and a damp handkerchief clutched in her hand.

"At the Temple of Music, of all places! Why didn't President McKinley's security team halt the shooter?" She didn't wait for his answer. "Well, mercifully, poor Ida McKinley didn't have to witness the calamity. And thank goodness they captured the madman responsible." Her tone softened. "Burford, there is something about the president that I need to tell you."

"What is it?"

"I met him. I had a private audience with him. It happened a couple of days before the shooting."

Burford leaned towards her in the exacting manner he used to a witness withholding evidence crucial to the defense. "And you chose to keep that a secret from me?"

"Well, you know my sister Odette and I took the streetcar to spend a weekend holiday in Niagara Falls."

Pharo had promised her younger sister a tour of one of the wonders of the world and had returned with a gift of a rust green painting of the cascading waves of the Falls which Burford had slipped into the bottom of an office drawer.

"It turned out that President McKinley and his wife chose the same weekend for a visit to Niagara Falls."

"I still don't understand how the two of you happened to meet?"

"Be patient," she demanded. "There is a section of the Falls that isn't protected by a railing and you can get reasonably close to the edge. I dared Odette to join me, but she told me that I was crazy."

"Because you *are* crazy."

"Oh, Burf. Don't fret over a trifle. I'm here to tell the tale, aren't I?"

"Don't fret over a *trifle*." Burford recalled the last time Pharo resorted to the same dismissive phrase during an overseas trip taken for her thirtieth birthday. An art exhibit at the Paris Exposition had inspired Pharo to locate a gallery on the Seine where she purchased paintings by Cezanne and Picasso. Next morning, she stumbled on Cezanne himself, dining at a Parisian bistro and returned with his piece of artwork and a courteous request to inscribe the back canvas with a personal message. "You disturbed the peace and serenity of Cezanne's breakfast," Burford admonished her, and Pharo returned a stern lecture about the assumed risks of fame.

"I can understand why you never shared this story with me. What if you'd had another fainting spell, Pharo?"

"You're right. You would have been livid with me. I stood at the edge of Niagara Falls and the powerful roar of the tumbling water against the rocks had the most marvelous hypnotic effect on me. I could have stayed watching it for hours --- but then I felt a hand clenched around my wrist. A man's hand pulled me away from the edge. I turned to see through the mist the silhouette of a man nattily attired in a suit. His strength surprised me. I could hardly see his face in all the foggy mist that sprayed around us. He caused me quite the scare! I asked him who he was, and he mouthed the words: 'Don't do it. Please don't do it.' We moved back. When we got about twenty feet away, he gently reminded me about life being precious and the virtue of faith. When it dawned on me that the silly man thought I was about to take my own life, I began to laugh. My reaction surprised him, and he began to laugh with me. I assured him that I had no plan to hurl myself over Niagara Falls. I introduced myself and he told me that he was the head of security for the president. He took me to meet President McKinley at a safe landing above the Falls and we had a pleasant chat and time raced by. He was such a lovely and gracious man. He has these piercing blue eyes that I couldn't look away from. He asked me about my cane, and I told him that I had an automobile accident and foolishly collided with a tree. He became concerned when he learned that the damage to my leg was permanent. He invited me to meet with a specialist he knew in Washington. He joked that a disproportionate amount of his time was devoted to consulting with doctors. A couple of physicians were even stationed on his train tour to attend to his medical needs and his wife's. Ida had been ill, and the travel across the country had been a burden. He expressed his reluctance to serve out his term as president if she required his steadfast care."

"President McKinley told you he might resign his office, did he?"

"Yes, of course he did. It's the truth! I wasn't planning on being a babbling brook about it. His secret was safely hidden in my diary. Well, until he got shot, of course --- I almost forgot to tell you something else."

Burford wondered what extravagant new surprise awaited him.

"I invited him to tea when he visited Buffalo for an opportunity to convert my maverick husband to be his supporter. He'd have embraced the challenge, he told me, but his schedule was packed so tightly that a bathroom break was an intrusion." She looked up, her eyes welling with tears. "And now he's almost been murdered. The thug who ambushed him with a revolver will need a proper lawyer, of course. Just your kind of trial, Mr. Simmons, I imagine."

"Yes, I'd already considered it."

He regretted the admission instantly, as his wife sprung up from the office chair.

"Now listen to me, Burford!" (The affectionate nickname Burf discarded.) "You must give me your word that you won't represent the president's shooter." Her eyes bore into his, the rest of her face a frozen scowl, as she continued. "No good will come of it. There are plenty of other attorneys in this city to represent him! We both remember what happened to your law school classmate when he spoke up for those killer anarchists in the Haymarket bombing."

"Pharo, you're assuming that the president's shooter is an anarchist." Burford pretended to be dubious, but he shared his wife's opinion. "Darrow spoke up eloquently in support of free speech. I am justly proud of my erudite friend."

His law school classmate and closest friend, Clarence Darrow, a well-known labor lawyer in Chicago, had publicly denounced the injustice of executing the anarchists charged in the Haymarket case. It began with a protest at the McCormick Works in Chicago by a group of workers clamoring for better work conditions including a shortened eight-hour day. After the police opened fire, several of the protestors were killed. The next night in a vegetable mart in Haymarket Square, a small rally of protestors gathered in a peaceful demonstration. When the police charged forward, a protestor hurled a dynamite bomb in their direction. Eight officers were killed in the mayhem, and many more wounded. Most of the defendants charged weren't even present at the scene of the explosion. It hardly mattered. Their charged crime involved inciting the assassin with their ideas of seizing power violently from the ruling class. The trial, overseen by a harsh judge steering the ship for the prosecution, turned into a sham and public spectacle.

"Clarence's career hasn't been tarnished by the Haymarket case," he told Pharo.

"Tarnished? What of the chief attorney involved with defending the damned anarchists? Don't think I forgot what Clarence Darrow told you --- the anarchists' lawyer was a decorated officer in the Civil War, and he's treated as if he has the flu plague. He lost everything: his clients, his fortune and his good name. What good came of it? And do you seriously believe that defending a man who tried to kill our president will attract a less hostile reception?"

"But it's my professional duty if I'm called upon," he said; the type of calibrated lawyerly answer that enraged Pharo.

She deflected this. "Why? Just to inspire your classmates and your law partners with your dedication --- what about the impact on me, on our family? Does that have the slightest influence on your decision? Do you accept that I have a stake in this? We'll need to build a towering wall around our house to guard us. Is that the life you want for us?"

Burford shrugged and pretended to ignore his wife's concern. But Pharo had raised a legitimate point. He might plausibly be a leading candidate to defend the man charged with the attempted assassination of President McKinley. He was the dean of the criminal bar in Buffalo, one of the most respected defense attorneys in the city. His recent defense of a widow who had shot her younger lover after he blackmailed her, had garnered much publicity culminating in a feature story in the *Strand* explaining his strategy to secure an acquittal from the jury. The deceased lover, variously described as wicked, conniving and a devious schemer, was portrayed as deserving his fate and Burford's brilliance in exposing him at his client's trial was acclaimed.

"I don't think you need to concern yourself with my involvement in this sordid crime," he told Pharo with a broad smile. "This fellow, Czolgosz, who shot President McKinley, is described in the paper as having lost his job and unemployed. I haven't met a poor defendant yet who can afford my fees."

"Shake on it," Pharo insisted. Her hand, still covered in mud from pulling roots from the garden plot, was firmly extended. She waited until Burford reluctantly shook it.

"I understand that the senior partner of my law firm showed up at the house this morning. What could he possibly want?"

"I forgot to tell you. Alex arranged for a carriage to pick both of you up at one-thirty for a partners' meeting this afternoon. He said that it's urgent."

Chapter Eight

The expert witness for the prosecution enters the courtroom with oval spectacles, a spry gait, and a padded resume. His role, bequeathed by eminent jurisprudence, is
to impart his unique wisdom to a jury of twelve ordinary
men. The defendant's lawyer's task is simply defined. To
find an equally skilled expert to present a countervailing
opinion to expunge any lingering damage, like a sandcas-
tle washed away by the spray of the ocean.

*

Signs painted on the varnished sides of horse carriages to
promote commerce --- another regressive sign of modern
life in a new century, Burford mused. This striking sign
contained the caricature of a pirate's face, a bandana
around his forehead and a cigarette dangling from his
mouth with puffs of ring-shaped smoke drifting upward.
'The sign read, PANJAMIN CIGARETTES – A SILKY
SMOOTH FLAVOUR.' Burford studied the advert as he

waited at the curb for his uncivil law partner's arrival. "Just like Proctor to call an emergency meeting and then leave him dangling like the lonely extra on the dance floor."

He added up the mistakes in the ad: the rings of smoke were perfectly concentric, forming the halo of an angel above the pirate's head; the artist had neglected to draw the pirate's lips; the nose didn't align with the chin and the ashes from the cigarette would have dropped on the pirate's striped singlet and scorched a hole through it. He checked his watch again. Fifteen minutes had passed since his arrival at the carriage station. The carriage driver, with buck gloves and an ulster, idly tended to the horses with a pail of water and straw under the wagon's canopy.

"He'll arrive shortly," Burford said, as the driver appeared primed to unstrap and unbuckle the harnesses.

He himself regretted hurrying his breakfast and skipping the luscious piece of chocolate cake that Bessie specially baked.

"Shine yer boots, Mister? Only two cents." A boy had snuck up from behind and perched himself, a brush and cloth in his left hand, at Burford's feet.

"Two cents you say?"

The boy appeared deflated. "I'll do it fors a penny if that's all you can pay."

"Oh no, I'll pay full price."

Fully committed to his work, the boy pulled out a tin of blacking and a mirror from his pocket and knelt beside Burford, dabbing blacking on the cloth.

"What you do, Mister?"

"Oh me? I'm a lawyer in the city."

"Tell me. Think I'd have the smarts be a lawyer like

you?"

"I'm quite certain you could. What's your name, son?"

"Sammy, sir."

"Well the first thing is hard work. You're already there. Read all the books you can."

"My mom reads me from the Bible at bedtime."

"Good --- and ask lots of questions. If you see a star at night, ask yourself, how did it get there? Why can I only see it at night-time? Why are there so many stars?"

"And why do some stars shine brighter than the rest?"

"Exactly, Sammy. Why do you have a mirror sticking out of your pant pocket?"

"Oh, a nice customer gave it to me. I use it fer the fellows who're a bit in the rounded way, can't see their feet over their belly. My mom taught me it's not polite to call anyone fat... You have a spot of blood on your shirt collar. Want to use my mirror to check?"

"Thank you, Sammy. Your mother is a wise woman."

Burford took the mirror and scrutinized his face. A couple of razor cuts, sagging skin on his cheeks and dark foreboding marks beneath his eyes. He needed to heed Pharo's advice and take a vacation. She continually reminded him of her cousin in Cheshire, England, with a furnished guest cottage, who extended the recently married couple an invitation to visit for the summer months. He could seize the opportunity to take a side trip to London to tour the grand Old Bailey. He'd seen the curious photograph in *The Standard* of an English barrister in his courtroom regalia of gown, wig and appropriately dark trousers.

Alex Proctor appeared at his side, panting, his shirt untucked and his wired spectacles lopsided.

"Sorry, I'm late, Burford," he said, with the conviction of a repentant pickpocket. "I expect you not to be tardy and then I'm delayed." He held a sheaf of papers tightly against his chest, as if expecting a sudden gust to blow them away.

Burford pulled a dime from his pocket and dropped it into the grateful boy's palm. "Here, Sammy," he said. "That's the best shine my boots ever had."

As they mounted the wagon, he asked Proctor. "What's the purpose of calling a meeting today? I assume that you're aware that President McKinley's been shot."

"Of course --- but I'll reserve my comments for the partners' meeting if you approve."

No further word passed between the law partners. Proctor sat reading a series of figures separated into lined columns, shielding the numbers from Burford's view with an outstretched arm. As he read, he sputtered and nodded in disapproval. When Proctor became angry, his face turned aflush, and he observed it beaming like the rosiest radish in a grocer's basket.

'This can't be a good sign,' Burford speculated.

The law firm of Proctor, Simmons and Sykes could be found on a muddy boulevard between a firehall and a saloon. The road didn't attract an established or business crowd like some of the stodgier law firms downtown. Proctor, the senior partner, handled estate and family litigation with a specialty of representing gilded, scorned wives. The mere sight of his name as counsel on a divorce paper signaled combative litigation to a philandering or scamming spouse. Burford represented the stock of criminal defendants, and Raleigh Sykes handled the firm's commercial and corporate law department. A fourth lawyer, Fig Golem, specializing in wills and trusts, shared space with the firm.

"I'm worried about our law firm's future," Alex Proctor stated in a taciturn tone at the outset of the boardroom meeting. "We all need to watch the bottom line, especially with a new associate being hired. It might have been helpful, Burford, if you'd approached us before deciding to hire a new lawyer."

"Don't worry about Mitchell," Burford answered assuredly. "He stood third in his class and he might be the brightest lawyer in the office. I'll keep him occupied. I'm expecting to be retained very soon by a wealthy businessman who's been charged in a fraud scheme as thin as an angel's bedsheet.

"Angels don't sleep," Raleigh put in mockingly.

"Precisely," Burford shot back. "Look, gentlemen, let's recognize Raleigh's true objection to young Mitchell's hiring. It's the color of his skin. He might benefit from knowing that a Negro waiter from the Plaza Restaurant, James Parker, was responsible for grabbing Leon Czolgosz by the throat and hurling him to the ground after McKinley's shooting."

Proctor denied the besmirching charge. "It's entirely a matter of profit and loss. Race is not the issue and it's unbecoming of you to accuse Raleigh. Let's confront an uncomfortable fact: we've faced a dry spell in the firm over the past few months. I've reviewed the balance sheet and accounts receivable." Proctor held up the papers in his hand. "We're mired in a slump, and we need solid paying clients, or the firm won't survive much longer."

Raleigh Sykes took over the scripted questioning. "What about your new client, this flying trapeze artist? How does he propose to pay your fees?"

Burford understood that the meeting had been called on his account.

"I have a promissory note," he replied. "I can cash it after my client joins a new carnival."

His partners shrugged in unison.

"Worthless," Raleigh declared. "Who would dare work with that circus performer again? Face it, your client is a torn shoelace, regardless of any unlikely favorable result you achieve."

"That's a cynical view of defense work."

"Cynical perhaps, but accurate," Proctor said. "A reputation soiled is forever spoiled. Look, let's get to the pressing reason for this meeting. Raleigh and I have spoken privately, and we're united in opposition to you assuming the defense of the president's shooter. It will spell an unmitigated disaster for the law firm."

"I'm grateful to learn that my partners are privately consorting against me! But let me remind both of you that I haven't been contacted to defend the culprit."

"Excellent. And let us hope that it stays that way. But if you are asked to be his lawyer, which is entirely possible, we demand that you to turn it down."

"And if I don't?" Burford asked angrily. An academic question, perhaps, but he wasn't accustomed to having his choice of cases challenged.

"Then this firm will disband, and Alex and I will be gone," Raleigh replied. "You'll have the nest to build with your educated associate."

Proctor nodded.

Burford pursed his lips and said. "While the vultures fly off. Notice taken," he added. The secretive plan to oust him, also duly noted.

The partners retired to Alex Proctor's office. The brittle tension in the meeting continued to simmer, and the discussion turned to a testy rugby match on a schoolyard that had left Raleigh missing a couple of front teeth. He flashed his open mouth like a cagey boxer unfazed by a flurry of blows. The three men leaned back on the circular white leather couch, feet up on a coffee table once owned by Benjamin Franklin, and sipped brandy from teacups.

"No court today for you, old man?" Sykes inquired. "Proctor told me it's another birthday."

"I took a relaxing day off to spend with Pharo. I wasn't expecting to be attacked for representing a non-existent client."

Proctor slapped Burford's lap. "Let's not be overly sensitive, my dear partner," he said. "We share a common interest to see each member of the firm thrive and prosper."

Raleigh Sykes' contorted face suggested that he had mistaken soap wash for wine. Proctor lifted his glass and made a toast to the American president's good health.

"Here, here!" they shouted, clanging their glasses.

A ringing bell at the entrance to the office alerted Burford and he rose to check. A runner from the courthouse handed Burford a folded note. Cases at the downtown courthouse assigned for the next day were to be adjourned. Burford rang up a clerk at the courthouse to probe the reason for the delay.

"Is it a sign of respect for the wounded president?" Burford asked.

"No, it's strictly a matter of security."

On the mayor's direction, the clerk said, an engineering crew had hastily drafted plans for a private cell area to hold Czolgosz. City officials, with the vocal support of the police chief and the warden of the local jail, recognized that the president's assailant wouldn't last more than a couple of minutes mixed with a general population of patriotic inmates. A rowdy group of angry protestors outside the jail might escalate to a violent outburst.

"I apologize for keeping you waiting. Court will resume on Wednesday," Burford informed his partners. "I have a cross-examination of a fire expert that will need to be put off. Leon Czolgosz is to be brought to the courthouse tomorrow. The presiding judge has ordered that his case will be the only one on the docket."

"I expect that he's only being cautious. With the press and an angry public, it will be pandemonium for certain. The courthouse is the last place in the world that any lawyer would want to be. I myself will remain in the office. I am negotiating a sizable settlement for my client in a divorce squabble tomorrow," Proctor added.

"Not much of a defense here for the lawyer he picks, in any event, is there?" Raleigh Sykes stated with feigned authority.

Sykes had spent as much time in the courtroom as the feeding pen on his Uncle Gus' pig farm near Albany. Proctor had appointed Sykes to be the newest partner to the firm and Burford found his haughty manner chafing. He claimed to prefer a bare-fisted duel to settle scores in conflicts rather than costly litigation that fattened the pockets of greedy trial lawyers. "And who exactly do you think you are?" Burford had asked. "Joan of Arc?"

Burford had questioned Proctor as to the precise reason that he'd strenuously advocated for Raleigh's introduction to the firm.

"I promised his uncle on his death bed. I can't break my promise, Burf," he'd replied.

"Why?" Burford asked. "Not as if he will ever know."

A point of deft sarcasm wasted.

The heated tension with Raleigh had erupted after Burford intervened to force the younger partner to dismiss a client who stipulated that a contract include a covenant barring Jews, Negroes and Italians from purchasing his golf course property. Raleigh had never forgiven him for dropping the client's fee for the firm.

Raleigh's father owned a flourishing tobacco business and provided a hefty monthly cheque to Raleigh, who therefore considered the money earned from his law practice as a bonus. He had clerked for one of the older judges on the New York Court of Appeals, who always spoke in rhythmic cadence as if reciting Tennyson, and Raleigh emulated the unsettling habit of his mentor after his clerkship ended.

"You have as much chance of winning Czolgosz's trial as punching a hole in the air," he stated now, lighting a cigarette. "The fellow was apprehended at the scene with the gun in his hand with a score of witnesses to the shooting. He was overheard claiming that he had done his duty. He was proud of the attack. It will be a straight path to the electric frying pan for Leon Czolgosz. I admit I'll be wildly cheering when it happens."

"I agree wholeheartedly," Procter chimed in. "I hope he rots in hell. McKinley was a distinguished leader and fine president. I can't say that I agreed with his politics, but what president is entirely virtuous? The country risks descending into utter chaos now. And for what *possible* gain to this fellow, Czolgosz? What do these traitors expect to achieve in the end?"

"You mean he *is* a fine president," Sykes said. "He's not gone yet." He sipped his brandy. "I feel sorry for this fellow, Wally Chapman, who owns Walbridge's Main Street store. I hear he sold the Iver Johnson revolver to Czolgosz. Perfectly legal, mind you. His wife plays croquet with Francis --- and she told her that Wally's afraid to leave their home and venture into the public."

"Does Czolgosz have a lawyer?" Burford wondered.

"There's nothing in the paper about anyone chosen to represent him." Proctor shook his head disapprovingly. "I can't imagine defending the scoundrel who shot our president." The senior partner looked directly at Bradford as a firm reminder of his earlier warning.

"We didn't take a loyalty test when we passed our law exams!" Burford exclaimed. He was ready with a lecture about the professional responsibility to represent the most loathsome and despised class of people, but he recalled his vow to his wife. "Even the president's attempted assassin deserves a defense, I suppose," he declared, absent any conviction.

He then changed the discussion to a fishing trip in northern Ontario they had planned for the end of autumn. The discussion about the attack on President McKinley was replaced with a lively debate about the frigid temperature expected on the trip and the plentiful supply of perch and bass reported to be awaiting their fishhooks.

As he left the law office, Burford encountered Fig Golem at the door, holding a damp handkerchief and patting his nose between bellowing sneezes.

"Another bad cold?" Burford asked. Fig suffered from an interminable cold and gasping cough that kept the lawyers in the office at bay. Burford often wondered how his perennially sick associate attracted any clients.

"The streets are bare this morning. Is there a civic holiday that I'm unaware of?"

"You don't know?... The president has been shot and wounded."

Golem collapsed to his knees and covered his face with the palms of his hands until he spoke. "Will he recover?"

Burford pensively stared back as he mulled the answer.

Chapter Nine

Giovanni Bocce, the owner of the Alberto Construction Company, had been requested by telegram to meet the Buffalo Superintendent of Police at his office in the downtown precinct. Bocce recognized that an order from the police, disguised as a mere request, could only be ignored at his peril. The telegram had been delivered to him, absent an explanation, by a uniformed officer at the crowded Gladstone Restaurant one block from his mistress's borrowed apartment. The circumstances understandably alarmed him. Bocce surmised that the police must have surreptitiously followed him to his girlfriend's apartment the night before and patiently waited for him to leave in the morning.

The officer didn't even bother to confirm his identity.

"Who else knows that I'm here?" he thought, frantically scanning every table in the restaurant and on the sidewalk outside of the beveled windows.

The officer exited alone. Bocce turned up the collars of his trench coat to partly obscure his face. The other patrons stared at him. He read their minds: 'What type of man is handed a telegram in a restaurant by a policeman?' 'What misdeed is he involved with?'

He read the last sentence as an intended threat: 'It is of utmost importance that you do not disclose this appointment with anyone.' He had one-and-a-half hours' notice to cancel an early morning meeting with an electrician, to wash the embedded lipstick stain from his collar and to vitiate the effects of a wild, sleepless night with jugs of coffee.

"Another, large," he said, cup in hand, to the waiter serving the next table.

The waiter turned and defiantly jerked his head to the counter, to say get it yourself!

Two minutes before the appointed time, Giovanni walked into the superintendent's office, accompanied by a detective notable for his brusque introduction and his stiff strides, like a soldier in procession. "Too many dabs of the perfume I think, *monsieur*," he commented before leaving the office. Giovanni appreciated that he reeked from the cologne that he'd splashed on his face, but he lacked the time to bathe.

"Superintendent Horace Grant." A perfunctory greeting, followed by a command. "Sit down."

Four-square boards with miniature military figurines filled the desk. "I'm a war games aficionado," the superintendent stated proudly. "It's my hobby. The army is in my blood. General Ulysses S. Grant, the commander of the Union army, was a distant cousin."

"My family lived in Italy during the war. I don't know much about it."

Bocce's remark sparked a curt rebuttal from Superintendent Grant. "You should take the time to learn about it. I lost a few relatives fighting in the Civil War for the cause of freedom." He poured two cups of black coffee and handed one to his guest.

"I'm sorry about the mysterious way that we brought you here. But I do appreciate you coming on such short notice."

The apology, cordial and apparently sincere, alleviated Giovanni's concern about trouble with the law. He proceeded to chastise the police for their slippery approach at the Gladstone Restaurant. "I didn't have much choice, did I, Superintendent?"

"I'm sure that you could have returned to the apartment to consult with Alicia about the propriety of the police request."

Giovanni raged visibly at the mention of his mistress' name.

"You must be wondering how I received a tip of your nocturnal rendezvous with Alicia. It's useful to the police to have a retired detective working as the concierge at the building."

"How dare you bring her into this! My personal affairs are no concern of the police."

"Yes, you're quite right. You alone are accountable for your perfidy. Up to a point, of course."

"Up to what point?" Bocce demanded.

"I suspect that Mrs. Bocce has an interest in your affairs."

The veiled threat hit its mark precisely. Bocce's shoulders sagged and he looked contritely at the floor.

"I may have to interrupt our meeting if I get a call about the president," the police superintendent cautioned

Giovanni. "I'll get directly to the reason for your attendance here, Mr. Bocce --- and unfortunately, there are matters of *national security* at stake and I won't be able to answer questions. I expect that you may have a few."

There was a survey map spread across a side table and the chief set his pointer at a spot in the middle.

"Come over here," he said, motioning to the table. "This is where I want it built."

The street names on the map were unfamiliar to Giovanni.

"You want what built?" he asked in bewilderment.

The superintendent's tone turned surly, like a principal to a disrespectful student.

"Please be patient and listen," he commanded. In a rapid-paced, tic-tac style, the details of the proposed project were described. Giovanni's construction company's expertise in building warehouses, factories and office buildings had resulted in a decision by city officials that he be selected --- and be paid at fair market value --- to construct a prison cell, bathroom and interview room in a secluded wooded area about twenty-five miles north of Buffalo close to the Canadian border. The brush at the site had already been cleared for access and the soil on the foundation had been tested for its firmness for construction.

"This isn't the London Bridge you'll be building. Just make sure that the walls and floor are secure and don't collapse. The prison cell will have iron bars in front. You'll have forty-eight hours to complete the operation."

"Two days? I can't meet that deadline, Superintendent. It's simply not feasible."

"My dear man, it's not optional. You'll have to make it work. We both know the identity of the high-profile prisoner that this unit will hold. I can't risk leaving him at the police precinct much longer. I've received calls from the governor and the mayor expressing their concern. If the president dies, there will be unruly, violent mobs attacking the station where he's being held prisoner. We needed soldiers and the police to beat back the horde of people congregated outside the Temple of Music anxious to lynch the anarchist."

"And what are the consequences if I refuse your offer?"

"You can leave right now if you choose, Mr. Bocce. The door is open, no-one will stop you. I'll never set my sights on you again. But when the story is told, after this terrible ordeal has ended, about which citizens stood bravely behind their leader in a time of grave crisis to this nation and which citizens cowered in shame and hid in a corner, I will certainly make it known where Giovanni Bocce..."

He was interrupted mid-sentence. Giovanni's resistance had waned, though his hands shook like a breezy sail. He preferred the label of philanderer to a traitor to his country.

"I'll agree to the terms," he declared.

"Smart decision," Superintendent Grant replied. The one-page agreement placed on the table for Giovanni to sign, contained a series of strict conditions. Any existing building contracts that the company was working on were to be temporarily shuffled aside. He could hire as many workers as the construction required but everyone associated with the project was required to be bound to a tightly worded confidentiality agreement. This provision included Giovanni and his son, Rupert, the company's vice-president.

*

Within seconds of Bocce's departure, Detective Eli Jacob rushed into Superintendent Grant's office.

"That was quick," the superintendent said. "I made a most persuasive case to Mr. Bocce."

"*En effet.* Indeed. I was standing outside the door and heard Bocce's voice quiver at your proposal, Superintendent. I couldn't hear the entire conversation though."

"You should have seen the veins in his neck bursting when I informed him that we knew about his little dalliance with Ms. Alicia Tucker."

The detective hid his chagrin at the thought of the police resorting to blackmail. He believed the police must distinguish themselves from the riffraff.

"Yes, terrified of a leak to his wife, I'm sure. Tell me, did Bocce agree to construct Camp Bogden in a couple of days?"

"Of course. He's scared to death of being branded another Benedict Arnold."

"A bit of dirty pool. But perhaps necessary under the circumstances," the detective replied. He had been assigned to lead the criminal investigation into the president's shooting. His use of the word 'perhaps' troubled the superintendent. Jacob wouldn't have been his first choice to lead the investigation, but his name had randomly turned up on the blackboard at the station to be assigned the next major case. Jacob had a reputation as a detective who fiercely advocated for the police to operate within the bounds of the law. "It's a dirty business, police work," he said. "But we must fight our enemies with one hand tied behind our back. The other hand is held back by our democratic values."

Horace Grant preferred a two-handed approach, to pummel a confession from a brutal thug like Leon Czolgosz. He'd bang the prisoner's head repeatedly against the wall of the interview room until he surrendered the names of his rogue confederates.

Eli Jacob stood out as an anomaly on the Buffalo police force. A foot shorter than any of the other detectives in the Major Crime Squad, he had barely passed the eligibility requirements. A portly, bald middle-aged man with an unmistakable French accent, the detective had lost the sight in one eye from a gun range accident. Jacob – he put the stress on the final *cob* – had studied languages at the Sorbonne and developed a mastery of English. A night owl, his curious hobbies included reading the Greek classics and the philosophers of the Enlightenment, Shakespeare, and baking bread. Jacob was often mistaken for a banker or accountant, an advantage in surveillance operations.

Jacob arrived from France at the turn of the century. As a detective in Paris, he had attended the court-martial of Alfred Dreyfus, as one of the assembly of gendarmes covering the semi-circle of the Place de Fontenoy, where a crowd of twenty thousand watched Dreyfus's humiliating court martial, the buttons from his uniform ripped off and his sword smashed in half before his sentence was pronounced. Dreyfus had been found guilty of delivering to Germany confidential documents that jeopardized the national defense of France. As the court ordered Dreyfus to be deported to the utterly remote Devil's Island for life, the surging crowd began to shout: "Death to the Jew! Judas! Death to the traitor!"

Worrying that he'd be crushed in a stampede, Jacob

had returned to his apartment by the Seine consumed with shame and fear. The vile, robust display of antisemitism; the lack of a credible case mounted against Dreyfus; the sense that he represented a convenient sacrificial lamb, propelled Jacob, himself a Jew, to uproot his wife and two children and move to America. Choosing the city of Buffalo, as his destination, rose from his fascination with the vivid story of the adventurer, Buffalo Bill Cody, read to him as a child. He hadn't realized that harsh winters, with swirling winds and mountains of snow, marked Buffalo as a destination of last resort for a man who enjoyed long contemplative walks in the open air.

"Did you interview Detective Garcy?" the police chief asked.

"Last night in his cabin on the train. He co-operated fully with my investigation, of course. I have met Garcy once before at a training course on fingerprints in Manhattan. He remembered me as the French Jewish copper. We laughed about that. Detective Garcy is blaming himself for the president being shot. I tried to assure him that the phony bandaged arm would have duped me too, but he wears his sadness like a weighted coat of armor. He's a broken man, I fear."

*

Immediately after leaving the police headquarters, Giovanni Bocce began plans for construction of the prison cell. Frosty temperatures could abort the project, but the weather co-operated.

The first step involved establishing a campsite with tents, digging a ditch for latrines and setting up a plentifully stocked kitchen. The campsite would serve as the outpost for the police officers assigned to guard the prisoner. The carpenter, masons and concrete pavers constituting the eight-man construction crew, chosen personally by Bocce, agreed to remain on site until the completion of the project. They worked long shifts until the last fleck of daylight faded. The first day was devoted to digging a trench and pouring concrete for the prison cell's foundation: three block walls of concrete, followed with a row of measured iron bars staked firmly into the ground. The next steps in the construction: dirt compacted to create a secure floor; a shallow hole dug for the prisoner's latrine and a timber roof set overhead. Bocce walked around the site holding a hammer and nails, on call as necessary, to lend a further pair of hands. President McKinley's picture, pinned to the kitchen cupboard, reminded the men of their mission.

Half a day early, Bocce returned to Buffalo to proudly announce to Superintendent Grant that the prison grounds were up and operational. Leon Czolgosz was moved to his private cell, surrounded by endless trees and shrubberies, later that night.

Chapter Ten

Detective Jacob had received strict orders from Superintendent Horace Grant to provide daily reports from Camp Bogden, the code name accorded to the prison base where Leon Czolgosz spent his captivity. The detective took charge of four separate interviews of the prisoner at hourly intervals. Determining whether the president's shooter acted alone, or as Superintendent Grant believed to be indisputable fact had been aided by a band of unscrupulous helpers, became a priority.

In his first telephoned report, Jacob inquired about President McKinley's condition. The news comforted him: the superintendent read from a confidential report, just delivered to his desk, indicating that a minor infection in the president's stomach had healed, a glimmer of an encouraging sign to his treating physicians.

"Our enemies underestimate our president's grit," Grant declared.

Conspiracy theories had sprouted around the country about the president's attack. The detective spurned them all. One speculative account promoted Czolgosz's connection to the American anarchist who assassinated the Russian Tsar. Rumors abounded that the shooter had visited a para-military group with ties to China. Another unsubstantiated theory involved a revenge attack planned by a group of disgruntled Confederate soldiers.

Unrelenting public pressure on the police to refute these expansive conspiracy theories became an unwelcome distraction for Superintendent Grant. The most pressing investigation to be actively pursued related to further arrests of Czolgosz's accomplices. The pressure mounted.

"Get to the bottom of Czolgosz's motives quickly and get me the names of every anarchist tied to his dastardly crime," Grant barked to Detective Jacob in his final instructions, before abruptly ending the call.

As lead detective, Jacob had insisted on meeting the prisoner with only a single officer taking notes. Now he studied the prisoner.

Czolgosz's handcuffs had been removed and he shook his hands, like a fish struggling with a hook, in an effort to get the blood in his arms circulating freely. Cavernous blue eyes, pallid skin and those long, flappy arms were paired with a wispy frame that looked as if it might tilt in a windstorm. He hardly fit the image of the world's most notorious criminal.

The detective began with some friendly chat. "Are you satisfied with your conditions?"

A list of complaints followed: the downpour of rain trickling onto the beveled floor of Czolgosz's cell forming a messy puddle, a request for an extra blanket ignored, the small portion of potatoes served at dinner.

Jacob struggled to understand how this callow, wispy misfit had managed to avoid the scrutiny of the vast security apparatus in place to protect President McKinley. "*C'est dommage*," he reflected. There surely would have been no *catastrophe* if Detective Eli Jacob received the assignment to guard President McKinley at the Temple of Music.

He banged the table alarming the officer at his side. "*Je suis certain.*"

Within minutes of his initial interview at a table under the main tent, Czolgosz took a pencil from Jacob and printed the reason that he killed the president.

"I killed President McKinley because I didn't believe one man should have so much service and another man should have none."

The answer puzzled the detective. "What do you mean that the president had so much service?" The prisoner stared at him in silence.

"The people of this Republic chose this president to serve them as their leader. Are you aware of that?"

The detective shifted tactics to break the prisoner's stoic silence. He stooped down from his chair and peered into Czolgosz's face. "Do you admit planning to kill President McKinley?"

"What's the use of talking about that? I killed the president. I simply did my duty."

Czolgosz treated the president's death as a foregone conclusion. The detective chose not to discourage the prisoner's boasting, but listened as he blurted out several times that he'd done his duty, a confession he had already made minutes after the shooting.

The answers varied: a duty to cure the supreme injustice of American society; a duty to prevent the exploitation of the poor; a duty to snub the gorging wealthy class and a duty to remedy the plight of the common man. He rejected the present form of government or any of its supporting institutions.

"How did you expect to achieve your goals by shooting the president?" the detective asked. For the moment, he didn't betray his deeply set anger.

"I killed the president because he was the enemy of the good people – the good working people."

"The good working people of America voted twice for William McKinley to be their president. He isn't their foe. Do you appreciate that? He had a single sworn enemy and that enemy was you, Mr. Czolgosz."

Czolgosz closed his eyes and yawned.

The detective stood and pressed his face close to his prisoner.

"Are you an anarchist?"

"Yes, sir."

Jacob listened as Czolgosz described being a student for several years of the Doctrine of Anarchy.

"Do you have any regrets about shooting the president?" the detective asked.

"I am not sorry for my crime," the prisoner casually replied, "but I'm sad that I won't be able to see my father again."

"Was it your plan to kill the president at the Temple of Music?"

"Nope. I was watching him for three or four days. I waited near the railway gate and I was there for his speech to a big crowd of people. I was looking for my chance to shoot him."

"Did you plan to shoot the president twice?"

"No, I was going to fire more shots, but this colored man jumped me and grabbed my gun."

Detective Jacob repeatedly asked Leon Czolgosz for the identity of his accomplices and confidents, but he stuck to his unwavering account that he'd acted alone.

"Who suggested that you shoot President McKinley?"

A blank stare – followed by a stern denial. He'd arrived in Buffalo a couple of days before the shooting and purchased the .32 revolver. He planned to shoot the president during his President's Day speech at the bandstand, but a tall police guard stood in front of him blocking his view. His plans to assassinate President McKinley were kept secret.

"Did you share your scheme with anyone?" the detective asked.

Another denial from the prisoner.

In long-winded speeches Czolgosz told the detective of being born in Detroit and growing up in Cleveland. He described himself as an abysmal loser in life, a failure in every job and business venture he attempted. The detective connected Czolgosz to a primary school classmate of his own, Simon, mocked by the other students as a loser for his failing grades, his slovenly grooming and for his stooped gait: Simon had ended up stalking and killing a prostitute in the port of Marseilles.

Leon Czolgosz described the events that shaped him into a hardened anarchist, from meetings with ardent believers to reading every book and pamphlet he could find, and attending several lectures by Emma Goldman, the reviled American anarchist. Detective Jacob knew from his own research into the anarchist movement that Goldman called for the assassination of all rulers. It was Goldman's fiery lectures about overthrowing government, Czolgosz explained, that had set him on his *heroic* path to kill the president at the Pan-American Exposition in Buffalo, New York.

Jacob telephoned Superintendent Grant to inform him of the prisoner's startling admission. The connection to anarchists' clubs ignited the superintendent's fury as did his mention of being a disciple of Emma Goldman. An order was issued for a complaint and warrant charging Goldman with conspiracy to murder President McKinley.

"Round up all the anarchists you can identify," the superintendent directed his staff, "and arrest them immediately."

A plan was readied to dispatch the urgent news to police stations across the country.

During the interviews, Czolgosz had complained about being in severe pain, with cramps in his stomach and his limbs where he had been repeatedly punched and stomped. His clothing was stained with swaths of dried blood from his severe beating. Both eyes had been blackened and his face was swollen.

Finishing the update to the police chief, Detective Jacob requested a doctor.

"You expect me to care about the prisoner's pain?"

"No, Superintendent Grant. But it is in our interest to present a trial with an able-bodied and healthy defendant. We don't need untreated injuries to fester and give him an excuse to complain to the judge."

He managed to overcome Grant's initial misgivings. The next morning, two policemen arrived at Camp Bogden in the company of Doctor Craig Melvin, who wore his white medical cape and carried a medical bag. The doctor introduced himself as the Head of Emergency Medicine for the Belleview Hospital and Czolgosz was escorted from his cell for examination.

Dr. Craig Melvin met with Detective Jacob to report his findings. "Your prisoner is fortunate to still be alive."

"His injuries didn't seem that serious to me. I didn't realize they were life-threatening."

"They are not, Detective Jacob. A broken nose, a few missing teeth, a broken jaw, some bruising to his chest and arms where he was attacked and a couple of black eyes. Migraine headaches that persist. I've cleaned and treated his wounds."

"*Je ne comprends*. I don't understand your conclusion that it is his good fortune to be alive."

"Czolgosz tells me he had accepted the president's defenders would pummel him to death, until he overheard the president say: 'Let no one hurt him.' President McKinley likely saved his life. Temporarily, I suppose, until his execution."

"Did Czolgosz share anything else with you?"

"Not really. He didn't seem sorry at all, if that's what you're getting at. He was less nervous than patients of mine getting a needle injected in their arm. He seemed almost relieved that the mission had been completed. I told him that President McKinley hadn't perished, and that enraged him. I had to hold myself back from punching him."

"Please remember our agreement, doctor. No-one is to know that we're keeping the prisoner at this location."

"Let me see if I have this correct. You send two officers to my home, who order me to get dressed while they stand watching me; then accompany me to this outpost in the wilderness without a word spoken on the way. And now you want me to help you keep my attendance here a secret?"

"Exactly. Look, I didn't ask to command this investigation, *monsieur le docteur*, but it is assigned to me. We shall have an angry mob at our door wanting Czolgosz's head chopped off if the news of our outpost gets out. He will not be killed on my watch. It's the safety of my officers that I must ponder. Any *imbecile* determined to kill my notorious prisoner will not be the least concerned about taking a few police officials down with him."

Dr. Melvin hesitated before answering. "I'll prepare my notes and put them in a locked drawer at my home if they're needed. The secret of Leon Czolgosz's whereabouts is safe with me."

Chapter Eleven

Friends, allies and loyal subjects of the Ottoman Empire called him Sultan Hakan; the burgeoning list of his enemies mocked him as Hakan the Wicked. The officials and uniformed guards on duty at the sultan's palace had been placed on notice that an honored guest would be feted by the sultan. The tinged sweet scent from a tanned copper incense burner with an arabesque Ottoman motif wafted through the Sultan's coral blue and white tiled Audience Chamber. A crystal chandelier, the size of a rose bush, and a gift from a European monarch, glistened brightly, surrounded by pedestals with marble statues of sultan rulers of the past century.

"Attention," a voice shouted from behind the emerald green curtain.

Sultan Hakan entered and sat in a throne adorned with golden leaves. "Bring in Planter," he commanded.

The back doors swung open, and Robert Planter marched into the chamber with a uniformed guard on each side. In his drab grey vest and matching grey bowtie, the guest bowed his head deferentially to his exalted host, then sat upright on an Egyptian mat in front of the sultan, his arms perfectly folded, and legs crossed.

The Sultan's arms opened into a fashioned embrace. "Robert Planter, my dear Cana...dian friend, how are you?" Hakan's English improved dramatically on each visit, the result of daily lessons, but he struggled to say the word 'Canadian' in his rapturous greeting to his visitor.

"Robert, what good *news* do you bring me today?"

Planter understood 'news' to be a code word for a delivery of an impressive cache of weapons --- guns, knives, cannons and munition. He used the alias Robert Planter to disguise his shadow identity. A set of official documents for his alter ego was secreted in an inside jacket pocket. He had served as a reliable arms merchant for the Sultan for several years, bringing weaponry to assist the sultan's efforts to defeat the militant uprisings of rebel factions seeking to chip away parts of the Ottoman empire. In the latest skirmish, a restocking of arms was needed to defuse dissent in Syria.

"I have a boat filled with the merchandise you requested. It's secured at the harbor in Istanbul, ready for pick-up, Sultan. My men are waiting to assist with the delivery."

"Planter, you have made the sultan a happy man today. You will be richly rewarded, my valued friend... as always." He snapped a finger at an assistant, signaling him to bring the salver of gold bars to complete the transaction.

His guest placed the treasure into a satchel. The sultan clapped twice, and a pair of burly guards appeared, lifting the satchel and standing beside Planter.

"My guards will carry the gold to your boat. Perhaps

you can stay for the night at the palace and share the lovely fruits of my harem."

"I thank you, Sultan Hakan, but I must return to my business in Canada. My ship leaves to cross the Straits of Bosporus this afternoon." Planter had arranged to make a call on the telephone to Ottawa from the palace before he embarked.

"Tell me, Robert. Have you heard about the surprise attack on President McKinley? The president has been shot twice. He's lucky to be alive." The sultan laughed in a snide, mocking tone. "Is this the way a grand imperial power protects its president?"

"How do you know about the attack on the president, Sultan?" his visitor asked.

"My counsellors showed me the message received in the palace. The sultans residing in this palace have a long history using the telegraph machine... Have a safe voyage, Robert," the sultan declared, waving his hand. "Chagatai will escort you out."

A man emerged, lurking in the shadows of the chamber, dressed in black and brandishing a dagger and jeweled handle in his waistband.

"Chagatai!"

"Hello, Planter." The two men tightly embraced and departed the sultan's Audience Chamber.

Chagatai was the head of the intricate spy network Sultan Hakan had created to handle the menacing threat to the Ottoman Empire. Chagatai and the Canadian shared a similar ruthless constitution. *Target, search and destroy.* The Ottoman spymaster had tutored his Canadian pupil on the critical stages of being a successful spy: Target: Any enemy, opponent or perceived opponent of the regime;

Search: Utilize reliable informants to track targets and follow up with surveillance and capture; Destroy: Extract information by torture to identify additional targets and eliminate original target.

On his arrival at the throne room, the spymaster requested permission from the sultan to meet privately with Robert Planter. As they walked down a wide, velvet carpeted staircase, Planter noticed a deep cut on Chagatai's left cheek near his left eye.

"The sultan appeared pleased with my visit."

"Very pleased. He only regrets that you cannot spend the night at the palace. Juliet inquired about you," Chagatai said.

"Ah, yes, Juliet...the harlot intrigued me. She is different from the other girls in the harem. Fair-skinned, golden tresses, aristocratic bearing and an English accent."

Chagatai opened a door and ushered Planter into a stately office at the front of the palace, with a polished desk and two bronzed chairs covered with embroidered pillows. Photographs of the sultan on his exotic travels lined a wall.

"Juliet is quite unique, you're right about that, my friend. She is originally from Australia and was touring the country alone when my men noticed her in Bodrum. The sultan had requested a blonde girl for his harem. My men tricked her to get into their car as she walked to the Castle of St. Peter. She was fortunate to be brought to the sultan's harem," Chagatai added.

"Why?" Planter asked.

"The Castle of St. Peter is an Ottoman prison."

Planter's eyes drifted to the window and the guards carrying his satchel. "What is so pressing that you needed to speak to me, Chagatai?"

"Listen to me, Planter. I'm not as optimistic as Sultan Hakan about the United States being hobbled. The attack on the president will shake up the world order. A sleeping giant has been awakened. It's not an ideal time to be secretly shipping arms to our empire and upset the Americans. The sultan can't afford to lose you as his valued supplier. My advice to you is to keep a low profile. I'll let you know when it's safe to continue your enterprise."

Chapter Twelve

The abbreviated morning session of the House of Commons had a single item on the agenda: an address by the Prime Minister regarding the shooting of President William McKinley.

Wilfred Laurier rose to speak earnest, heartfelt words, flowing in his customary smooth cadence. Over the course of years, Canada's leader had earned an unembellished reputation for oratorical flair. His international rivals could fit on a park bench.

"It is with a solemn heart that I address you about the tragic events at the Pan-American Exposition. I have sent a message to President McKinley extending him our country's fondest wishes and a hasty recovery from his injuries." Laurier paused for a sip of water. "We must never forget," he continued, "that the United States is our most durable and reliable ally, along with England, and that a vicious and unprovoked attack on its leader of government is an attack on the Dominion of Canada. The firm lesson from recent events in Buffalo we must carry is that we must be guarded and vigilant, for as government officials, we continue to be on the front lines of attack. The shooting of President McKinley has caused me great personal consternation as a fellow leader and a friend."

The Prime Minister pointed to Borden Tupper and Martin Beliveau seated at his side. "I particularly wish to commend the dedicated bravery of Canada's Governor General and our Minister of Railways who were present at the Temple of Music, in the near vicinity of this calamitous shooting. Both men conducted themselves with great distinction by aiding and comforting President McKinley. Canadians are rightly proud of the exemplary actions of our government officials."

"Hip, hip, hurrah!" A spontaneous cheer erupted from the back rows.

Members of Parliament streamed towards Martin at the close of the session, clapping him on the back and congratulating him until he had a sudden desire to flee the parliamentary chamber.

Beliveau had woken that morning nauseated, and the sick feeling in his stomach only increased after Laurier's undeserved tribute. Newspapers around the world had carried a drawing depicting Martin resolutely helping to carry President McKinley to the ambulance. His name and title appeared in the caption.

Borden Tupper, genuinely worthy of praise and commendation, according to Martin, heaped praise instead on the railways minister. The Governor General rushed to the President after the shooting, with the prisoner's attacker thwarted from further harm. He held McKinley's hand offering him soothing words of comfort --- whereas Beliveau had stood frozen for several seconds, in shock after the two gunshots were fired. As Czolgosz was led away, his face bloodied and bruised, he passed within a couple of feet of Martin. Their eyes met briefly and Czolgosz sneered at him with cold contempt.

The *Toronto Globe's* headline story that morning revealed Leon Czolgosz's declaration that he was an anarchist. The piece carried the assassin's story as recounted to the police. One item stood out for Martin --- Czolgosz described bringing a gun to the Esplanade on the day of the President's speech.

Martin recognized instantly that his suitability for a targeted assassination had been considered by Czolgosz. He must have determined that a meagre Minister of Railways from Canada would fail to garner the kind of worldwide attention an American president would command. The line on his tombstone should properly read: 'Saved in his Lifetime by Obscurity.'

*

In the afternoon, Laurier requested a private conference with the Minister at his official residence. A flurry of requests from the media for interviews had all been diverted to Borden Tupper, and Martin had a couple of hours to spare. Desperately needing time on his own, he clambered carefully down the rocky cliff behind Parliament and the Supreme Court building to reach the bank of the Ottawa River. A soft winding path guided him along the twisting shoreline. As he walked, he focused on the dim brick houses, gothic churches and Kingston limestone buildings across the river in Quebec and pondered the treacherous climb back up the hill that discouraged fellow walkers from attempting this excursion.

Descending into the still valley below, Martin felt alone in the universe. A decision loomed that could seal his doomed political fate and destroy the Beliveau name. Should he do the morally correct thing and acknowledge to the Prime Minister that he could have prevented President McKinley's shooting? A simple flicker of his wrist could have called the attention of the detective guarding the president and assured a quick apprehension and arrest of the perpetrator. Martin hesitated over the impulse to confession, knowing that he must heed the repercussions to Canada's future relations with its southern neighbor, and not wanting to jeopardize the harmonious co-existence that bonded the two countries.

He had failed at the critical moment, effectively aiding and abetting Czolgosz' s grotesque crime. His political adversaries might credibly argue that Martin had behaved no differently than a co-conspirator. But it would be Laurier's untenable responsibility to send the harmful message to the American vice-president. Foreign relations between the two nations would necessarily suffer.

The negative consequences of disclosure must override his sense of honor. Martin resolved that the murky storm must be permitted to pass. Recalling Lincoln's saying, he knew he must protect Canada's interests at all costs. He'd lie if necessary, even to his friend and political leader.

In the distance, someone was waving in his direction. He looked behind to see who was following, but there was no-one. The waving person continued to approach, her physical features familiar. It was his unwelcome suitor, the reporter from the *Brooklyn Daily Eagle*. She flagged him to stop.

"Minister Beliveau! Hello! By good fortune, a couple of your government colleagues tipped me off to your whereabouts."

"I'm on my way to meet with the prime minister. Why did you seek me out?"

If Czolgosz had advised the Buffalo police about his encounter with a Canadian minister, Willow Hooper would likely be aware of the details. Martin listened to the reasons for his interview.

"Our paper is doing a feature story on you, Minister, and I'd like to interview you about your background. Are you married? Do you have children? Where did you grow up? What are your hobbies?"

"Anything else?"

"Our readers will be interested, of course, in everything that happened at the Temple of Music. You've become quite famous in America, Minister Beliveau. You were so brave helping our president after he was shot."

"Brave?" But he was satisfied that he wasn't even remotely implicated in wrongdoing. "I will agree to an interview in a couple of hours," Martin said. "Wait in the lobby of the Parliament building and you'll be brought to my office. I will not agree, however, to be asked about any of the events at the Temple of Music."

"We can save that for a follow-up story," Hooper said.

Martin turned from the persistent *Brooklyn Daily Eagle* reporter and set off to meet with Laurier, arriving at the Prime Minister's office more resolute than ever upon secrecy.

Appearing distracted, Laurier stood gazing out the window and ignored Martin's mild question about purchasing ice skates for the upcoming winter skate along the Rideau Canal. "Martin," he said, "I'm about to share some highly sensitive information with you. I need your word that you'll keep it confidential, even from your colleagues."

"You have my word, Prime Minister."

"Good. Early this morning I received a somber call from Vice-President Roosevelt, who advised me that the physicians have discovered an infection in the President's stomach and are unable to stop it spreading through his body. The effect will, of course, be disastrous for McKinley's health. I commiserated with Teddy about his compatriot's dire condition. I also guaranteed that I'd keep it private, although he agreed that I could share it with you, Martin. You and Tupper are highly regarded by the vice-president. He looks forward to thanking you in person for your commendable actions with President McKinley."

Martin Beliveau looked down at his trembling hands. "Prime Minister, I'll be seeking your permission to attend Leon Czolgosz's murder trial."

"Newspapers will cover the trial extensively. Reporters will seek you out for interviews. Why do you need to be in the courtroom?"

"I was on the ground at the time that McKinley was shot. It has affected me deeply."

"Precisely the reason to stay as far from the trial as possible. It's an unusual request, Martin... Is there something that you're keeping from me?"

"Not at all. I'd like to be present when the jury declares the President's murderer guilty." He clenched his fists to stop their trembling betrayal.

"Let's put your request off to another day, Martin. I will defer to your wishes, but it's entirely possible that you and the Governor General may be prosecution witnesses. I have another piece of grim news to share. The Canadian consul general to Scotland died in his sleep last night. Eighty-two, he lived a full life. Please give some thought to his replacement. I'll be soliciting suggestions from the rest of the Cabinet."

Chapter Thirteen

For an early lesson in Mitchell Harris's fledgling apprenticeship, Burford Simmons had summed up the secret of great advocacy in one succinct sentence: "You must artfully persuade your audience that a nail is a screw." His mentor's point, delivered with a curve of a smile, conveyed the labouring challenge of the trial lawyer, confronted by damning evidence, to proceed undaunted and with authority, to obtain the client's desired result. Mitchell felt chagrined, but the senior lawyer reassured him. "One day, a jury will return a verdict that will dismay you, and your head will continue to shake in wonder as your elated client embraces you tightly. You will have convinced the bunch of them that a nail is a screw."

After defending one trial where the magic of turning a nail into a screw eluded him, Mitchel had attended church. In the basement of the Michigan Street Baptist Church, Pastor Hutch had asked Mitchell, a regular congregant of his church, to run an after-school series for the boys' club. "The boys all admire and look up to you." The pastor wanted the boys' club modelled after the Club of Colored Women at the church. Led by the indefatigable effort of a community organizer, Mary Talbert, the women's club had campaigned to include a Negro Exhibit at the Pan American Exposition, showcasing the strides of progress of Negroes in the decades since Emancipation.

"This won't be any Aunt Jemima booth," Mary had promised Pastor Hutch, referring to the booth at the Chicago World's Fair with a mammy in an apron and red bandana, gleeful and flipping pancakes.

Mitchell's first guest to the boys' club was W.E.B. Dubois, who brought his photographs and charts of the American Negro Exhibit displayed at the 1900 Paris exposition. The boys learned of Negro business men in the United States who were grocers, bankers, undertakers and druggists.

James Parker, the towering, gangly waiter working at the Plaza Restaurant during the Exposition, had made a glowing second choice for the program at the boys' club. He had heroically subdued the president's shooter at the Temple of Music and prevented further carnage.

After his talk, one of the boys received permission to ask Parker a question.

"What are you going to do now?" the boy inquired.

"Do? Nothing," came the modest reply. "Ain't I working?"

Mitchell's third foray into church programming came about by chance. Alex Proctor had created a bulletin board in the office kitchen to post interesting lectures and programs for the lawyers. One program devoted to mob law attracted Mitchell's interest. The description read:

Conference on Mob Law at Chautauqua

Chautauqua, September 10 – A conference will be held here Sept. 13-14, at which recent manifestations of the mob spirit in this country will be discussed. Men of note will deliver addresses on feud assassinations, lynching, labor lots, their cause, and the means to stamp them out.

Mitchell had read the frequent reports of lynching in the southern states, of Negro men being hauled like wild creatures to dank forests by festering mobs and hung by their necks as the mob sportingly cheered on the spectacle. The victory of the Union soldiers and the end of slavery had not halted the throes of oppression. Mitchell had just read a book by the great emancipator, Frederick Douglass, and felt that any conference run by 'men of note' genuinely searching for a solution to end lynching must qualify as a worthy program for his church boys' club.

Pastor Hutch warmed to the idea immediately. A special Sunday church drive raised enough money to hire a couple of wagons to take the boys to Chautauqua, a lakeside resort town in western New York and to book rooms at The Athenaeum Hotel. Eight boys eagerly signed up for the trip with their parents' permission and brought their Sunday best to wear at the conference. The joyful mood during the ride began with the boys singing hymns, guided by Hutch's mellifluous harmonica. Hand pies and muffins dripping with melted butter prepared by the church's Sisterhood group were gobbled up.

"Do you think they'll show pictures of a lynching?" one of the boys anxiously asked Mitchell.

"I don't think so, Jimmy. Civilized men and women don't need a photograph to move them to action."

At the ticket counter, a man in a cream white suit with an oblong face, bushy eyebrows and a shiny bald head shaped like an egg, approached Mitchell and Hutch.

"You the one in charge here?" he asked Hutch with a pronounced southern drawl.

"Yes I am. Is there a problem?"

"My name is Furnifold James --- I'm one of the organizers of this mob conference." He spoke sternly. "You've brought a bunch of Negro children with you. I believe that it's a mockery of the serious topics we're going to be examining here. I think you should leave right now."

"Thank you, Mr. James. I appreciate your concern, but it's misplaced. These are mature young men who grasp the important nature of this program. You see Wilbur here," he said, pointing to a boy across from him. "His great uncle was horse-whipped to death by a sharecropper in Macon, Georgia. The boy standing beside him had two cousins lynched in New Orleans. They were strung up close enough to hold hands as they were hanged together. Booker," he said, "tell Mr. James about your older brother Gatesby's fate in North Carolina."

"Yessir... Gatesby was a reporter at a colored paper, *The Daily Record*. A clan of men burned the building and shot my brother in the back when they chased after him. My daddy and me found my brother's body on the bank of the Cape Fear River. We brought Gatesby home to bury him."

"Those white rioters massacred scores of Negro men in Wilmington that day," the pastor steamed. He turned abruptly towards the ticket counter. "Now Mitchell. Please purchase our conference tickets."

Mitchell and Pastor Hutch escorted the boys into the hall and took their seats in the front row. Mitchell stood and scanned the full room. By his count, they were the only Negroes present.

A couple of men jabbed at Mitchell and told him to sit down. Furnifold James, Hutch's words still stinging, shook his fist in the pastor's direction.

The first speaker, John Temple Gravestone, from the city of Atlanta, waited by the lectern as Hugh Lording, the conference chair, introduced him:

"Permit me to say a few words before Mr. Gravestone starts his talk. The alarming increase of mob spirit gives intense national importance to this conference. The national standing of the speakers ensures sane and rational treatment, and the fair play shown in the free-for-all discussions at Chautauqua gives opportunity for honest statement of the most diverse views."

Hutch shot a concerned look at Mitchell. Atlanta had been the site of Grant's great conquest of the Confederate army. The burning, ravaged city symbolized the destruction of the southern dream for domination. The topic of Gravestone's address, 'The mob spirit of the south,' might provide legitimate cover to the inhumane act of lynching.

"We all know that lynching is a crime." Gravestone spoke in a booming sepulchral voice augmented by a wagging finger. "But it is justified by the crime which provokes it."

A smattering of applause in the second and third rows followed.

Mitchell exchanged an ornery stare with Furnifold James seated a few rows behind him. He recalled the admonition of Frederick Douglass that with freedom, there is a mountain of prejudice to keep the Negro down.

The speaker continued: "Lynching will never be discontinued until that crime is eliminated. The response to lynching must be the elimination of criminal assault."

Mitchell correctly predicted the insipid solution suggested by the racist speaker.

"The only way that we're going to achieve that, is by the separation of the two races in the United States."

Mitchell found himself on his feet, waving his right hand incessantly, demanding to be heard. "May I be permitted to ask a question? You did promise free-for-all discussions." He could hear a couple of men complaining about the uppity Negro.

"Go ahead," Gravestone declared in a resigned voice. "I don't expect my talk is too popular with your folk. I don't mean any offence."

"None taken, sir. But I do want to know if you'd support the lynching of a Caucasian man who assaults a Negro woman. If we follow the line of logic directly."

"I just don't think you're being realistic, son."

Mitchell remained undeterred. "Sir, can we agree for the moment that it is one spoiled apple in the barrel who beats the Negro woman. You must acknowledge that every group known to humankind suffers from spoiled apples in its membership. Would you approve if the boys' group from my church sitting here, should acquire a rope, haul the offender to the woods and hang him on a tree until he's pronounced dead?"

The murmuring and angry chatter in the hall became notable. "How does it feel to be a problem?" a woman at the back shouted.

"I know excellent colored men in Atlanta, young man," Gravestone said angrily.

"It's the ballot of the colored man that scares men like you, Mr. Gravestone. A lynched colored is one less vote cast."

Catcalls humming with rage swelled around the rim of the hall. A minute or so passed and then a couple of burly men in uniforms approached Mitchell in the front row and grabbed him by each arm.

"You're going to have to leave the hall," the larger one said. "You're being disruptive to this conference."

"Then we're all leaving together," Pastor Hutch interjected. "Boys, we will follow Mitchell out and leave this room quietly, and with our heads held high. Does everyone understand?"

The boys nodded in unison.

"Separation of the two races!" Mitchell exclaimed after returning to the wagon. "Doesn't this fool recognize that the year is 1901 and that his side lost the war?"

"The war is not over, Mitchell, according to his racist leanings. He doesn't accept the surrender of the Confederates. The Negro travels on a separate road, never crossing the line."

"What a colossal waste of time. I'm sorry, Pastor Hutch. I've made a mess of things."

"On the contrary, Mitchell. You've given every one of the boys in the church group a memorable lesson about standing up to negro baiting. Your dear father Rufus, God rest his soul, never had the chance to resist racial injustice. You showed mighty courage with those folks. It might be blasphemous for a preacher to say, but right now I think Jesus got this wrong. *The meek shall never inherit the earth.*"

Just then, Booker approached, his shirt sleeves peeking out of his black three buttoned jacket, adorned with a white scarf and smartly placed pocket square. His eyes were brooding and still, a curtain to the sadness stirring inside.

"This was Gatesby's suit, Pastor Hutch," he said dolefully.

"I'm proud of you, Booker. That was plenty righteous to tell that story about your brother back there." The pastor had performed two of the funerals for the young men slaughtered in Wilmington.

"You'll sit next to me on the wagon, Booker," the pastor said, cupping his hand over the boy's shoulder.

Chapter Fourteen

Tucked beneath a grassy heath in the rolling hills of the Poconos beside a still and glistening lake is a dining room, boathouse and a row of log cabins known as Camp Falls Be-Leaf. Every year, on the first Tuesday of July, hordes of boys and girls merrily descend on the camp. After the early morning bugle call and nourishing breakfast, the campers disband into small groups for outdoor daily classes. Each lesson is dedicated to erode the myths milling about like shiny counterfeit coins: one religion is superior to the others; a person's skin color shapes character; avarice and greed are the optimal paths to riches; words expressed in rancor cause no pain and a person charged by the police with a crime is presumed and plainly guilty. "Why would the police charge an innocent man?" one cherubic camper eagerly asked. "It's a waste of time." "To err is human," was the perceptive response.

*

They lingered on the curb of the road to check for any sign of being followed. A couple of vagrant pigeons floated by, landing on a puddle in a muffled splash. The electrical streetlight outside the vacant shop illuminated the smokey grey facade of the building; the silhouette of an empty table could be discerned through the ribs of the windowpane.

The assembled group included the twin brothers, Goss and Ludwig, and two women younger by a couple of years, Candice and Marie. At Marie's direction, they crossed the barren road and slipped in through an unlocked back door.

A burning candle carried by Goss provided enough light to guide the four young comrades to the printing press. Its purchase the previous year had followed a stirring debate about fiscal responsibility and fascist symbolism. Practicality had prevailed. A new model of press, it had depleted half of their working budget for the year. But their message of stifling government oppression reached its targeted sympathetic audience. The membership of their anarchist den doubled to a list of one hundred and fifty within a couple of months. On this night, however, their burgeoning membership mattered little to the huddled group. They had congregated on this late night for the urgent business of deciding the future of the *Buffalo Anarchist Wayfarer*, their monthly magazine covering the writings and speeches of anarchists from around the world. A resolution to temporarily suspend publication passed without a hint of dissent and no-one bothered to discuss a date to publish again. They resolved to disband their association and to adopt the safe course of leaving Buffalo for different regions across the country. They were likely gathering for the last time.

Leon Czolgosz! Each member of the group recognized that Leon Czolgosz's affiliation with known anarchists prior to the president's shooting branded them equally as traitors and pariahs in their community. The governor of New York had announced his goal of ridding the state of every anarchist. They now wore the sign of Judas pasted onto their foreheads. Old friends became foes and even family members couldn't be trusted not to turn them in. Around the country, reports were spreading of fellow anarchists under siege by law enforcement, the focus of the spewing anger of the nation which held their movement accountable for the president's attack. The headline in the morning newspaper was foreboding: "*Talk of a Plot – Was Emma Goldman at Buffalo with Czolgosz?*"

The decision to meet had resulted from a conversation fortuitously overheard by Ludwig that morning at his barbershop. As he lay prone in the barber's chair, face masked in creamy lather, Ludwig heard the uniformed policeman in the next chair boasting of plans for a series of raids on anarchist mobs in a couple of days. Ludwig watched him spit in his hand and brush it through his hair for a sheen before donning his cap.

Marie, the lead columnist for the *Wayfarer*, stacked the back issues of the magazine in a couple of cardboard boxes; Goss helped her carry the boxes from the shop.

"Halt right there. On the ground with your hands behind your heads. Now!"

Six police officers brandishing their guns pushed Marie and the others face-first to the ground, handcuffed them tightly behind their backs, and heaved them into the back of a police wagon like coal being shoveled into the belly of a ship. The cardboard boxes were seized and transported to the wagon for evidence. One of the officers snickered as he pulled the canvas aside and peered into the back. Ludwig recognized him as the policeman from the barbershop and knew that they'd been set up.

"What are we being arrested for?" Marie protested.

"You're all dirty traitors," the officer said.

A booming explosion followed, and the wagon shook, almost toppling over to its side. "What in the dickens was that?" one of the uniformed officers asked in disbelief. He patted his body to check for injuries.

Across the street, the vacated shop had vanished, reduced to smoldering rubble and ashes.

Marie looked through the back of the wagon at the wreckage, feeling no relief that her life had been spared by seconds. No-one in the group appeared elated. They had survived, but the venom of their enemies would not subside, and the threat of a deadly attack loomed in the days, weeks, and months ahead. They were hunted prey.

Chapter Fifteen

In his role as Mitchell's mentor, Burford had cautioned against descending into personal attacks against the wayward prosecutor. Unseemly, undisciplined, and clouding the court record, it served no useful purpose. For the unreasonable prosecutor, the accusation of being an ostrich with his head buried in the sand was regrettable. For the excessively argumentative adversary, the claim that the prosecutor was treating the court like a stamp and trading club, quibbling over the value of vintage stamps, was avoidable. Burford advised a firm and respectful approach, citing the following example: "The prosecutor's position is untenable and without legal precedent."

*

Grey plumes of clouds arched over the sky of Buffalo like a blanket. The bleak grey canvas filled the early morning, interspersed with pattering rainfall. Sparkles of sunshine arrived as the day's second act, matching the lifting mood of the bustling city. The rhythm of life returned.

The president was convalescing, his recovery expected and reports of the police swooping up and arresting anarchists, like plague-carrying mutants, calmed fears of another attack. Government buildings and schools re-opened; croquet teams returned to compete at lawn clubs; bakeries filled their shelves with apple pie and peach cake with whipped cream; fishmongers haggled with customers about the price of cod; swooning lovers danced in dimly lit living rooms to phonographs playing Viennese waltzes.

In front of the oval cathedral doors of the Gothic Tudor courthouse, Burford Simmons bounced anxiously from side to side, waiting to be the first lawyer admitted entry.

"Can't wait for court to resume, Mr. Simmons. I share your bounding enthusiasm." The speaker's familiar haggard voice placed the lawyer on guard.

Caleb, whose rotund-shaped hips wobbled like a penguin as he climbed the courthouse steps, acquired gossip like a scavenger picking through trash for lost treasures. His imposing briefcase might as easily be filled with samples of cotton as law books. Lawyers frequenting the courthouse knew the garrulous Caleb didn't represent any clients or defend a single trial, he only paced the courthouse accumulating tidbits from the lawyers and court staff he encountered.

"Here comes Caleb the Crab," watchful counsel would exclaim, as Caleb plodded and approached, waving his slinky arms like pincers.

"Any word on the lawyer acting for Czolgosz?" he asked with a curious grin.

"I have no idea," Burford replied warily.

"Well, you must let me know if you learn the lawyer's identity for the plum case. Who knows? He might choose you." Caleb studied the lawyer for clues of any tell. "Your client will be appearing before Judge Mirth on the second floor. I checked the court docket yesterday."

Judge Pontius Mirth, an ill-fitting name for a jaundiced jurist devoid of any sense of humor, wouldn't be Burford's first choice for this case. Nor the second, third or fourth choice either. In one of their early cases, at a stirring juncture of a jury address, Burford's peroration had been followed by rain pelting against the window, and he waved a hand towards it, saying, "You see, God is signaling that he agrees with me." But Judge Mirth interrupted the jurors' laughter. "Mr. Simmons," he said in a shrill intonation, "please restrict your comments to the evidence and avoid mention of the deity. This jury is judging your client's case, not God."

Burford watched Mitchell escort the client and his chagrined mother to a bench outside the courtroom and went to greet them.

The mother appealed to him. "Please, Mr. Simmons, don't let them put Wilbert in jail. He's a good boy."

Wilbert Clay, the nineteen-year-old client, had been arrested after attempting to steal a couple of chickens from the farm owned by a church vicar. He ran like a gazelle from the chicken coup with the chickens noisily flapping their wings. The farmer's two sons, panting and out of breath, caught up with him half a mile from the farm and tackled him to the ground.

"There sure are some nice windows here," Wilbert said, staring at the stained-glass windows adorning the east side of the courthouse.

Burford agreed. "That's right, Wilbert. And in a few minutes the judge will start court and you will plead guilty to theft. Mitchell will be there to help. I'll be there too. Remember what I told you."

"Sit there and listen like I'm in the front row in class," he said. "Did I say that right, Mr. Simmons?"

"An excellent effort, Wilbert," the lawyer replied.

Mitchell Harris had prepared diligently for the client's sentencing hearing. "Every lawyer has a first case," Burford reminded him. He described his own experience where a haughty prosecutor neglected to have his client identified as the offender. "It was my easiest win," he stated.

Judge Mirth peppered Mitchell with questions during his submissions. "Shouldn't your client have been in school at the time of the theft?"

"That's correct, Judge."

"Well, I certainly take a harsh view of your client's conduct. This was a planned and deliberate theft and I don't detect a hint of remorse from this young man."

Mitchell called Wilbert's mother, Louisa, as his witness.

"Louisa, what grade is Mitchell in at school?"

"He's in the tenth grade. My son is a slow learner. School's hard for him. He does his homework, but he can't keep up with the other boys and girls in his class."

"Does he perform any work?"

"He got a summer job stocking grocery goods next summer. Wilbert has long arms and can reach the top shelf."

"Where's Wilbert's father?"

"I made him leave a few years ago. He used to whip

Wilbert with his strap all over his body. I tried to stop him, but he threw me to the ground. One day I came home from work and Wilbert's head was bleeding bad. He told me that his father hit him with a brick. I took my gun from under my mattress and I told his father to get out of the house. I would have shot him if he didn't go. Right in his temple. My papa taught me to shoot."

"Did your son change after that beating?"

"He was never the same." Tears flowed down her cheeks.

"Let me show you a couple of pictures, and you tell Judge Mirth if you can recognize them." Mitchell placed the pictures on the table at the witness stand.

"They're pictures of my boy. The first one here shows the deep welts on his back. You can see the mark on the other picture where the brick hit the back of Wilbert's head and made a hole."

Judge Mirth held up the pictures. "Why did he need to steal the chickens, Mrs. Clay?" he asked.

"He was trying to help put food on the table, Judge. It was a struggle to survive when it was just the two of us. I have a job cleaning at the hospital, but I have a house to keep and I need to pay for Wilbert's extra care."

"It's still not an excuse to steal."

"I know that, sir. I believe that my son has learned a valuable lesson and understands." Wilbert nodded in agreement as she spoke.

"I'll listen to Mr. Winkler's submissions on behalf of the prosecution, but I'm inclined to give this young man a chance and sentence him to probation." Burford marveled at the judge's sudden turn, like a sail catching a pocket of wind, shifting in an opposite direction.

Wilbert embraced his lawyers outside the courtroom.

The senior counsel warmly congratulated his young associate.

"You managed to achieve something from Judge Pontius Mirth in less than an hour that has eluded me for over ten years."

"What's that?"

"Justice," he declared. "Remember that there are hills and valleys in our profession. Resist basking in the glory of your wins or despairing in those crashing moments of defeat."

"Will you share a pint of lager at the pub? Does that meet your obligatory standard?"

"Absolutely," he replied. "And I'm gladly buying a round of drinks to celebrate."

*

"Is that you, John?"

"Yes, it is, Mister President. It's me, John Garcy."

"Let me turn around now and see you."

"Be careful, William," his wife Ida interceded softly.

A couple of attendants rushed to the president's bedside to gently roll him over. Detective Garcy had received an unexpected telephone call at his hotel requesting his attendance at Milburn House in the upstairs bedroom where President McKinley convalesced. He discovered a room full of attendants, nurses and doctors when he arrived. Vice-president Roosevelt stood to the side with George Cortelyou. A chaplain hovered over the president's bedside reciting hymns of prayer. The president appeared gravely ill.

The president clasped a hand around Garcy's wrist.

"The surgeons couldn't remove one of the bullets," he said in a muffled whisper. "The doctors are worried about the possible damage to my vital organs. Looks like I'll be keeping a souvenir from the Pan-American Exposition for the rest of my life." The president's attempt at laughter converted to a choking sound. "Sorry about that. How are you managing, Detective Garcy?"

"Perfectly fine, sir. But I do miss our checkers matches."

"I miss them too. I miss ice cream more! Listen here, it's been reported to me by my personal secretary that you're taking this shooting quite hard and blaming yourself."

Garcy glanced toward Ida's steely gaze.

"I'll have none of this nonsense. Do you hear me?"

"Yes, Mister President, but if only I..."

"Shush, and that's a direct order from your president. I've dictated a letter that I've asked Ida to share with you. It will be delivered to the captain of the Greenpoint police station tomorrow. Ida, please read my letter to John."

Ida unfolded the piece of paper in her lap, her eyes straying from the detective as she read:

Dear Captain Williams,

I am writing to you in my capacity as the President of the United States. I had the distinct privilege to cross our wonderful country by train and greet thousands of its patriotic citizens from all walks of life. During the many days of my trip, I have enjoyed the company of Detective John Garcy, a fine detective under your command. The admirable and exceedingly pleasant detective has served me as the head of my security team with consummate dedication, proficiency and bountiful skill. As your nation's president, I give Detective Garcy my highest commendation.

Yours sincerely,

President William McKinley

Attendants hurried again to his bedside as the president coughed again, a racking sound.

"You'll have to excuse me, John." His voice faded to a grainy whisper.

"I'm weary and do need my rest. Please give my best wishes to your lovely wife."

Garcy turned to leave in silence, like a doleful moment in a church service. There were no fond farewells or wishes of good tidings. Cortelyou doffed his hat as he passed and the gruff vice president turned his back. Garcy reproached himself for failing to thank McKinley. He recognized that there wouldn't be a second opportunity.

Chapter Sixteen

The driver stopped the hansom cab on the tree-lined boulevard of Johnson Park to let his elderly passenger, elegantly dressed in a top hat and cape coat, descend. The passenger asked the driver to wait for him: "My business here will occupy no more than a quarter of an hour."

Upstairs, Burford Simmons wiped the beads of sweat from his face with a towel after completing his morning regimen of stretching and strenuous exercise in his bedroom. He dipped his face in a basin of cold water.

Pharo shouted from below, "Burf, come downstairs at once!"

He bounded down the set of stars, still in a jersey singlet and loose flannel bags.

She was draped in a luxurious kimono, a simmering cup of coffee in her hand. "There's a guest in the living room to see you," Pharo said.

"Please don't keep me in suspense. Did this mysterious guest provide a name?"

"He told Bessie his name is Judge Wilbert Champion."

"The grand jury judge, here?" Burford was incredulous. "It must be serious."

"He's waiting for you in the living room, go on."

Deciding not to change out of his athletic gear, Burford went in to Judge Champion, to be greeted by an embracing smile. The senior judge, with his distinctive twirled mustache and cropped cloudy grey beard, was neatly dressed in a vest and suit with a gold watch peeking from his pocket. Burford regretted not taking the extra time to change his slovenly attire.

"I apologize for keeping you waiting, Judge."

"Nonsense, I'm sorry to surprise you with a house visit. There's some urgent business we need to discuss. Can we speak in private, Mr. Simmons?"

Burford directed the judge to the office beside the kitchen, a quiet room that he used to rehearse his addresses to the jury.

He locked the door and upon turning around, discovered the judge slumped in his chair with his eyes firmly shut.

"I haven't slept in a couple of days," Champion said, when Burford tapped him gently on the shoulder.

"Please sit down, Mr. Simmons," he requested. "Messy stuff, this shooting of the president. The country is under siege from these anarchists. There is no assurance that the attack will stop with our leader. Every branch of government is at risk."

"The country will surely withstand the attack. McKinley's alive and recovering. He'll soon return to Washington and the government's business will resume as before."

"Not alive for very long, Mr. Simmons." The judge spoke in the grave tone of a mortician at a funeral. "The gangrene in the president's stomach is not receding. His doctors have informed his wife that his condition is grave and imperiled. The entire family has been summoned to his bedside post haste, and Teddy Roosevelt is waiting patiently in the wings to take the president's oath of office. The American nation will soon be moving into a dark period of mourning."

"Is there no possibility that he'll recover?"

"None, unfortunately. You must keep the grim news confidential while McKinley's yet alive. I'm counting on your discretion."

"Of course, but why are you telling me?"

"I'm getting to that. A meeting was called for the judges yesterday by the presiding judge. We appreciate that the anarchist who shot McKinley will be charged with murder --- it's simply a matter of time. I may ask to witness his execution personally. Enough, however, with my indiscreet revelations of grievance. We agreed that the entire world will be scrutinizing the trial. It cannot be allowed to form a rallying point, to foment dissent and plant seeds of support for Leon Czolgosz. As the grand jury judge, it is my responsibility to ensure that the murder trial is seen to be inscrutably fair. That's why I need your help."

"My help?"

"The judges privately took a straw vote and the result reached was unanimous; you are going to defend Czolgosz and carry his brief."

Burford found his mind tumbling into freefall with the judge's stark declaration. "Wait a minute, Judge!" I gave Pharo my firm commitment that I would have nothing to do with this man's trial. Why, my partners have threatened to shut me out of the law firm if I dare to take the case!"

The judge sat up in his chair, in command of himself again. "Look here, Burford, I have absolutely no interest in impairing your domestic bliss or disrupting your firm. This isn't a casual request I'm presenting. The future of the entire administration of justice will rest squarely on your shoulders. It's your patriotic duty to defend the anarchist. I don't expect you to take the brief for free, you'll be paid a small stipend..."

"Most reassuring. I'll risk losing my home, my marriage, my law practice, have my reputation pilloried, but be paid a pittance."

"I'm sympathetic to the sacrifice you'll be undertaking. Your colleagues and the judges on my court will, no doubt, appreciate your valiant effort. You will be acting in the highest tradition of the legal profession, of course. And let's confront the immutable facts here. It's not much of a trial, is it? There are over fifty eyewitnesses to the shooting, as I read in the newspaper."

"I'll fight to win the trial if I take it," Burford cautioned.

"Jolly good, that's the spirit. Give the damn rascal your usual skilled effort. You won't regret taking the case."

"I'm quite certain that I will." His words concealed his fury. The trial had been foisted on him like an emperor's edict. He could easily imagine Pharo's unforgiving reaction to him reneging on his promise.

"There's no backing away from this brief," the grand jury judge admonished Burford. "The arraignment will take place in a couple of days. We're setting up a special court at City Hall across from the jail. City Hall will serve strictly as a courthouse during the trial. We'll delay the arraignment in the unlikely event that the president is still alive. I'll expect you to be there at the prisoner's side as his attorney. I'm assured that you'll be afforded a wide berth to present your defense."

Before Burford could respond, the judge hastily left the room. Burford watched him grab his hat from the bronze hat rack and depart the house with a pleasing gait.

The grandfather clock sounded a series of chimes.

He marked the time, ten o'clock as the moment that Burford Simmons' battleship struck an iceberg.

Pharo entered the room as the image of the battleship crashing lingered.

"Well that was quick," she said. "What did the judge want?"

Burford hesitated. "Just court business." The impending storm, a deserved stern rebuke from Pharo, was temporarily delayed.

"Court business that required an unannounced visit by the judge at your home. Did your shabby attire impress him?"

"The judge claimed to be unconcerned about my state of dress. Or should I say undress?"

"Very gracious," Pharo said unconvincingly. "Don't forget that we have my cousin Edwina's dinner party this evening."

"You mean Marie Antoinette's gala ball.'

"I only wish both of you would make a genuine effort to get along. My cousin can be fun and charming if you'd give her a chance."

"Charming as a viper", he replied. "She might start by abandoning her foolish notion that she's a descendant of royalty." Her visit at last year's Thanksgiving Day dinner had been an unmitigated disaster. Sharp nose perched upward, Edwina regaled the guests with her connection to British royalty. Her husband, Wilson, she boasted, was the fifth cousin of a duke who lived on a lavish castle in Yorkshire, wrote unpublished poetry and shot pheasant from the sky as a hobby. Burford dismissed her pretensions: "In America, lineage of privilege ended with the revolution."

Over the course of the dinner, Edwina scoffed at a museum exhibiting ancient artifacts unavailable for purchase; disparaged American products after buying an umbrella in Binghamton that collapsed at the first hint of wind; and brandished an autographed novel by the British statesman and soldier, Winston Churchill, about a Balkan tyrant tripped up by a daring political reformer named Savrola. "We had tea and crumpets with Winston's father, Lord Randolph Churchill, on a trip to London years ago," Edwina added. "Wilson, read aloud a passage of Savrola," she said, thrusting her finger at the page:

> "'In spite of such tactics,' Savrola continued, 'and in the face of all opposition, whether by bribes or bullets, whether by hired bravos or a merciless and mercenary soldiery, the great cause we are here to support has gone on, is going on, and is going to go on, until at length our ancient liberties are regained, and those who have robbed us of them punished.' Loud cheers rose from all parts of the hall. *His voice was even and not loud, but his words conveyed an impression of dauntless resolution.*"

"Young Winston has the makings of a fine English barrister," Burford interrupted. "An advocate will never win over a jury by shouting like a clanging bell."

"Savrola is not an account of lawyers!" Edwina grumbled.

At dessert, Edwina turned her contempt on Burford: "A toast to the great defender of the dregs and vagabonds infesting our communities...Burford Simmons!" She raised her glass with a derisive laugh.

"If by dregs, you're referring to the poor, hapless and oppressed," he fired back, "I'm proud to defend them in my chosen vocation. Stifle dissent and society is diminished; allow injustice to fester and society is destroyed."

Edwina just lifted a fork menacingly and began to devour her souffle and strawberries.

*

The impending trial of Leon Czolgosz pre-occupied Burford for the duration of the day. As he adjusted the collar of his dinner jacket, he examined the framed wedding photograph on the mantle. His second anniversary with Pharo had recently passed and today he seriously questioned that they would reach a third. He rued his tacit agreement to defend the president's shooter. What could these judges do if he refused? Shackle him in chains to the counsel table?

He arrived with Pharo at the opulent home of Edwina and Wilson at seven, to find the festivities underway. A harpist serenaded them at the door and waiters in white gloves adroitly balanced silver trays filled with caviar and sardines weaving their way expertly through the pockets of guests.

A gushing fountain in the center of the room, littered with pennies and speckled goldfish, splashed onto Burford's pants. Pharo twisted a penny into his palm. "Make a wish, Burf."

"I wish that Sammy, the shoeshine boy, could be here to collect all the pennies," he said with a hint of mischief, hurling the coin into the pond of water.

Edwina, lord-like, hovered over her feast on the fifth step of a circular staircase in a pale watermelon pink gown of silk lace, an imposing peacock feather in her hat, her hair neatly tucked beneath it. After a contemptuous snarl aimed at Burford, Edwina shifted her gaze and waved affectionately at his wife. He imagined a gleeful Edwina, with a giant broom, sweeping him from her abode through the grand French windows.

Pharo was already greeting her father, Mervin, across the room, and interrupting his animated conversation with the mayor about the rising cost of petrol.

This raucous celebration jarred Burford's sense of decent behavior, with the imminent death of President McKinley. He abandoned the party's roar of conversation and gaiety and set off to discover the dining room, separated by a velvet rope, with an octagonal dining room table of hand-carved Cuban mahogany.

Burford gingerly stepped over the rope and sat at the table, reflecting on the day's events. He faced a glass cabinet filled with ornamental porcelain jars with distinctive Chinese lettering. A mandarin duck was etched onto a large, ornate bowl. Edwina had boasted to Pharo about acquiring the ornaments on a trip to the Far East.

"Do you mind if I join you?" Pharo's father entered and handed him a glass of claret. "Have a drink. It will revive you."

"Is my downcast mood so obvious?"

"Listen up, Burf. I know you're taking on the defense of this wretched anarchist." He watched Burford's startled reaction. "I play poker once a month with the presiding judge. I'm keeping tabs on you --- you're married to my livewire daughter, remember. Who else but Pharo gets a tattoo of a snake on her wrist? I still love her to pieces though." He sipped his champagne and continued. "I shouldn't be so quick to disparage her. Rockefeller claims that she's a 'true chip of the old block,' you know."

"You didn't give me fair warning of that handicap," Burford shot back.

"Look, Burf, I'm fully aware you've been cornered into this defense. I told the presiding judge they weren't playing fair or in accordance with the rules, and I flashed a full house in his scoffing face as I said it. But there's no cause to be downcast or glum. You'll give it a whirl in court, like a play where the audience is already alerted to the desired closing scene. You didn't choose your part. You're a conscripted actor. Everyone will be aware of that crucial fact. You'll recover from this debacle."

"Do you sincerely believe that?"

"I'm not given to gratuitous encouragement. But, of course, if I'm wrong, there's always a desk waiting at my oil company." Mervin clasped Burford's hand tightly. "Be sure to let Pharo know about Czolgosz after the party. The lid won't be kept tight much longer. Now come back into the party. A bit of revelry to buffer the pain."

"I'll be there in a couple of minutes," Burford answered. He strolled about examining the contents of the lavishly designed room. Magnificent treasures of art accumulating dust in a cloistered room like an empty cupboard. These ornate surroundings didn't suit him, like his soon-to-be-former partner, Raleigh Sykes.

Defending the despised criminal class was unsettling and disfavored. He'd never shirked his duty to defend a ghastly client in a robust manner, regardless of daunting stakes. As the erudite Clarence Darrow once told him, the lawyer's professional obligation included the defense of the defenseless. Now, Burford considered, there was not a criminal defendant in the entire country as weak and defenseless as Leon Czolgosz.

"What were you and my father discussing in here?" Pharo stood, her hands clasped with a steely stare, as if she'd caught a rustler snatching a hen's eggs.

"I can't deceive you Pharo. I've been asked to defend the president's shooter."

"And you've agreed, I presume."

"Yes."

"Will Mitchell be assisting you?"

"It will be his choice."

"I hope you'll take the time to share with your young associate what a fool's adventure this trial will be. I had assumed that the grand jury judge asked you to defend Leon Czolgosz. I've arranged to stay with my sister at her home in Maine during the trial. Bessie has been informed. I can take relaxing walks along Moosehead Lake with Odette's spaniel. And please don't expect me to wish you success with your trial."

"I'm meeting my new client tomorrow," Burford said, "and I expect the news about my defense of Czolgosz will circulate quickly."

"Do as you wish. The anarchist traitor needs his great defender. Gallop to his rescue, Burford Simmons."

Chapter Seventeen

The Prime Minister wired his condolences from Quebec, where he awaited the arrival of his guests, the Duke and Duchess of Cornwall and York. The heartrending and tragic news of the president's death produced a signed wired message of shared commiseration from Wilfred Laurier:

> *"The uncontrollable sorrow of the American nation will be almost as keenly felt by the people of Canada, who being so close neighbors of the United States, have had many an opportunity of becoming familiar with the noble qualities which characterized Mr. McKinley in his private as well as in his public life."*

The flag at the entrance to the House of Commons flapped at half-mast and Canadian banks and government buildings soon adopted the same symbol of solemn respect. The stunning news of the popular American president's death cast a shadowy pall over the country. A letter to the editor of a prominent Canadian newspaper prompted a trend of men in cities and villages to wear black ties as a visible sign of bereavement. Many citizens of Canada had traveled by boat and by train to tour the Pan-American Exposition and passed by the Temple of Music on the Esplanade --- a few had been present on the day of the momentous shooting. The *Globe's* prominent bulletin board at the corner of Yonge and Melinda Street in Toronto carried gloomy updates to scores of interested citizens and American visitors. One message included a report of lines extending for miles to view President McKinley's body at the Buffalo City Hall. Another report described pieces of black crepe bound to every mourner's sleeve. In a myriad of churches dotting the landscape of both countries, the tolling bells rang a doleful chime through the day and into nightfall. An American president had died at the hand of an assassin.

The sentry stationed at the guard box at Camp Bogden dreaded the ten-hour shift ahead. The frigid temperature in his tight quarters, the tedium of standing guard, and the silence all contributed to Officer Finnegan's disquiet. He left pieces of bread outside the box to entice an animal to keep him company. The next day he observed a squirrel on its hunches devouring the breadcrumbs. Finnegan chatted with the squirrel, christening him Disraeli. He recalled the name of a former British prime minister from a history class. "Come back again, Disraeli," he urged the furry creature.

Finnegan despised the camp's prisoner, Leon Czolgosz; all the officers at Camp Bogden shared his evident disdain. Unperturbed, the prisoner delighted in bantering with his guards. Insults and curses bounced off the prisoner without stirring a reaction, as if Czolgosz' s moral conscience was tied to an off switch. Finnegan concluded that anyone capable of murdering President McKinley, must be swiftly destroyed. The other three officers privately discussed a sneak midnight attack on the prisoner, but Finnegan reminded them of Detective Jacob's explicit caution to avoid a physical confrontation. The consequences for breaching that order would be severe and Finnegan had no desire to test the limits of the crafty detective's temper. In a wistful moment in the guard box, Finnegan imagined being placed in charge of the prisoner. The indelible image of Czolgosz handcuffed and alone in his company, as he pummeled him into unconsciousness, comforted him.

Finnegan brought the comics from the Sunday newspaper to the sentry box, savoring each frame like a spoonful of a delicious soup. He wrapped himself in blankets, lit a candle and set his ham sandwich next to it to prevent it from freezing.

The noise started as a faint rumble but grew into the discernable sound of pounding in the distance. Alarmed, the officer pulled a set of binoculars from the shelf. His first impression peering at the gulley ahead, was a herd of cattle on a stampede. His view sharpened. The binoculars focused on a line of horse carriages, fifteen by his count, approaching Camp Bogden on a direct route.

He must notify Detective Jacob at once. Exiting the sentry box, he stepped on the sandwich and candle.

Finnegan found the detective in the stock room preparing a food order to the grocer and butcher.

"Fifteen carriages descending on the camp! How much

time do we have?"

"Hard to say, sir. My estimate is five minutes. Seven minutes at a maximum." The constable wobbled and appeared to be on the verge of collapsing.

"Pull yourself together, Finnegan. You did a splendid job here. Gather the rest of the men and meet me in the lunchroom. I must make a telephone call first."

Jacob hurried to the telephone and called the detective's office in Buffalo.

"Is that you, Boulder?" he asked. He'd given his mountainous former partner the nickname.

"Yes. Is that you Eli? I miss you buddy."

"Me too. Listen, there any news about President McKinley's condition?"

"News! Didn't anyone call you to tell you? The president died in his sleep last night."

"Did the story make the papers this morning?"

"It made the headline of the *Buffalo Morning Express*. 'PRESIDENT MCKINLEY IS DEAD'."

"Does it tell the location of his killer?"

Jacob rapped his knuckles nervously on the table as he waited to confirm his premonition.

"Here it is. I found it --- a story about his secret prison cell including a map of the location. Not much of a secret now."

"*Mon Dieu*," Jacob exclaimed. "Who leaked it, I wonder?" Listen, Boulder, I want you to get an ambulance to our site as fast as possible, *tout suite*."

"What should I give as the reason?"

"Tell them one of my officers had a seizure, an epileptic seizure and requires immediate hospital care."

"Consider it done," Boulder replied.

Detective Jacob entered the lunchroom where the group of four officers had congregated. "Get Czolgosz in here," he ordered one of the men. "We have no precious moments to spare. Do any of you have acting experience?"

"I was the lead in my kindergarten Christmas play."

"You're the lucky prize winner, Officer Jennings. I'll soon explain." The detective held up his right hand. "Listen, everyone," he said. "We will take our weapons and ammunition from the stock room to the sentry box. You'll receive your instructions from me there. We're being confronted by an angry mob ready to kill our prisoner. I have some dreadful news to share. President McKinley died last night."

Entering the room in time to hear the update of the president's demise, Czolgosz smiled.

"Let's move. Jennings, a quick word alone --- you'll remain with the prisoner. Remove his handcuffs. Keep your gun pointed at his head. Fire it without hesitation, if necessary."

Detective Jacob and the three officers in his company returned to the sentry box at precisely the time the carriages reached the fenced camp. Jacob counted forty-five men carrying rifles and revolvers as they proceeded towards the camp. The rage evident on their faces sparked a memory for Detective Jacob of the rancor visible in the faces on the Paris streets at the Dreyfus court-martial.

"We want the president's murderer," one of them shouted, followed by several cries to lynch Leon Czolgosz.

Detective Jacob addressed the rowdy crowd in a steady, measured voice:

"Good morning," he told the unsettled group. "I've put in a call to my unit sergeant to receive instructions. We took a vote among the officers, and we've decided to turn the prisoner over to you. As far as we're concerned, you can hang *l'assassin* right here. We'll supply the rope. But we must obey police protocol and proceed through the proper channels of command. Be patient. I expect to get word back within the next hour."

"Do you expect us to sit here twiddling our thumbs while we wait for you?"

"Why should we trust you fellows?" another man shouted, his rifle firmly pointed at the detective. "You're the ones who hid him in the first place."

A chorus of shouts came. 'Kill him.'

"We don't want anyone to get hurt," Detective Jacob said with authority. "My men are instructed to shoot anyone who tries to get past this sentry box. But good news! I counted, and we have only forty bullets. Of the forty-five members of your group present here, five of you are assured of surviving the blast of gunfire."

The three officers' guns were leveled at the crowd. No-one dared to step forward.

Jacob worried that a loud sneeze could tip the standoff into a blast of bullets.

"I'm going to make another contact with police headquarters for an update," he said calmly, and then ventured back to the lunchroom with a plan to involve the prisoner in his scheme.

"Listen!" he directed Czolgosz. "There is a pack of raging men out there anxious to maul the skin off your body and hang your carcass like a trophy. You will follow my lead. An ambulance is arriving shortly. You will leave the prison camp in that ambulance."

Jacob saw Officer Jennings' perplexed look but continued to Czolgosz. "I'm determined to get you out of this place alive."

"Why should I care? You only care about saving your public show of roasting me in the electric chair? What if my preference is to die here?"

The detective shuffled aside Czolgosz's outburst. "You'll obey my orders as my prisoner. It's that simple. Do you understand?"

Czolgosz was silent.

As the men continued to wait outside the fence on the camp's perimeter, murmurings in the hostile crowd mounted.

"How much longer?" one man yelled.

The shouted question was followed by a rock smashing a window a couple of feet from Detective Jacob. He motioned for the officers to hold their positions.

Jacob stepped outside again. "I expect a call from headquarters any minute! There's an officer inside the building ready to brief me immediately. Please be patient. You'll have your hanging."

Minutes later he heard the sound of ringing bells approaching with some relief.

The leader of the group stepped forward. "Do you think that you can trick us? You're not getting Czolgosz out of here in that ambulance."

The crowd surged closer to the fence perimeter.

"Now listen up," Jacob replied. "One of my officers had a crippling seizure. I'll prove it to you if you give me the chance."

The detective had to move forward with his plan quickly. The ambulance arrived and the paramedics were directed inside. "Jennings, get onto the stretcher."

The two ambulance men appeared stunned, and one approached Jacob. "Those men have guns. What's the commotion outside about?"

"You're not to administer any medication to my officer, do you understand? My name is Detective Eli Jacob." He instructed them to bring the ambulance to an adjoining garage.

Inside the garage, he told the driver. "You'll be staying with me." Turning to his men, he snapped. "Warsaw, get in the driver's seat. And now for the prisoner."

The remaining officers brought Czolgosz out, hands securely cuffed.

Jacob ordered." Czolgosz, you go with him. You're being delivered to the courthouse. You have a court appearance this afternoon."

The prisoner obediently crouched on the floor of the front passenger seat, Warsaw's gun pointed at him. Jacob directed a paramedic to sit in the passenger seat, his legs dangling over the prisoner.

The ambulance lurched out of the garage and past the gate at the fence and halted amid the angry mob. The back of the ambulance was open for display, where Jennings lay supine on his back shaking like an autumn leaf in the wind. "*Bon acteur*," Jacob thought.

The ambulance pulled away from Camp Bogden, the jingling bells fading as it traversed the pine-grown hillside. Leon Czolgosz left unnoticed.

As soon as the ambulance safely passed the gate, the detective began to count to one hundred. "*Quatre-vingt-dix-huit, quatre-vingt-dix-neuf, cent.*"

The remaining officers and paramedics climbed into two rattling open vehicles and started off. At the gate, the detective stood, gripping the roof rail, and waived the impatient mob into the grounds.

"He's all yours, lads. Please think of President McKinley when you tighten the rope around his neck."

The crowded motor cars accelerated forward, and Jacob waved farewell to Camp Bogden. "*A bientot*," he declared. "Finnegan, drive us to the Buffalo courthouse."

Chapter Eighteen

Robert Planter had a few hours of delay waiting on the ship's deck to claim his cabin, as his ship embarked from London, bound for Canada. At least he was dry. As pellets of misty rain began to collect in puddles on the wharf bordering the ship's hull, a steward had handed him an umbrella.

Planter had picked up the latest issue of the *Daily Telegraph* to occupy his time. There, on the third page, was the familiar picture of Burford Simmons with an accompanying article describing the lawyer's role as the lead attorney for Leon Czolgosz. The picture of Simmons startled Planter. With rising scorn, he read the *Telegraph's* description of the respected attorney and his lofty stature in the Buffalo legal community. He preferred to read a fawning obituary.

The account of Burford Simmons' dutiful defense of the president's killer enraged Planter. His body shook in anger and he banged a metal post with his fist, bruising his thumb.

But the mounting pain faded as the rage converted to elation. A perfect opportunity presented itself to exact his revenge. He walked around the promenade deck hatching his plan, rereading the drenched newspaper article and his clue. A band of American anarchists were blamed in the article for inspiring Czolgosz's insipid crime. A diabolic idea flashed into his mind. He devised the message to send to his trusted assistant in Canada.

*

Burford Simmons examined the slight prisoner frowning and shaking his head as if to thwart a persistent bee.

"You're wasting your time here," he said. "I don't need any lawyer."

"You haven't allowed me to introduce myself. I didn't ask to be assigned to defend you, Leon, but you'll get my best representation."

Burford's questions about Czolgosz's background were dismissed with an arch of his eyebrows.

"I need to know everything about your life before you shot the president," the lawyer said. "We can start today."

"Why's it matter to you? I don't want your help."

Burford resisted a lecture about the lawyer's role as the doomed prisoner's only salvation and savior. He wondered how Czolgosz strode into the Temple of Music undetected and shot the president. Yet he shared some sympathy for President McKinley's protectors. Czolgosz appeared utterly simple and guileless, that disguised any threat of an approaching assassin.

"I will see you upstairs." The lawyer observed Czolgosz looking forlornly at the floor.

"This room needs sweeping," he said.

*

Judge Benjamin Pickett, known as Sour Pickles to the lawyers appearing in his courtroom, gazed irritably at the crowd of spectators squeezed inside.

"Is there a public event proceeding here that I'm not aware of? I don't know why everyone's bothered to show up," the dour judge complained. "We're only setting a trial date today. Mr. Simmons, I assume that you're prepared for trial."

"Judge, I had the first opportunity to meet my client this afternoon in a room --- without a table or chairs --- in the basement of the courthouse. I explained to him that I was the lawyer assigned to defend him at his murder trial, but he steadfastly opposes my representation. Indeed, it's his fervent wish not to have any lawyer."

"Is that so? We'll see about that." Judge Pickett sneered at the prisoner. "Stand up."

"Are you Leon Czolgosz?"

The prisoner, dressed in a dark grey suit and light-colored pink bow tie, rose slowly.

"Yes," he said.

"What's this foolhardy talk about not wanting a lawyer? Do you appreciate that you are facing the death penalty?" he asked, flashing a conqueror's grin. "Will you accept Mr. Burford as your lawyer?"

Czolgosz looked away from the ornery judge without a reply.

"I'm not prepared to leave this courtroom until I get your answer. Now do you want a lawyer to defend you?"

"I don't want anyone's help."

Discernable gasps came from the gallery.

"Tut, tut, the nasty murderer doesn't need help," a man seated in the front row said. "He'll be straight to the electric chair."

Representatives of the press penned every word, as they surveyed every mannerism of the prisoner.

"Silence," the judge demanded. He leaned forward to scold the prisoner. "This lawyer is acting for you whether you like it or not. I'll not permit my courtroom to be turned into one of your kind's wild charades. I will see that you receive an eminently fair trial, and Mr. Simmons will ably represent you. Counsel, you'll both return to pick a jury two weeks from today."

The prosecutor didn't wait for her counterpart's protest. "That only provides Mr. Simmons with minimal time to prepare for a murder trial. Perhaps a later trial date might be considered."

"And what date are you proposing, Miss Sharma?"

"At least a month or two, Judge."

"I'll see both lawyers in my chambers," he directed, bounding from his chair on the podium and exiting the courtroom.

In Pickett's chambers, the lawyers sat across from the judge as he sipped a glass of water. The walls of his chambers were lined with photographs of birds.

"I didn't enjoy being embarrassed in my courtroom, Miss Sharma."

"That wasn't my intent," she answered back.

"Is that a robin?" Burford asked, pointing to a sketch on the desk. "And behind your chair. A goldfinch and a couple of mockingbirds? The hybrid male goldfinch is notable for its coat of yellow in the summer and olive-colored hue in the winter."

"You certainly know your birds, Mr. Simmons."

Burford had stumbled on Judge Pickett's birdwatching hobby in a passing conversation with Caleb and immersed himself in the study of birds at the library. A few weeks later, he had followed the judge into a hardware store, and had displayed his profound interest in the study of birds. Judge Pickett was impressed.

"Burford, I'm arranging a birdwatching trip with my club to Connecticut in the spring. It would be wonderful if someone with such a keen interest in birds might join the group."

"I'd be honored to attend, Judge. Now about this trial date..."

"I'm sorry, counsel. Your client came very close to a public lynching this morning. A detective notified the presiding judge about an hour ago. I'm obliged to move forward to trial with all haste. Two weeks is more than ample time in this case. And if he's adamant about hindering his legal representation, defendant Czolgosz has free will, of course, and I'll abide by his decision. Let's return to court and get the date fixed."

"Can we meet in my office after court?" Neeru asked, as they sauntered back to the courtroom. "I didn't realize that you enjoy birdwatching as a hobby."

"A discussion for another time," Burford said, distracted by the prospect of the imminent trial.

At the end of court proceedings, the handcuffed prisoner was moved from the courtroom with an escorting officer on each side and transported down the stairs to the basement of City Hall and through a tunnel under Delaware

Avenue to the jail.

Burford and Mitchell exited the courtroom into a throng of media that surged forward to surround the defense team.

"How can you defend the President's killer?" one reporter inquired.

"What possible defense can you offer the anarchist?" another interrupted.

Burford resisted the journalists' bait. "I'll do my talking at the trial," he remarked, before turning away.

Neeru Sharma had been the first woman admitted as a lawyer by the New York Bar Association. She had also been the first Indian American member of the Bar. Many of her colleagues warmly welcomed her, but she had been shunned by a few who took umbrage at their white male bastion being trampled upon. "Tuff, tuff to them", she declared, spurred by their rejection.

Neeru ushered Burford into her office and locked the door. The defense counsel had acted as her mentor after she graduated in the top half of her class at Fordham Law School. Neeru had immigrated with her family from Jaipur, India. Her father, a banker with Barclays, the British bank, managed a northeastern office in Buffalo. After her graduation from law school, Neeru, five years younger than her mentor, became his protégée. She eventually left his practice and opened her own law office, receiving referrals from an admiring Burford. She developed a reputation for blistering cross-examination and was as an unrelenting advocate. One police officer famously fainted on the witness stand during her obdurate questioning at a trial.

"Burford," she said. "I'll get straight to the point. We've

received a steady flow of threatening messages directed to your client. The police are carefully monitoring them. We'll have extra security in the courtroom during the trial. However, one note dropped off in the night mail, was of interest to me. Here it is." She handed him a crumpled piece of parchment.

The note was composed of cut-out letters, cobbled together from a newspaper and pasted onto the paper. Burford read it aloud:

> To the princes and kings and queens and presidents and prime ministers who rule in dominion over this world, we have a dire warning for you. We will succeed in overthrowing you. It is only a matter of time. Leon Czolgosz is a hero to our valiant cause and anyone who blocks his path to martyrdom will perish.
>
> The Anarchist League of America

"Have you investigated this anarchist organization?" he asked. He requested a scrap of paper and made a copy of the note.

"The police checked, and it doesn't exist. We have no leads on who sent the letter. My concern is that the lawyer defending Czolgosz --- against his wishes --- will be accused of blocking his path to be a martyr. With fatal consequences. Be careful, Burford. Please take precautions for your safety. Your life may be in grave danger. If you want police protection, let me know. These anarchists are lethal and ruthless."

"Neeru, I appreciate your genuine concern, but I will not be impeded from providing a vigorous defense to my unpopular and beleaguered client. These anarchists will fail resoundingly if their goal is to intimidate me. They've chosen the wrong lawyer to scare."

"That's precisely the answer I expected to receive," Neeru replied. "But please heed my warning and take precautions."

*

Although he deemed the exercise as eventful as an extra turn on the merry-go-round, Burford had arranged to meet Mitchell in the court cells for a second session with the client.

Animated by his brief court appearance, Leon Czolgosz railed at the lawyers about the judge's labelling the trial as a "wild charade."

"Tell me, what does he take me for, a raving fool? My mission improves the plight of the common man. The gulf between the despots and the peasants is narrowing!"

Mitchell began the interview as planned. "Why did you tell the police that your name was Fred Nieman when they arrested you? You declared that you killed President McKinley because it was your duty. Why bother to give the police your wrong name?"

"I chose the name Nieman because it translates to *nobody* in German. Even a nobody like me can do something heroic for the anarchist cause that I admire. Just like Gaetano Bresci did when he killed the Italian king."

"Bresci is dead and buried." Mitchell shook his head in bewilderment. "This is the hero you hold up to follow as a role model?"

"Leon, we need to devote our time to focus on your

defense," Burford said. "The window to your trial is narrowing."

"There is no defense to prepare for. I'm resigned to my fate. I have nothing further to say to either of you."

Mitchell said. "Mr. Simmons is desperately trying to save your life. You don't really want to die, do you?"

"I've performed my duty and I'm not afraid to die for my cause."

Clanking his shackles, Czolgosz called for the guard to remove him from the interview room.

"We're not quite finished yet."

"Oh, let him go, Mitchell. We can't foist a defense on an unwilling client. Mr. Czolgosz, I can assure you that Mitchell and I intend to put the government to strict proof of its case, regardless of your participation. The task may be daunting, even insurmountable, but I will be undeterred. You may be the defendant least deserving just treatment in the history of our Republic, but you will receive equal justice under law."

Czolgosz appeared unmoved as he shuffled in leg irons past his lawyers.

*

Burford arrived home determined, for one evening, to remove Czolgosz's trial from his thoughts. Fig Golem had delivered a pot of white chrysanthemums with a card wishing him good fortune at the upcoming trial. Burford had promised to see a film with Pharo starring a blooming French actress, but Pharo called for him to take a telephone call in the hallway to the kitchen.

"It's Clarence Darrow," she said, handing him the receiver. "He's called twice looking for you."

"Clarence," he said, taking it. "How is my old law school comrade?"

"The brave fight continues --- but, more importantly, I admire the courage you're displaying, my good fellow. I'm proud of you for representing Czolgosz. You have earned the admiration of every lawyer I respect in Chicago. Trial lawyers are the only real lawyers, you know."

"Kind words of encouragement, Clarence. I wish my client had a sliver of insight into his serious predicament."

"I gave Pharo my telephone number. Call me anytime if you need a cheery boost of support."

"Thank you. Pharo has been extremely helpful, especially when she learned that my law partners had abandoned me and fired my new associate. She cancelled her plans to stay with her sister during the trial. I had a raucous conversation with the senior partner. He accused me of being an agent of the anarchists' movement."

"Strike out on your own! You're an outstanding lawyer, and I have no doubt that your new practice will flourish."

"That is high praise, indeed, coming from you, Clarence. Are you still giving those unfathomable four-hour jury addresses?"

"Five hours. I maintain that the most important attribute for a trial lawyer is a pair of strong legs. I've joined the Medinah Athletic Club on Michigan Avenue, and swim in the pool a couple of times a week."

"My jury address will be considerably shorter than five hours this time. More likely in the range of five minutes."

"I suppose you're left to argue insanity as your client's defense."

"It's the only avenue available. I'm meeting with a defense psychiatrist tomorrow. But enough of my travails. Where are you living in Chicago?"

"I'm staying at the Langdon sharing the rent with a hardy cousin who is devoted to rousing fun. Have you heard the Chicago Blues? I'm off to a costume ball tonight dressed as a police officer. Just imagine. You and Pharo must take the train to Chicago and plan a visit. I'll find you proper accommodation."

"Grand idea to consider after the murder trial."

After his call with Darrow, Burford showed the threatening note to Pharo.

She examined each word on the piece of paper, becoming indignant as she reviewed it.

"The prosecutor is trying to intimidate you! It's quite a stretch to conclude that you're the target. I don't understand how being Leon Czolgosz's lawyer places you in jeopardy. The jury decides the case on the evidence presented --- it makes no sense to blame you for performing your duty and putting up a defense."

"Your perspicacity is welcome, and I agree with you," he said, "up to a point."

Burford harbored lingering concerns that he genuinely remained in an adversary's firing line, but he overcame the portending menace for the evening. Candles, roast beef with gravy and an open bottle of Chablis awaited them at the dinner table. A delightful evening at the movie theatre followed and any lurking danger dropped to the rearmost part of Burford's mind.

Chapter Nineteen

The law office of Darrow, Thompson and Thomas hummed with the voices of lawyers jostling to meet pressing court deadlines: "Where's the appendix to the motion record?" "Did you find the citation for the appellate decision in the law library?" "Can you confirm the mailing address of the courthouse in Springfield?"

Amid the cacophony, a timorous man in his early twenties, bursting out of a wrinkled suit with a stained shirt collar and a ruddy complexion, haggard eyes and nervous twitch, approached the reception desk.

He spoke quietly. "I'm here to see Mr. Darrow."

"Do you have an appointment?"

"I don't, and I apologize for not making one. My life is topsy- turvy right now and I didn't get a wink of sleep last night."

Emily, seasoned keeper of the law partners' appointments, looked up. The prospect of gaining time with Mr. Darrow compared evenly to shifting the alabaster pillar in the hallway.

"It will not be possible to meet Mr. Darrow, then," she reproached him. "Look around at the waiting room."

He observed a row of chairs, notable for the despairing faces of the people filling them. An elderly man, eyes closed, leaned against a wall with framed investigative articles highlighting appalling social conditions in Chicago. A 1900 calendar open to the month of May and a Chicago lawyers' magazine with Clarence Darrow's picture on the cover rested on an oak table in the center.

"Mrs. Jasper, Mr. Thomas' office is straight down the hall and then turn right," Emily called out.

"It's critical that I meet with Mr. Darrow as quickly as possible. Please," the young man implored her. "My father is a longstanding friend of Mr. Darrow and needs his help. My father's life is at risk."

The desperate plea of imminent harm hit its desired mark. "Just a moment. What is your name?"

"Pete Isaak."

A couple of minutes later she emerged with Clarence Darrow following, a dangling cowlick covering his right eye and his brows arched, curiously surveying the young man in the reception area. "Are you one of Abe Isaac's sons?" he asked, his tone genial, and didn't wait for a response. "Come with me."

Pete struggled to keep up with the strides of the lawyer.

Darrow directed him to a plush leather armchair with a soft cushion on the seat. The musky odor of cigar smoke clashed with the sweet embers of burning incense.

"Please sit down and tell me about yourself, and what poor fate has befallen my good friend, Abe."

"I'm a student at Northwestern. I'm in charge of the

university's newspaper."

"A successor to your father's publishing business, I see."

"Yes, Mr. Darrow, that is my career aspiration." He took a deep breath and continued. "I went to visit my parents in Oak Park for a couple of days. I had settled into my old bedroom for a night of studying when I heard loud banging at the front door. I heard someone shouting to be let in. My parents being out at the opera for the evening, I put my slippers on and opened the door. A couple of belligerent police officers rudely demanded to see my father. They refused to answer my questions and insisted on waiting inside. I was frightened, Mr. Darrow. The officers asked me questions about my university newspaper—one of them called me a traitor and described the paper as subversive junk. They threatened to return to arrest me, and then just sat with their arms folded, waiting for my father to arrive. When he did, they manhandled him, while my mother looked on in fright. I watched him being shoved to the ground like a sack of potatoes and then handcuffed behind his back. One of the officers proceeded to arrest him."

"What possible grounds did the officers provide your father to justify his arrest?"

"He was accused of aiding the president's assassin."

Darrow furrowed his brow.

"That's an unreasonable stretch," he said. "I'm aware that your father publishes an anarchist weekly. I've read the *Free Society* myself. But Abe Isaac doesn't condone violence of any kind --- certainly not the murder of the American president. I chaired a gathering last year where a group of militant radicals spoke. Does listening to radical thought make me guilty of every crime that any of them might commit? Not in the United States of America. Where is your father being held in custody?"

"My mother confirmed that the police transported him to a downtown precinct. They plan to take him to Joliet Prison tomorrow. His final instruction to me before being hauled from our home was to get in touch with Clarence Darrow. That's why I'm here."

"It's good that you came, Pete. Your father is innocent of any crime, but he is in grave danger of being swept up by the tide of blind hatred in this country to anyone branded with the anarchist label. The *Chicago Tribune* ran a front-page story recently about 'the high priestess of anarchy,' Emma Goldman, accusing her of inciting the attack on President McKinley. I shall do all that I can to assist Abe. I'm in the final day of a trial but I'll visit him at the police station tonight. Leave Emily your contact information on your exit and let her know that I'll need a quarter of an hour before my next appointment."

Darrow returned to the blotting paper on his desk to map out his jury address, but first ruminated for a few moments about the arrest of his dear friend. He recalled a speech he once delivered to a group of workingmen at the Sunset Club, about William McKinley's war against the Philippines. He called the war "murder" and "robbery" and told his audience that "if this war be called patriotism then blessed be treason." Perhaps he'd be the next casualty in the sweep of arrests.

He returned to the formidable task of outlining his jury address. Darrow's capacious mind permitted him to be radical and practical at once.

*

A criminal trial starts as a blank canvas. For the non-partisan judge, the Latin term *tabula rasa* applies. The lawyers, one assigned for the government and the other, chosen by the innocent (at least until proven guilty) defendant, are the artisans filling the canvas with the evidence in the case. On occasion, the evidence produces incisive words and poignant pictures. In other instances, the canvas remains starkly white and sparsely filled. The fault, it must be acknowledged, does not lie with the lawyer. The lawyer is not entrusted with creating the evidence like an artist dipping a brush into palettes of color, but is instead the designated gatherer, selecting available witnesses and pieces of evidence to promote an advantageous position. The case may be supplemented through the probing engine of cross-examination of the adversary's witnesses. There are cases, however, where the cupboard of evidence is empty and beyond the ken of even the masterful lawyer to control; the shunned category of the overwhelming case where a doomed verdict is uneagerly anticipated.

Clarence Darrow plunged into the fifth day of such an overwhelming case. His thirteen-year-old client, Thomas Crosby, struggled to keep his tiny head above the prisoner's box. Darrow instructed his client to give him a holler if the witness's face evaded his view.

The criminal trial marked a world beyond the scope of the teenage defendant. But even at his tender years, he did appreciate the grave charge he faced of murdering Deputy Sheriff, Frank Nye. The sensational trial had produced a divided reaction in the vast community of court-watchers avidly following the case in Chicago and around America. Thomas Crosby represented the victim of extreme hardship valiantly defending his family's shelter --- or alternatively, he had fired the gun deliberately, as the prosecutor outlined, and thereby committed murder.

Thomas Crosby's mother, thrust suddenly into the life of a widow, struggled with the daunting task of keeping her house and maintaining the obligatory mortgage payments. She had sued her dead husband's firm for a tidy sum and that legal contest awaited judgment. The bank, with its feverish dedication to profits and losses, foreclosed on the mortgage.

The story then moved to its conclusion, an unsavory one in the prosecutor's virtuous opinion. Thomas, in the company of his mother and sister, had remained in possession of the house, with a padlocked gate and nailed boards covering the windows. Their food was running low, the interior unheated, and the house patrolled and protected from intruders by a brandished loaded revolver.

The inevitable time for eviction arrived, with Deputy Sheriff Nye allotted the task of prying the nailed boards apart with a crowbar. Thomas Crosby fired one shot from the gun and the blast killed his evictor.

Clarence Darrow stared one final time at the notes jotted on the blotting paper and shuffled them aside. The jurors must feel the palpable pain and fear that young Thomas felt, confined to a home with depleted coal and impoverished conditions.

Darrow seized on the tender age of his client to craft a central message to the jury. It would be bold and daring, even by his skillful standards, but in the case of a brazen shooting of a deputy sheriff, vital and necessary.

"I must forge ahead with my plan," he resolved.

One hour later, Darrow rose before Thomas Crosby's jury with a plea draped with conviction:

"Gentlemen of the jury, rather than have you send this boy to the penitentiary or to the reform school, to be incarcerated among criminals, where his young life would be contaminated... I would have you sentence him to death."

After the jury recessed to ponder their verdict, the judge addressed the defense lawyer:

"You do appreciate, Mr. Darrow, that you've just invited the jury to find your client guilty of murder." The trial judge stared from his perch at the defense lawyer's feckless act in dismay.

"On the contrary, Judge, I invited the jurors to be wise and merciful and return with a true verdict." Clarence Darrow's strategy, left unexplained to the baffled judge, involved presenting the jury with two stark and opposing choices. A disjointed submission might brook a wholly unsatisfactory compromise verdict. The jury, according to Darrow's compulsory script, possessed the choice of two contrasting alternatives. It could accept either the extreme verdict of murder or a not guilty verdict. He banked his client's freedom on the jurors' moral conscience shielding a boy from the fate of a hanging.

"We shall soon see if your tactic works with this jury, Mr. Darrow," the judge stated smugly.

*

Abraham Isaac sat slumped in his cell, eyes half open. He caught sight of Clarence Darrow's face through the bars and immediately sprung up and leaped a couple of strides to face him.

"Hello Clarence," he said. "I'm so happy that you came.

Pete told me that you had a jury trial ending today. What was the jurors' verdict?"

"Not guilty, Abe. I came straight from the courthouse to meet my friend. How are you managing?"

"I do worry about my family, but I'll be fine. The police provided me with a separate cell. The detective told me that I wouldn't survive longer than a minute in the main cell with the rest of the prisoners." He paused and stared intently at the lawyer. "I did meet him, Clarence."

"Who did you meet?"

"Czolgosz, the president's killer."

Darrow nodded, urging him to continue.

"He traveled from Cleveland and showed up unannounced at my house in July. He said that Emma Goldman referred him. She told him of her plans to leave Chicago for Buffalo to visit the Pan-American Exposition. Ironic, isn't it?"

There, Darrow interrupted the client's recitation. "I once attended a lecture by Goldman. At the end I told her that when I was younger, I hoped to reform the world, but I gave it up. Now tell me everything about your encounter with Czolgosz."

"Leon Czolgosz asked me a number of basic questions about the anarchist movement. I suspected that he must be a spy trying to extract damaging information about the movement. When I asked him what he wanted from me, he said he was soliciting assistance for acts of planned violence."

"What was your response?"

"He left without a lick of support. I believed even more strongly that he was trying to infiltrate the anarchist movement. Before I asked him to leave, I assured him that our views on the American flag didn't coincide. He just shrugged after I said that."

"Yes," Darrow said. "But predictably, he told the police about your meeting. We have no idea what else he's said."

"But I did take prudent action. At the beginning of September, I published a notice in the *Free Standard* calling on my anarchist comrades to be warned about this man making the rounds in Chicago whose fraudulent identity was a government imposter. I included a physical description of the man. Pete can locate a copy of the pamphlet in my desk drawer at home."

"Did Czolgosz mention to you that he planned a trip to Buffalo or anything specific about his plans for the president?"

"Absolutely not, Clarence." He held his face in his hands. "No-one will believe me, will they?"

"Stay strong, Abe," Darrow said as he packed up to leave. "I believe you, and it's my responsibility to make a prosecutor believe in your innocence and relieve you of this travesty of justice. I won't rest, Abe Isaac, until your liberty is regained."

Chapter Twenty

"*J'accuse*! I accuse you, my son, Eli Jacob, of abandoning your nation and being lured across the ocean for paltry riches. You forsake French culture for American capital. I accuse you of leaving when France needs you most, as it continues to recover from the smoldering ashes of humiliation of a lost war to Germany and the coronation of the German emperor in the Hall of Mirrors in Versailles. You were a distinguished police officer with an enviable, meteoric career in Paris and you foolishly chose to become an American stooge detective."

Disconcertingly, Eli Jacob sat with his mother and older sister, Louisa, in the Restaurante Botin overlooking the banks of the Seine River. Mama had summoned Eli to attend an urgent family meeting to save her crumbling family. She despaired at losing her only son.

"But *maman*," he protested. "I haven't abandoned you or France. America offers me a temporary residence, not a country that my family adopts."

Mama shrugged off his denial with a dismissive wave.

"*J'Accuse*! I accuse you, my brother, Eli Jacob, of discarding your people and your heritage. The splintered divisions in France left by the Dreyfus affair, the punctured lies implicating an innocent Jewish military captain, are continuing unabated. It is the destiny of the Jews of France to stem the tide of antisemitism and racism. Your meek and timid decision to leave your people at this time of need brands you as a coward, and I'm ashamed to call you my brother."

"*Mais non*, Louisa. I've not forgotten my roots. We light the Sabbath candles on Friday night. We attend synagogue services and fast on the Day of Atonement."

"A few token displays of your religion and, bravo, you pathetically believe that you're entitled to label yourself a proud Jew. If you have a religious spine, heed the call of Theodor Herzl and join me in December as a delegate to the Zionist Conference in Basel, Switzerland."

Detective Eli Jacob awoke from his trance and scrutinized his bedroom.

His wife lay still, peacefully asleep in their bed. The room remained intact. These nightmares were occurring more frequently, and he awoke each time with a sense of longing to return to French soil. The feeling quickly dissipated. In truth, the adjustment to life in America for the Jacob family had been relatively seamless. The scourge of antisemitism eluded them in Buffalo. The stinging condemnation in his dreams of abandoning France seemed illusory. A one-month trip to Paris to visit Mama and Louisa was planned for the spring and he'd spoken to his mother the day before on the telephone about the trip and agreed to take the train to Lyon with her to visit her brother, Phillipe.

"Mama, the trial for the president's killer starts today. I will be sitting beside the prosecutor in the front of the court."

"I'm proud of you, Eli," she had said. He imagined her comforting smile from afar.

During breakfast, he recalled a pleasant conversation with Theodor Herzl about their cycling clubs. He'd been introduced to Herzl with his old-fashioned bushy beard and piercing eyes. Herzl arrived at the police station in Paris in his suit riding a bicycle. The Viennese journalist had covered the court-martial hearing for Alfred Dreyfus, and Jacob's captain had arranged for Herzl to interview the detective.

"Eli," he said, "this pesky reporter wants to speak to a French policeman about the German spy and traitor. *Tu est un juif.* Let him see that the fidelity of a French Jew is with France."

Herzl struck him as an odd sort, a quacking duck in a settled pond of restful ducks. Rather than conducting an interview, Herzl lectured the Jewish detective.

"Dreyfus' plight is the clearest warning to our people that we are not safe," he declared ominously. "We're not safe in Austria; not safe in France, not safe in Germany and not safe in England." Before leaving, he slipped a scrap of paper into Jacob's hand. "Read this," he whispered. "It's from the prophet Ezekiel."

Jacob kept the paper as a charm, tucked under his police badge. He'd memorized Ezekiel's message:

Thus saith the Lord GOD; Behold, I will take the children of Israel from among the heathen, whither they be gone, and will gather them on every side, and bring them into their own land: And I will make them one nation in the land upon the mountains of Israel; and one king shall be king to them all.

Now Jacob hurried to dress for court. At Miss Sharma's request, he'd arranged for Detective John Garcy to meet them at her office at eight o'clock that morning. The prosecutor planned to call Garcy as her first witness at the trial. Fifty-five witnesses were slotted into separate days and times of the trial. The detective had devised the tight schedule; eye-witnesses first, followed by the police evidence and Czolgosz's statements and the various medical practitioners treating the president and addressing his cause of death.

Superintendent Horace Grant and Assistant Super-intendent Wilk paced outside of Neeru's office. "Good morning, Detective Jacob. We've been waiting for you," Wilk said, impatiently. "I know that you're pre-occupied with the trial. We only require a brief word."

"Yes, Assistant Superintendent. How may I be of service?"

"I understand that James Parker is on your witness list."

"That is correct."

"Well, we'd like you to convince the prosecutor to drop Mr. Parker from her witnesses," Grant said.

"For what possible reason, Superintendent?"

"You don't require him. Secret Service Agent Albert Foster is primarily responsible for the assassin's takedown. He wrenched the gun from Czolgosz while ten policemen and secret service agents subdued him. It will not reflect well on law enforcement if the jury hears that a civilian was the first person to rush to defend the president."

"But won't Foster say that Parker subdued Czolgosz?"

"I've spoken to him. He'll testify that he never saw no colored man in the whole fracas."

"So, we are to pretend at this trial that Parker wasn't even at the Temple of Music?"

The assistant superintendent nodded.

"And one more item, Detective Jacob," Superintendent Grant said. "We're pursuing these devilish anarchists all over the country. We've arrested a batch of them and are holding them in jail. The objectionable fact is, we can't keep them behind bars forever. The problem is, we're drawing a blank connecting any of them to the president's murderer. I receive daily reports by telegraph and the updates are disappointing."

"What are you proposing that I do, sir?"

"I had an idea that your prisoner might be interested in some form of a deal."

"A deal, Superintendent? Why?" Jacob shouted. "I will not negotiate with the prisoner!"

"Please stay calm and keep your rambling down. The last thing the police need is some press scribe recording our conversation. Leon Czolgosz knows that he will die. By God, the bloody fool is looking forward to the electric chair. But he must have some family member, a woman friend or parent, who he wants to meet. Make a deal with him to give up the names of his accomplices and you'll agree to extend him some private time in exchange."

"Superintendent Grant and Assistant Superintendent Wilk," Jacob replied curtly, my considered opinion is that the president's killer acted alone. There are no accomplices to his crime. I am quite certain."

This answer stunned his commanding officers.

"I must leave now to meet the prosecutor. She's waiting with a witness."

There was no farewell or "good luck" from the superintendent and his assistant as they went stomping down the hallway.

"*C'est dommage*," he thought. Superintendent Grant's unyielding search for a confederate of Czolgosz was akin to a stroll through a dark tunnel, rejecting any beam of light.

Detective Jacob updated Miss Sharma on the surprise visit from Grant and Wilk.

"And what are your thoughts about not calling Parker as a witness?" she asked. "He's here, ready to testify as our first witness."

"*Je pense* --- I think the assistant superintendent may have a valid point. It is harmful that the President's security staff allowed a misfit to slip through their fingers and shoot President McKinley. Why pour more kerosene on the fire?"

Sharma argued strenuously against cutting Parker, but ultimately relented. "All right," she declared. "Thank Mr. Parker and let him know that his services won't be needed." She picked up a sheaf of documents from her desk. "I've received the reports of the experts in mental disease. They have effectively eliminated the defense of insanity."

"Then what is left to argue?" Jacob asked the prosecutor.

"I can't foresee any defense being successfully mounted." Sharma implicitly understood why the New York attorney general had selected her as the prosecutor for this murder trial. The world's media hovered around the courtroom to cover the high-profile case. The trial would be widely followed, and presented a marvelous opportunity for the attorney general to showcase his progressive northern state; a woman prosecuting Czolgosz was a suitable prop to achieve his goal.

Sharma knew that her daughter in grade school could as successfully prosecute Leon Czolgosz. The verdict in this case would never be in doubt.

Chapter Twenty-One

The handcart swerved out of the man's path at the last moment, barely missing him. A loose sack of loafers emptied and scattered across the road as the handcart abruptly stopped.

"Hey, watch yourself, Mister, I nearly nicked you."

Clarence Darrow ignored the snarling driver and glanced idly at the sign on the handcart's side. 'SHOES RE-PAIRED', it read. His own career, he thought, could similarly be described as repairing reputations. The solace he restored to a defendant's bleak misery, beset with a tarnished good name, engaged the craft of mending. Darrow crossed the streets of Wabash and Monroe until he reached his bustling law office on Dearborn. He'd been up before sunrise for the brisk walk, guided initially by hazy streams of light from swinging lamps.

"Emily," he said with a dash of swagger upon arriving at the office. "I've decided. Please cancel my appointments and shuffle my court hearings for the next three days."

"Do you have a fever, Mr. Darrow?" she asked, with

concern. The notion of her venerable employer choosing to be unoccupied by the law for three days seemed as likely as her corrupt local city councilman turning down an enticing bribe.

"I'm grand, feeling splendid, Emily. The most wonderful thing occurred last night. Dare to guess what it is?"

"I'm not very adept at guessing."

The usually earnest lawyer practically bounded off the floor in glee.

"What is it, Mr. Darrow? I can't recall seeing you in such a state."

"Abraham Isaak has been released from jail." Darrow raised his fist in exultation, before embarking on a wisp of rhetorical flourish. "The freedom to express boundless speech and to expound infinite thought are the pillars sustaining a democracy. The powers of capital will not succeed at stamping out all radical thought."

In the waiting room, a young man with curled locks and a faint beard and moustache, a whimpering baby cradled at his side, raised his hands to applaud this silver-tongued soliloquy.

Darrow continued, his eyes sparkling with delight. "But Emily, there are more good tidings. A tender thirteen-year-old boy mercifully heard the most precious two words in the English language: '*not guilty*'."

"You won Thomas Crosby's trial, Mr. Darrow! This is welcome news, indeed." Emily recalled her first encounter with young Thomas. She had scolded his mother for bringing a mere child to the lawyer's office and was mortified to learn of his perilous criminal charge.

"The story improves, Emily. Thomas's mother was notified yesterday that she has won a judgment of almost eighteen thousand dollars against her dead husband's firm. The family can't save their old home, but Thomas's mother can find a new house without resorting to nailed shutters. You see, Emily, it's a spectacular morning. And I'm consumed by a celebratory spirit. I'm visiting that new Art Institute on the lakefront. A friend at a costume party recommended that I see a Rembrandt painting of 'The Accountant.' I asked her if Rembrandt painted any lawyers and she wasn't sure. It will be my first inquiry. I plan a stop at a saloon on Walton Street on the way for a pint and rye bread with some cheese and a sour pickle. I defended the owner years ago and he'll open early for me. And for tonight, I've purchased a train ticket to Buffalo to witness the finest lawyer in that grand city fulfill the highest calling of our profession."

"I will speak to Mr. Thompson about handling your appointments this morning." Emily grabbed the appointment book and pencil from her desk and began to circle the list of names to contact. "I'll juggle your schedule, Mr. Darrow. Don't fret about your cases being ignored."

"It will be accomplished with consummate skill. I'm certain of that," he said.

*

Caleb, with a surname unknown to any save the Bureau of Census, (it was Smerchanslove), secured the last chair in Judge Pickett's packed courtroom. The courtroom doors were locked.

"I can't believe how close I came to missing the trial," he blurted out, brushing past the gangly young man squeezed beside him in his row. Even lining up a couple of hours early for court at the City Hall entrance had not guaranteed a spot. Caleb's cherubic cheeks folded into two distinct creases as he spoke, symbolic of the clashing facets of his personality: vivid and curious and venal and cruel. He called over to the court constabulary, jabbing his finger at the front row. "Why did that *Negress* get a seat over there?"

"The defense lawyer was given three chairs to reserve. The two ladies in the front row are his guests."

"And what of the empty seat beside them. Who is that saved for?"

"That seat, I'm advised, is for a famous Chicago lawyer, Clarence Darrow. He'll be attending the courtroom this morning."

Seated beside the Negro lady – Bessie Harris, Mitchell's mother – Pharo passed the ticking minutes until trial reading a pamphlet for a manual training school for the children of the less favored and fortunate. Five hundred children populated the school on Buffalo's north side which combined education in grammar and arithmetic with modern methods of manual training. The school relied on the charitable contributions of the city's wealthiest patrons and Pharo had agreed to hold a fund-raising gala at her home in a fortnight; Burford was to help with her introductory greeting.

She heard sniffling and looked up to find Bessie dabbing her tears with a tissue.

"What can possibly be wrong?" Pharo asked.

"Nothing at all... I was just thinking, Miss Pharo, that you could offer me a seat at the throne of Jesus or the King's coronation, and I'd turn it down if I had to give up my seat in this here court. Mitchell came to the house yesterday to work on the trial with your husband. I saw Mr. Simmons with his arm wrapped around my son's shoulders, and Mitchell beaming like a choir boy in heaven, he was so thrilled. You know, I think that the greatest gift you can give someone is self-respect."

"You're a wise woman, Bessie," Pharo said. She reached over and delicately straightened Bessie's flat straw hat.

"Who's this handsome gentleman beside me?"

"I'm not sure, Bessie. Why not ask him?"

The man bowed slightly in his seat, saying, "My name is Martin Beliveau. I apologize, but I overheard your conversation."

Pharo saw Bessie blushing and intervened.

"Why are you here? Do you know my husband?"

"Who is your husband?"

"Burford Simmons, the defense lawyer for the murderer. Bessie's son, Mitchell, is assisting Burford."

Beliveau shook hands with Bessie and Pharo.

"Yes, of course. I'm familiar with your husband and his stellar reputation. And as to why I am here. I am a Canadian politician and I witnessed the shooting at the Temple of Music. I've come to court as a sincere token of my respect for President McKinley."

"You poor fellow. I've read all about you, Mr. Beliveau." Pharo took his hand. "You conducted yourself with admirable valor at the Temple of Music."

Beliveau sagged in his seat. That journalist, Willow Hooper, had prepared an effusive profile in courage of the Canadian railways minister after her abbreviated trip to Ottawa. Knowing the truth of his cowardice, he had refused to read it.

Bessie spoke. "You'll have to promise us that you won't

be cheering too hard for the prosecutor."

"At least not when my husband is speaking," Pharo put in.

Martin flashed a politician's practiced smile. "I have no stake in this trial's outcome, let me assure you ladies. I'm here strictly as an observer."

The deputy clerk stood in front of the gallery of spectators and raised one of his spotless white gloves. He carried a rod carved from walnut with a round knob at the top and spoke in a firm voice.

"The trial is to commence in exactly fifteen minutes. The prisoner will be brought into the courtroom shortly. Please do not make any noise, cursing or disturbance or I will be forced to ask you to leave. Judge Pickett will not tolerate any unruly disruptions in his courtroom."

*

The defense lawyers had plotted to enter the courtroom through a back-door staff entrance. Ten steps from the door, Burford directed his associate to forge ahead without him, since there was a pressing matter that Mitchell needed to address with the prosecutor.

"I'm going to the candy shop," he said in explanation. Burford's daily court ritual, almost forgotten in the brittle tension of this morning, was to indulge in a piece of chocolate. Conveniently, a candy shop was located a short walk from the City Hall courthouse. The owner had a bar of milk chocolate ready in the morning for pick-up by Burford. He'd read in the newspaper that he was the lawyer defending Leon Czolgosz.

Burford divided all food into a periodic table of food

groups. Food that was unhealthy for his diet, like pickled ham, was declared the enemy; permissible food, his ally. The basket at the grocery store was filled entirely with cherished allies. The enemy, constantly stalking him with temptation, must be adroitly avoided. Some delicacies, like pineapple, he declared as neutrals. He had declared chocolate to be his staunch ally, supplying the energy to sustain him in courtroom battle.

As he left the candy shop to a side road on his way to court, he failed to see a delivery truck pull up to his side. Two men in work uniforms approached. One dragged a pull-cart loaded with blocks of ice, and the other carried a huge cardboard box over his head. Burford felt a tap on his shoulder and turned around. Before blacking out, his last memory was a rag being shoved in his face with a tangy, acid smell.

He did not observe the ice hastily kicked off the pull-cart to melt on the street, his own limp body being dropped into the box and onto the pull-cart.

The workmen worked deposited their weighted load onto the back of the delivery truck and sped away.

Chapter Twenty-Two

The history of optometry records robust debate about which country was responsible for the origins of spectacles. Without any convincing evidence of a clear winner, India, China and Italy emerge as the leading candidates. In the vaster history of the common law, the science of vision developed as a critical component in the pursuit of justice. Justice, it is handily affirmed, must not simply be done, it must be *seen* to be done. The defendant, his accuser, the parties to a case and the general public must collectively arrive at an abiding and sincere belief that the balanced scales of justice are untainted by any element of bias or favor.

*

Mitchell Harris arrived at Neeru's office demanding an urgent meeting. Detective Jacob brought him a chair.

"I'll stand," he said testily.

"What's the problem, Mitchell?"

"I passed James Parker as he was leaving the courthouse --- he told me he won't be a witness at the trial."

"That's correct."

"So, you've decided to cancel the lone Negro witness at this trial. Do you expect me to believe that is a coincidence?" Mitchell's tone became indignant. "I can't think of any other reason you'd choose not to call the man responsible for thwarting Leon Czolgosz. Mr. Parker could have been killed trying to save the president. He stopped Czolgosz firing more bullets. This is the supreme gratitude he receives from the government for his act of courage."

"Calm down, Mitchell. You've misinterpreted my reason for not calling him."

"Really?" Mitchell answered in a cantankerous tone. "Don't take this young lawyer for a fool. You can't disguise the spittle of bigotry dangling from your lips."

"Mr. Harris, leave my office immediately," Neeru ordered. She motioned for the detective to escort him.

"I'm leaving on my own," he said defiantly. "I'll see you in court." He slammed the door shut on his way out.

*

"Where is Burford Simmons?" Judge Benjamin Pickett inquired, imperiously perusing every corner of the packed courtroom.

The trial of William McKinley's assassin introduced a freshly minted coin to the realm, that of the legal pundit. Such pundits insisted, for example, on introducing a caveat to the legal description of an assassin. The correct title it was strenuously argued, was an *alleged* assassin, as the batter of the trial had not yet been beaten. The practical response was that any description of Leon Czolgosz as an alleged murderer or assassin was an oxymoron in the extreme, as the defendant had proclaimed himself, in a bellowing tone, the president's killer.

Another tidbit of knowledge offered by the new brand of legal punditry was to be wary in law of stating a generalized proposition or an immutable rule. The expert pointed to a constellation of exceptions that invariably follow any legal principle. An intentional killing is murder, on the condition that it is not provoked; not the result of self-defense; not the product of an insane mind; and not borne of necessity.

There is, however, one rule that is a stranger to an exception. The criminal trial of the defendant cannot proceed in the absence of the retained lawyer.

The witness may be on the witness stand, Bible in hand, ready to be bound by solemn oath. The prosecutor may be holding a tablet of questions, prepared to advance a barrage. The bookish judge may be perched in a lofty chair facing the lonely defendant in the prisoner's dock. Yet, the trial will remain dormant and the parties, as still as the Statue of David, if the defense attorney is absent from the courtroom.

Mitchell Harris paused and looked back one last time before addressing Judge Pickett. "He is not here, and I have no reason to offer the court for his absence," he stated. "Mr. Simmons was in my company minutes before I entered the courthouse. I'm certain that my senior co-counsel intended to be here for the start of the trial. He would never disrespect this court or his client. I must say, Judge, his absence is confounding and a worry to me."

The judge pursed his lips and responded unsympathetically. "Most disappointing. I expect better from an experienced attorney. The morning is off to a bad start. I'll return to court when I'm notified of Mr. Simmons' return. You will expend your time locating your dilatory co-counsel, Mr. Harris, am I clear?"

If the purpose of the question was a disguised attempt to stoke an unmeasured response, Mitchell didn't rise to the flame. "Perfectly clear, Judge," he said. "I'll make my best effort."

The pronouncement in court of a lawyer's disappearance shrouded in mystery produced the effect of throwing a barrel of worms into the bay. Like a surging school of famished fish to the bait, the members of the press scrambled to unravel the reason for the defense lawyer's absence. Mitchell ignored their churlish questions. Noisy murmurings in the gallery included a recitation of wildly speculative theories. "It's Emma Goldman's crew," one reporter said brashly. "A band of anarchists scooped him up to create more chaos," another stated with feigned authority. A reporter from the *Washington Evening Star*, with old-fashioned round spectacles and red, white and blue suspenders, professed his opinion that the defense lawyer had panicked from the heightened pressure of the high-profile case and fled covered in shame.

Caleb overheard these speculative theories. "You're foolish and naive to expound such nonsense," he stated loudly, standing on the court bench. "Burford Simmons would never abandon his client. Regretfully, we need to consider that Burford Simmons might be seriously injured --- or even worse, dead."

The scribes and reporters recorded every word.

*

Detective Jacob discreetly asked Mitchell to meet him in the prosecutor's office. The junior lawyer stopped to offer a soothing message of support to Pharo and his mother, visibly distressed, in the front row. "He'll be back, Mrs. Simmons."

His eyes met an anguished stare. For Pharo, the idea that her exacting husband, who insisted on being spot on time for his bridge game, and ate dinner at the stroke of seven o'clock, would arrive late to a client's murder trial was preposterous. She had never known him to be dilatory in the whole course of their marital journey. The threatening letter and the prosecutor's menacing warning to Burford that had she summarily dismissed, now assumed a pejorative meaning and she began to fear foul play.

"Let's leave this wretched place and go home," she said to Bessie. "Mitchell, I'm relying on you to keep me informed of any development."

Mitchell steadfastly reassured her.

"What a shameful display from Judge Sour Pickles," Neeru exclaimed, in her office, her earlier acrimonious exchange with Mitchell forgotten. "He's treating Burford's disappearance like a delinquent child overstaying a curfew. I feel badly for Burford's wife --- I glanced at her in court and she appeared shocked. Mitchell," she continued, "I'd like you to retrace with Detective Jacob the route you and Mr. Simmons took to court this morning. It's important that you be precise. Mr. Simmons' life is likely in grave danger. And don't be troubled by our ornery judge. I'll protect you from that curmudgeon's wrath."

With each passing minute, the prospect of not finding

the missing lawyer heightened.

"Come with me, Mitchell," Detective Jacob said, rising. "Quickly."

A uniformed officer accompanied them, to confront any reporter seeking to obstruct their path. As they went, the detective probed Mitchell with questions about his principal's background. The identity of his wealthy father-in-law and the Rockefeller connection piqued Jacob's interest.

"What was Simmons' mood like today?" the detective asked.

"Quite calm, to my surprise. But Mr. Simmons is an extremely composed lawyer. The magnified profile of this trial didn't affect him in the least. I'm a lowly associate, and I found the heightened pressure suffocating."

"Did you notice anyone following you?"

They walked from the courthouse and the detective trailed Mitchell slightly.

"I didn't see anything unusual, but I wasn't paying attention to the surroundings either. Mr. Parker was the only person I spoke to. Here, down this road," Mitchell said, pointing. They walked along the roadway, as Mitchel outlined the exact route taken to the courthouse. "This is where Mr. Simmons and I agreed to part company. He headed in the direction of the candy shop over there."

He pointed to a shop with a basket brimming with candies on the sign over the window.

"Thank you, *monsieur l'avocat*. You've been most helpful. The patrolman will escort you into the courthouse."

Detective Jacob entered the candy shop through a chiming door. The shop's owner, Richard Bly, recognized the name of Burford Simmons instantly.

"He's my favorite customer," he said. "A real gentleman. He sent me a couple of regulars. One of them, a judge, buys a bag of Tootsie Roll candy every Friday. What's this about?" he asked the detective.

"He's gone missing. Tell me, do you remember anyone else in the shop with him?"

"No, he was alone. Missing, that's a darn shame. I sure hope he's not in any danger. I remember that he purchased a miniature box of chocolates and a couple of Hershey bars. One of the chocolate bars was a gift. I knew that he was defending President McKinley's murderer. It takes a strong man to defend vermin of that kind."

"Did you see where Mr. Simmons went after he left your shop?"

"He turned right. It took him through a curving street and alley."

"And to the back entrance of the City Hall."

"Yes, I believe so. It's a couple of blocks from the building."

Bly, his voice wavering, confirmed that he was sure that the lawyer had left alone.

Outside the shop, Detective Jacob turned down the side street. He noticed an object protruding from the plyboards lining the sidewalk. Approaching closer and examining it, he saw that the object was a block of half-melted ice. A fenced empty lot occupied this side of the unused road. Jacob stooped to touch the ice and had a sudden onset of queasiness. He identified the faint acrid odor as he was overcome with a discomforting sense of passing out. "Chloroform," he muttered, and immediately stepped away to survey the scene. A damp cloth lay on the ground behind the block of ice. *"Je comprends tout,"* he said aloud, shaking his head.

Burford Simmons had surely been rendered unconscious and kidnapped. The detective had discovered the precise location of the crime. The kidnapper had used the ice as a decoy somehow, he deduced. He must return to the police bureau at the courthouse immediately. Jacob made a cursory examination of the melted ice. Considering the temperature, he estimated that the kidnappers had about an hour head start.

The detective had investigated a few challenging kidnapping cases in his career in France. Unlike random crimes, kidnapping involved intricate and deliberate planning by the culprits. An idea flashed into his mind as he trotted to the courthouse.

Within moments of entering the police bureau, a group of seven attentive constables had congregated under his lead command. The detective was a maestro at handling a crisis, a prime reason that *les inspectuers* in Paris competed to engage the busy detective's services.

"Listen everyone," he ordered. "We must set up a series of police checks at different points across the city." Jacob pointed to a couple of officers in the front. "We're looking for two men travelling together with a third person in a hidden compartment." Jacob calculated that a pair of handlers had been necessary to carry the lawyer into the transporting vehicle. "We don't know if this is the crafty work of anarchists or not. But we must assume that the assailants are carrying firearms."

An officer was detailed to the crime scene to secure it until the exhibits were seized and Jacob dispatched a second officer to Pharo Simmons's house.

"Please be most gentle with the news about her husband," he said.

One possible motive for the kidnapping appeared to be a ransom demand --- Burford's father-in-law's business relationship with Rockefeller made his son-in-law a prime target.

"If requested, Mrs. Simmons should agree to the rendezvous and the kidnappers' terms. I must be notified at once of the call."

A patrolman was assigned the desk duty of contacting police stations in the vicinity to update them on the investigation.

Jacob gathered an assistant and prepared to leave. "Jennings, you're coming with me. Get a police artist on standby."

The distracted cashier at the grocery store, humming and dancing to a vaudeville song as they entered, told Detective Jacob that her store just started selling blocks of ice a month earlier. The owner of the grocery store had put a cardboard sign in the window informing his customers.

"Yes, I saw the sign. How long has it been there?"

"Two weeks."

The detective jotted a note.

The cashier remembered selling two men blocks of ice earlier that morning. She couldn't fix the time but recounted the men mentioning that they needed the ice for their catch and that they were fishermen. She had had no reason to disbelieve their story and never checked their mode of transportation.

"What's your name?" the detective asked.

"Patricia Clancy," she said, fidgeting nervously.

"You did nothing wrong, Patricia, but the police need your help. Are you willing to meet with a police artist at the station to describe the physical features of these men?"

"Sure, if it's important."

Jacob directed Officer Jennings to bring Patricia to the station.

"Where are you going, sir?" Jennings asked.

"I'm taking a walk to think. *Je pense*, I think, I'm missing an obvious clue..."

Chapter Twenty-Three

Pharo's Diary: *I have continued composing my diary. I'm not certain that the practice conforms to the model of overwhelming despair that belongs to the kidnap victim's spouse. I should probably be knitting or folding tablecloths and blankets and stoking the fire. But I am a writer at heart and the word exercise maintains the flow of circulation. I feel sorry for anyone who isn't a writer. I once expressed to my sister that the telephone is the greatest innovation in history. Odette's eyebrows flickered inwards dismissively. "I dare say I'd list the steam engine and electricity far ahead of a chatter box, Pharo." Odette always insists on the last word. The telephone has emerged as my companion as I wait for its clattering ring to auger the kidnapper's call. "He'll call you," the kind copper hovering in the doorway reassured me. But the kidnapper has not called, and a natural human impulse propels me to the most sinister outcome. I have begun to chart the funeral service for my husband. The pastor shall speak first; Clarence Darrow second; and the final tribute shall be mine.*

"Welcome to my country estate, Mr. Simmons."

"Where am I?" The words fumbled from his mouth, his eyes straining to focus. He felt groggy, his throat parched, and his fingers numb. Burford awoke and began assessing his surroundings, plotting his imminent escape. A middle-aged man with glittering eyes, a pencil-lined moustache and a circular birthmark on his Adam's apple, sat still, a victor's grin painted to his face and his legs casually crossed. The musty room, with faint vestiges of a wooden door nailed shut with rusty nails, held an imposing fireplace with burning logs and crackling branches strewn across. A cloudy grey sealskin carpet lay at his bare feet and a cot, blanket, and washbasin tucked into a corner. His hands and ankles were bound by rope that he pressed away from to keep the blood flowing.

He wiggled his fingers and toes and craned his neck. His body parts seemed to function.

Burford sat upright, his back hurting with the motion, perhaps from sprawling to the ground after the blackout. He scoured the room for an exit but found none.

"The chloroform has served a useful purpose. You've crossed the border into Canada, spent a few peaceful hours in Toronto. You're now in the basement of my farmhouse in Sutton, Ontario. It's surrounded by a barbed-wire fence, in case you're considering an escape. The wire glides through your skin like butter."

"What am I doing in Canada?"

Burford skipped over the obvious and pressing question of the reason for his kidnapping, but the remote location in a foreign country concerned him. The local police might be unaware of his plight. A search party of the Canadian Mounted Police wasn't about to show up for a daring rescue. These dimly lit surroundings seemed adequate but without an apparent escape hatch. Dingy dove-colored curtains blocked the windows.

Back in Buffalo, Burford surmised his sudden absence must be generating quite a commotion. Pharo would know some criminal misdeed had befallen him. But would anyone believe her? The murder trial focused sharply in his mind, generating a host of clashing thoughts. In effect, he had refused to conduct the defense of his anarchist client. The judge would be excessively perturbed, Mitchell devastated, the client indifferent and likely amused, and the rabid press whipped into a frenzy.

And what of dear Pharo? He imagined his anxious wife beset with unabated fright. He should have heeded her call and avoided Czolgosz's case like a cave of snakes.

How had his kidnapper managed to transport him to Canada without being foiled? The scheme couldn't be attributed to a rank amateur. Moments before the menacing beady-eyed man entered, Burford had heard a bell ring outside the house with a distinct gong-like sound, and concluded that the man didn't reside here, and that at least one other person occupied the farmhouse.

"Can we speak of my immediate release?"

Now the man, in his fifties, his voice unfamiliar, brushed his query aside. "This isn't the time for questions, Simmons. I've arrived back from a tiring trip overseas. I have several business ventures to run and I'm due to be in Toronto for an important meeting. I'll return to check on you tomorrow."

"And the topic of my return to Buffalo will be the first item on your agenda," Burford said, not flinching.

"Do you seriously contend that I'd take the considerable effort and risk to bring you this distance, only to let you vanish unscathed?" A sneering, mocking laugh followed, like that of a raving despot. Moving to depart, the man turned towards the lawyer. "You may be interested to learn that Czolgosz's trial is continuing in a few days. Two former State Supreme Court judges have been appointed to ably defend him. You're his *former, defunct* lawyer now, Burford Simmons."

"I'm not concerned with the trial or my law practice," Burford said defiantly. "I'm not aware why you selected to kidnap and hold me as your hostage and why you're not prepared to discuss releasing me. But please understand that I will be found, and you'll be held accountable. Don't consider for a moment that you'll evade punishment for this damnable crime."

"Bravo, Mr. Simmons, and persuasively delivered --- with the same robust flourish of one of your jury addresses. But I am not one of your impressionable jurors; I'm your kidnapper, in full control of your fate, and I have a firm plan to put in place." He left without another word.

"*A firm plan to put in place.*" The words were forbidding, but Burford resolutely refused to panic. He despaired when he thought of Pharo. She'd blame herself for not urging him to take precautions for his safety. The state of her health consumed him, and he resolved to escape. He accepted that the kidnapper's scheme must inevitably include killing him. Burford's ability to identify the man's facial features settled his fate.

He struggled to recall any contacts in Canada, but drew a blank. He searched the room in vain for a telephone. He realized that it would likely be in the hall upstairs. Burford noticed the bulge in his jacket pocket and recalled the chocolate bars he had acquired. He'd eat one squashed bar and hide the rest of the chocolate under the blanket on the cot.

A considerable time passed before a young man entered the room, balancing a tray of food. He had a taut frame and wore a white shirt with baggy slacks --- and Burford could not help but notice the revolver in his hand.

He placed the tray and gun on the cot and began to retie a loosened rope around Burford's hands. "I'm going to let you eat your lunch," he said. "Any funny stuff and I'll be forced to shoot you. Do you understand?"

"Yes, I understand. Tell me, what is your name?"

"I'm not permitted to answer your questions."

"If you're bringing me my meals, it's only respectful and proper that we exchange basic information about ourselves."

"Okay, but that's all. My name is Arthur Simon. I'm one of the guys who brought you here from the States. I borrowed the trolley from work. I'm a longshoreman in the summer unloading the big iron steamers on Lake Ontario."

Burford made a mental note: this scoundrel can be coaxed to volunteer information.

He said lightly, "I certainly made it convenient to pick me up, traveling on my own from the candy shop."

"Just like we were told. You plopped right into our laps as we planned it. And thanks for the box of chocolates."

A major clue, Burford thought... *Habits, habits...* His kidnapper had followed him at an earlier trial he had defended. "But why?" he wondered.

"That was a solid scheme you all worked out. How did you get me across the border into Canada?"

"That was simple. The guy in charge runs an export-import business. We had an invoice to show the customs officer that we were bringing a piece of furniture in the box."

A business for his kidnapper! "Expertly done and bravo to you for succeeding. Tell me more about this fellow giving orders," Burford urged Arthur. "What's his name?"

"Wait a minute, you're tricking me! I told you no questions are allowed." He rubbed the gun against Burford's chin.

Burford feigned amusement. "Listen to me Arthur. I've studied the law my entire adult life. It's my professional calling and I'm good at it. If I die in this house, you're going to be charged with murder as surely as if you pressed your finger on that trigger and blew my brains from my skull. You'll be executed in an electric chair along with your boss. Is that the way you want your life to end?"

Arthur dropped his head and his voice softened.

"I didn't want to be part of your kidnapping. You must believe me. H..." He paused. "The guy in charge, frightens me more than anyone I've ever met. I had no choice, or else."

Burford made a mental note of the first letter of his kidnapper's surname.

"Why didn't you have a choice, Arthur?"

"I have a bad gambling problem with poker and the racetrack. I got some credit advanced, gambled it and lost. The people who lent it to me threatened to break my legs and arms if I didn't pay them. A friend at work recommended this guy he knew. He seemed really understanding about my cash problem. He gave me five hundred dollars without me even signing a piece of paper."

"And then what happened?" Burford had once defended a similar extortionist who charged a thousand percent interest on a loan.

"A couple weeks later, couple of huge goons showed up at my house demanding ten thousand dollars. When I told them I couldn't pay it, they brought me to an office on the top floor of the Temple Building in Toronto. I was pushed up a stairway to the roof."

"And this guy in charge told you that you could pay your debt by running a few errands for him --- and my kidnapping in Buffalo turned out to be one of those meagre errands."

"Exactly."

"Tell me, Arthur, did this fellow you owed the money to ever tell you why he chose to kidnap me?"

"Nope, but I know that he hates you something fierce. You must have done something awful to get him so worked up. Listen, enough. Eat your food. You'd better not tell Mr. Ha... that we spoke. It will end badly for both of us."

The lawyer acted non-plussed. Another letter to add to his kidnapper's surname.

"Your secret is safe," Burford reassured him. "I like you, Arthur. I can tell you're a decent person who's been placed in an overwhelming position. I think I can help you."

He gazed with favor at the man pointing a revolver at his head. Arthur Simon could be the key to securing his freedom. The first step --- a letter delivered to Pharo.

Chapter Twenty-Four

Pharo's Diary: *A letter arrived this morning from the president of the New York Bar Association. At the annual dinner of the association a special prayer was recited for Burford Simmons. I discovered the paper slipped inside the letter on an unfolded piece of stationary. It will make ideal material to construct a paper puppet or an Eddy kite. I shall enlist Mervin's help after he returns from his lawn tennis match. I am anxious to ask if the prayer's insertion at the dinner came before or after the serving of the roast pork. Not a single colleague of Burford's (except for Mitchell Harris and Fig Golem --- who sneezed the entire time) dropped by the house to offer comfort or support. And now this distinguished group of lawyers dares to convey an inscription of fond wishes and solemn prayers. It makes my blood boil.*

In receipt of a motion to be disqualified for reasons of conflict, a budding lawyer proceeds directly to the senior member of the firm in bafflement. "Reasons of conflict? My training in law school prepared me for conflict!" he complains. "It's an adversarial system of justice and not a tea party. My criminal procedure professor emphasized that the prosecution and defense are locked in a combative struggle to secure opposing verdicts."

"This is a conflict of a different type," the scholarly lawyer says, after reading the motion. "You defended a prosecution witness in a trial last month. The prosecutor is seeking to remove you as counsel to prevent you from cross-examining your former client."

Unlike the driver of a cab for hire, who must accept all fares, a trial lawyer may be prevented, in rare circumstances, from handling a brief. In the case of a Lothario prosecutor sharing a bed with the officer in charge of the investigation, the appearance of fairness and propriety would be tarnished. The officer might nudge a witness's answers to favor his lover's side. Conflict may be a product of subterfuge. That perennial litigator, Barley Wiggins, traversed the city's top law firms on the pretense of retaining counsel, with the purpose of disqualifying the batch from acting for his adversary. When word circulated of his nefarious deed, no lawyer would dare represent him.

The issue of a possible conflict in the trial of Leon Czolgosz arose thusly.

Arriving at court in Buffalo, Clarence Darrow was bewildered to discover a locked courtroom and a deserted corridor. A caretaker dipped his mop in a pail of water and a yawning policeman sat idly on a chair guarding the door. "You're too late," he said. "Court's finished."

Darrow, flummoxed, checked his watch. "It's only 11:00. Why isn't court in session?"

"The trial couldn't proceed because the attorney went missing. He ran away. Poor fellow's feeling ashamed for defending the man who killed our president. I can't say I blame him. Are you a lawyer too?"

"I wear the title proudly and I'm a friend of the attorney who's gone missing. He didn't run." Flummoxed, Darrow pressed for more information and was directed to the prosecutor's office on the third floor.

His train had been delayed and he had come directly from the train station, after little sleep, and was carrying an overnight bag, valise and a copy of the *Chicago Tribune* tucked under the arm of his suit jacket. He bounded the stairs in giant leaps and knocked and entered the cramped office.

"Tell me it isn't true," he said, the formality of introductions skipped over.

"You must be Clarence Darrow. This is Detective Jacob," Neeru said.

"A diabolical deed," Darrow said. "There's an element of danger in defending the reviled and despised. But kidnapping a defense lawyer moments before the trial starts...that's a first."

"*Pardon moi*, excuse me, but why are you confident that Czolgosz's defender was kidnapped?"

Darrow cast a dismissive glance at the detective. "Because my dear friend Burford would never abandon a client. Do you hear me, Detective? Never!"

"I'm truly sorry, Mr. Darrow," Neeru said. "Burford had told me that you'd be attending the trial. Detective Jacob didn't intend to offend you. Is that correct, Detective?"

"But no. Of course. We have started *sur le mauvais pied*. How do you say in English --- on the wrong foot? Mister Darrow, how long will you be gracing us with your presence?"

"I'm attending the first two days of the trial, but I'll let my office know that my stay will now be extended."

A man with a jolly smile and radish red cheeks entered.

"Judge Kerfoot!" Neeru said.

"Glenn will do."

Judge Glenn Kerfoot, affably lavishing praise on the lawyers in his courtroom as dewdrops on a field, had been a commanding officer in the Spanish-American War and employed cunning military strategy to the prosecution's advantage. His lecture at a prosecutors' conference had been titled: "Lessons of the Trojan Horse". Kerfoot had a box-sized head with stubbles on top like manicured shrubs. His eyes opened at half-mast, conveying the false impression that he was mildly awake.

"Judge Pickett sent me here for a chat," he said. "His message, Neeru, is that he's prepared to forgive Burford for a bout of stage freight. He possesses human foibles like the rest of us. The judge is in a foul mood, but much calmer after I vouched for Burford's sterling character. I reminded Judge Pickett that this trial is a showcase for Buffalo and that Burford Simmons would play his part honorably." Wishing Neeru a good day, Judge Kerfoot abruptly departed.

"Thank God for juries," Darrow said. "The trial isn't a regal gala on display for the world."

"Where are you putting up in Buffalo?" the detective asked.

"Pharo Simmons has invited me to stay with her."

"That will not be possible," Jacob said. "I have instructed the policemen at that house to permit no visitors. We're monitoring Mrs. Simmons' home day and night for messages or telephone calls, hoping that she'll be contacted to pay a ransom for her husband's release."

"But there is no contact yet from the kidnapper?"

The detective checked for Neeru's approving nod before answering. "None, but it's still early. I'll be honored if you'd be a guest in my family's home during your brief stay in Buffalo."

"That's kind of you, Detective, but I'll locate a hotel in the area."

"I won't hear of it." Detective Jacob took the valise from the lawyer's arm. "I'll arrange for your bag to be transported to the house."

"You're most generous."

Early that evening, Clarence Darrow sat subdued and reflective, at the Jacob family dinner table, dabbing at a meal of roasted chicken in honey and plum sauce and baked sweet potatoes prepared by Chef Jacob. Slices of the detective's freshly baked sweet challah bread were passed around in a wicker basket. A carafe of French wine from Provence rested in the middle of the table.

"The chicken is exquisite, Francoise," he said. "I apologize for my lack of appetite."

"We do understand, Mr. Darrow, she said. "Eli and I are most distressed about your friend's kidnapping. I was looking forward to his defense of Mr. Czolgosz. I know this might sound strange coming from a police officer's wife."

"A question just occurred to me, Clarence," the detective said, chagrined. "Do you think there is a problem with the lead detective hosting the close friend of Mr. Czolgosz's lawyer?"

"It's evident that Burford can't act for the fellow if he's been spirited away, can he?"

"I agree," Eli said, sighing in relief.

Clarence Darrow and the detective retired to the living room with the red wine, two empty glasses and a tubular cigar. Darrow sat in a round leathern club chair next to a small smoker's stand. Lighting the cigar, he asked for the details of the police investigation into Burford's kidnapping "in the strictest of confidence."

Jacob told him that no fingerprints had been picked up from the crime scene. A sketch of the kidnappers had been delivered to the local newspapers.

"You're not expecting a ransom demand are you, Detective?"

"Very perceptive, Mr. Darrow. The motive of the kidnappers is a mystery yet to be solved," Jacob said. "But money --- no, that is not the goal of these kidnappers, I deduce. Why choose a time when the whole world is watching?"

"Then who is the likely culprit?"

"The prosecutor contends that the hands of the anarchist are responsible for Mr. Simmons' capture. What better way could be chosen to disrupt the trial of Leon Czolgosz? But I experience doubts. I'd expect an anarchist kidnapper to boast of his daring crime and puff out his chest, as you Americans say. Instead, we have *rien*, absolute silence. This fact concerns me."

"I am aware, Detective Jacob, that the anarchist Emma Goldman attempted to rally support for the president's shooter before she learned, to her dismay, that Czolgosz is reviled by most anarchists. He's blamed for the public hysteria and targeting of anarchists and the roundup of arrests by the police. He's caused incalculable damage to the movement that may never be recovered. The kidnapping of Leon Czolgosz's lawyer could only senselessly compound the problem."

Jacob sipped his wine as coiling rings of smoke drifted by. "I hadn't taken that into account, Clarence. But it does raise the possibility that the police are being steered to a dead end."

"Precisely, Detective. The kidnapping may deliberately camouflage the kidnapper's true purpose. His charade may be duping the police to believe that anarchists are responsible."

"We were taught in police college in France that the obvious answer is not always the correct one." Jacob stood and paced the floor before speaking. "I do have a policeman's theory, Mr. Darrow, permit me to share it with you. A man's fermenting rage may lead to manic and uncontrollable behavior. Are you familiar with the works of William Shakespeare?"

Darrow preferred Mark Twain but allowed that he had heard of Shakespeare.

"In Shakespeare's play, '*The Winter's Tale*', the King of Sicilia, suspects, on the flimsiest of evidence, that his childhood friend, is having an affair with his wife, Hermione. The king is filled with jealous rage, renounces his unfaithful wife and abandons their baby daughter on the coast of Bohemia, where she is raised by a shepherd. The faithful Hermione, falsely accused and misjudged, eventually dies of grief. But the oracle of Delphi vindicates Hermione's pristine virtue and the king, belatedly contrite, is rebuked by Paulina, a noblewoman of Sicily:

But, O thou tyrant!
Do not repent these things, for they are heavier
Than all thy woes can stir; therefore betake thee
To nothing but despair. A thousand knees

Ten thousand years together, naked, fasting,
Upon a barren mountain and still winter
In storm perpetual, could not move the gods
To look that way thou wert

"Is it your opinion then, Detective Jacob, that Burford Simmons committed an act so outrageous to prompt the kidnappers' vengeful actions? I'm not sure that I follow you."

"I apologize, Clarence. I did not intend to accuse your friend of committing a grievous deed. It is the perception of the offended party that dictates revenge. We need to examine the previous cases of Burford Simmons to check for possible clues. An old client, perhaps, disenchanted with his lawyer's result. His files are stored at his former law firm. I spoke today to a lawyer at the firm, Raleigh Sykes, who insists that Simmons' files cannot be shared with the police."

"I'll plan to take a side trip to the law firm to speak to Burford's former law partners. They likely will be more accommodating opening the files to another defense lawyer. I'm certainly aware of the principle of attorney-client privilege. But a man's life is at stake."

"I welcome your splendid idea. My time, of course is devoted to assisting Neeru with Czolgosz's murder trial. The judge will be most anxious to proceed with the trial. *En enfin.* My time will be occupied. Other officers will be designated to assist, of course."

Both men retired for the evening. In the middle of the night Eli Jacob awoke and replayed the conversation with Darrow.

"The obvious answer is not always the correct one."

He sat up upright in bed. "That letter," he exclaimed.

"I must check it again." Dragging his bathrobe, he hurried down the stairway to the study --- noticing on the way a candle was still burning in Clarence Darrow's bedroom.

The letter had been placed in a thin file titled: *Simmons Kidnapping*. He'd dismissed the threatening letter as a hoax after the police confirmed that the Anarchist League of America didn't exist. But had he been too hasty reaching his conclusion? He marched up the stairs with carrying the letter and tapped on Darrow's door.

"I hope that I'm not disturbing you," he said, entering.

"Not at all, Eli. I'm reading a book about a flying machine. I'm too concerned about Burford Simmons' well-being to sleep. Dark thoughts creep into my mind."

"Please --- look at this letter." Jacob filled him in on its background.

"And this Anarchist League is a ruse?" Darrow asked.

Eli assured him that the police had conducted a thorough check.

"Let's assume," the lawyer observed, "that this letter was sent by the kidnapper. If the actual identity of any anarchist or organization is included, the police would conduct a thorough investigation. Correct?"

"*En effet.*" Eli nodded his agreement.

"The targets may have verifiable alibis."

"And the investigation would be closed."

"What if the kidnappers wanted you to believe that the anarchists are connected to the kidnapping, but can't risk the police disproving it?"

"They'd use a fake name as a cover --- such as the Anarchist League of America."

"It's possibly a ruse. Exhibit A: the timing of the kidnapping on the morning of the trial; Exhibit B: the kidnapping in the vicinity of the courthouse and Exhibit C: this letter." Darrow perused the letter. "It appears to be a concerted campaign to blame the anarchists."

"Certainly."

"Is this the newsprint used by the *Buffalo Morning Express*?" Darrow asked.

"I'm not sure. I'd need the newspaper to compare," Detective Jacob replied after reviewing the lettering.

"Newspapers in the country are generally distinguished by different typesetting. The *Chicago Tribune*, the *New York Times* and the *Buffalo Morning Express* each have unique typesetting. Detective, it isn't the place for a Chicago lawyer to instruct the police on their investigation..."

"You are right," Eli interrupted him. "We must locate the newspaper connected to the typesetting of this letter."

Darrow pulled the blankets aside and blew out the dim candlelight. "We both have a busy day ahead, Detective."

*

Eli Jacob spent a restful Saturday morning before the trial, at the Park Heights Synagogue. The synagogue's rabbi, Rabbi Benjamin Woodley, fluent in five languages, possessing a thunderous voice, and capable of reciting a vegetable hash recipe like the Gettysburg Address, chanted a blessing for the new American president, Theodore Roosevelt.

Roosevelt's oath of office had taken place on a crisp afternoon in a plain ceremony laden with sadness, on Delaware Avenue, a few blocks from the synagogue.

"The smooth transition of leadership scored a double

eagle for America," Rabbi Woodley declared.

He routinely sprinkled his sermons with references to golf, his chosen sport. The rabbi's calendar in the spring and summer listed Saturday as a day of prayer and Sunday as a day of links. "Live each day of your life like an approach shot," he'd often preach, "as we advance steadily to the hole at the pin." The proverbial hole at *this* pin, Eli had learned, was a burial plot in the synagogue's cemetery.

Rabbi Woodley's sermon this Sabbath morning included the biblical story of Joseph and the lascivious wife of the Egyptian pharaoh. Eli listened raptly as Rabbi Woodley recounted Joseph's attendance at Pharaoh's palace and the failed seduction attempt by the Egyptian king's wife. "The Bible records that Joseph ran," the rabbi preached, "but not because he had been chased. Here stood a man alone in the foreign world of Egypt, sold repeatedly into slavery, deciding to imperil his freedom by fleeing. It led to a false accusation and wrongful imprisonment. So why then did Joseph choose to run?" Rabbi Woodley asked, as he pounded the lectern. "The answer is that a fallible man recognized that he'd surely succumb to his own human frailties. The visage of his father saved him at the moment of his reckoning. The message we must all take from Joseph's story is that we share Joseph's malleable nature. But the irresistible pull towards questionable and dishonest deeds must be perennially shunned."

The allegory touched a chord with the detective. He reproached himself for tricking Clarence Darrow into spending the night at his home. The ruse was hatched in Neeru's office. Darrow deserved a truthful account.

The morning before, Eli had been summoned to the Chief of Detective's office where the chief and his deputy awaited.

"You are taking an active part in the Burford Simmons investigation," the deputy chief stated.

The detective readily acknowledged his role.

"You're hereby ordered to dedicate yourself exclusively to the Czolgosz trial. The chief and I have assigned Detective Kunstler to the Simmons investigation. Do you understand?"

Jacob accepted this stricture, though knowing that Kunstler, newly promoted, had distinguished himself in the detectives' office for his abject level of incompetence. In his first month, he'd dropped his gun down a grain silo, called for a pathologist with the victim still alive, spilled ink on his police notebook and arrested the mayor of Buffalo for speeding in a horse carriage.

But Jacob recognized the import of the executive decision. The kidnapping of the lawyer for McKinley's shooter was only a token concern for the police, and unworthy of a senior detective to lead the investigation.

His invitation to Darrow was an opportunity to solicit the assistance of the renowned lawyer. There had been no discussion with Raleigh Sykes about attorney-client privilege. Indeed, the victim's former law partners were suitably co-operative. Jacob regretted the fib, but it produced the desired result of the lawyer Darrow's participation.

So, Clarence Darrow assumed the role of leading the investigation into his friend's abduction, but it might be too late. Neeru had pointed out that Burford Simmons could be dead, and Jacob shared her grim view.

Rabbi Woodley announced to the congregation the final prayer for the service, Jacob's favorite, *Masteur De Universe*. He searched upward in supplication and sang:

Steve Skurka

"*He is my God, my living Redeemer,*
Rock of my pain in time of distress.
He is my banner, a refuge for me,
The portion in my cup on the day I call."

Chapter Twenty-Five

Pharo's Diary: *Detective John Garcy called on me today. I gladly invited him in, recalling our fleeting encounter at Niagara Falls days before the president's shooting. Garcy told me the president was deeply concerned about my fate as I stood perilously close to the edge of the falls. "President McKinley was persuaded that you were prepared to leap to your certain death," Garcy said. "I certainly was not!" I replied indignantly. Garcy told me that McKinley's assassin was hovering around the president at Niagara Falls. I nearly fainted. Garcy told me of his police career after McKinley's death --- he has resumed his duties in the detective's office in Greenpoint. A letter from the president on his death bed relieved Garcy of any official blame for the tragedy at the Temple of Music. His life, however, has not been easy. We are kindred spirits sharing the cabin of despair. This perhaps explains his surprising visit. Senior officers shunned him at his detective's office. I offered him a glass of lemonade. "The president would approve of my visit, Mrs. Simmons. I will devote the rest of my life to meeting his lofty standards." I admired John Garcy's reverent affection for our lost president. In this bleak streak of misery, I have acquired the knowledge that loyalty is a paramount virtue. It earns no dividend; is wholly unselfish and is the surest measure of an enduring friendship. Garcy slipped me a note before departing. "Telephone me if you need to hear a friendly voice," he said.*

The word stubborn, it is stated, absent authority, is named after the mountain climber, Pinchas Eden Stubborn, whose sterling quality, it is remarked, absent affectation, was that when fixed on a decision he became immovable as a petulant mule. It happened that one day that Pinchas strode up an obscure mountain in the Italian Alps in the company of a business partner, Mr. Hamish Webster. Torrential rain pour soaked the mountain as the pair of climbers peered at the outline of the summit through their foggy goggles. Feet sliding like a circus seal, Hamish sensibly decided to return to the mountain base. Pinchas, however, continued to climb, reaching a distance of five umbrellas from the top, when he slipped. At his funeral, Webster, the nascent author of an English dictionary, introduced his dearly departed friend's surname as a descriptive adjective, depicting unwavering patronage to an idea. Webster neglected to consider that the new word's wingspan covered a broad spectrum of conduct, from the wickedly stubborn to the idyllic and heroic.

Pharo's lineage could be traced to Pinchas, the mountaineer. As the month of September in the year, 1901, receded into October, she sat transfixed to a bench next to a telephone, like a stubborn angel, for a call from her husband's kidnapper. At one point, she inadvertently knocked the receiver off the hook and let it hang; discovering the mistake, she cried in panic: "Oh no, I'm sure that I missed the call."

"Please, Miss Pharo," Bessie declared, "you must have your rest or get some fresh air. Let Mitchell and me take a turn on the bench."

"Thank you", Pharo replied, "but the caller" (any mention of a 'kidnapper' had been forbidden by Mervin) "will be expecting me to answer. I must be ready for his instructions."

She sat next to the phone, reading, conversing and praying. Mitchell and Bessie watched in wonderment. On a rising scale of majesty, there is first the Taj Mahal of Agra, followed by the Great Wall of China, topped only by a display of the unremitting love of one human being for another.

*

"Hooper! in my office." Shelby's sharp command could be heard through the premises of the *Brooklyn Daily Eagle*.

Willow Hooper crossed the floor, deftly hopping over boxes and wiggling through narrow aisles accentuated by the resonant sound of fingers pounding on typewriter keys. She planned to ask Shelby for a raise in the next few days. A couple of reputable metropolitan newspapers, including the *Buffalo Morning Express*, were enticing her to join their papers. She planned to tell Shelby about her rising status of a reporter in demand, meriting increased pay.

"Listen, Willow. This story circulating that the lawyer for the president's assassin is kidnapped is getting some buzz. No-one, including the police, seems to have a clue who is responsible. The mystery makes it an edgy story. I need my best reporter in Buffalo covering it. And we both know who that is."

"As a matter of fact, I've intended to…"

Shelby interrupted her mid-sentence. "I wonder if it's one of those crazy anarchists. Maybe it's a ploy to keep everyone guessing. Well guess what?" Shelby clapped his hands and laughed louder than a cutting buzz-saw. "It's working. Find yourself a live anarchist to interview. Our meeting is finished. Call me when you've typed your story, I want the first look. Okay, scoot." He didn't bother to raise his head from the sheaf of papers on his desk.

Willow overlooked his rudeness. The heady assignment of speaking to an anarchist intrigued her. Even a nitwit like Shelby could stumble occasionally on a masterful idea. This might be her big career break.

Chapter Twenty-Six

Pharo's Diary: *I have decided to resume my weekly book club with Edna and Gertrude so that my brain cells don't become as stale as moldy bread. Edna's assignment today was Huckleberry Finn. Edna elegantly read a chapter and then presented a neat summary of the book. We must have read different editions though, because Edna's comments missed their mark by a farmer's field. When my turn arrived, I struggled to humbly respond, balancing myself on the tightrope of veracity. "Riveting, Edna", I said, "You've given me a fresh perspective on Twain." I labor to smile. Not a peep yet from Burford's cursed kidnapper!*

"Good morning."

"It may be for one of us."

"It will not help matters, Mr. Simmons, if you use that surly tone. It is unappreciated and against your vested interest. But you're already aware of that. It's your lawyerly instinct to oppose authority and be the contrarian."

This marked the second occasion that his well-spoken

captor had resorted to an unprovoked tirade against lawyers. Another instructive clue for Burford to file.

The kidnapper, carrying a magazine, dropped a log of wood in the fire, examined the bindings on Burford's hands and feet, and pulled up a chair beside him.

"These are the rules of the house: you'll be fed morning and night and permitted one quick walk in the morning to relieve yourself. You'll be treated humanely. You will be permitted no contact with anyone on the outside. I will allow you to write a farewell letter to your wife which will be sent at the appropriate time. And finally, you will be killed on the same day that Leon Czolgosz is executed. It's not that I care about your former client --- he can rot in hell as far as I'm concerned."

"You want to link my murder to the anarchists. The police will be fooled into believing that I'm the victim of a revenge killing. That's the explanation for the timing of my death, isn't it?"

"Correct. An astute observation on your part." His tone turned wistful. "You know, my father hoped that I'd pursue the law and be a lawyer. I disappointed him. He sent me to Oxford to study humanities. Instead, I acquired an interest in enterprising criminal schemes, which paid handsome dividends. I live in a magnificent home on Jarvis Street with my wife and daughter. I've managed to build a half-million-dollar export-import business. I keep offices on the fifth floor of the Temple Building in Toronto; one office for my company, Phantom, and the other to manage our corporate donations. You'd be impressed with my commitment to philanthropy."

"Bronze plaques in hospitals and homes for the aged with the family name, I expect," Burford replied, surmising that his kidnapper would relish the chance to boast to his doomed captive.

"Tell me more about how you achieved Phantom's rousing success."

"My most recent business venture is an exquisite operation. Not a single piece of merchandise is brought into Canada or exported. Let's say I receive an order for a product with a cash payment of ten thousand dollars. I deliver a shipping order with an envelope filled with eighty hundred-dollar bills. No product is shipped, but if the money is traced, there is legitimate paperwork to support it."

"And you've made a couple grand by cleaning the dirty cash through a ringer, like a money laundry. The customer is happy because the money's source is from gambling, prostitution or a drug racket, and eludes the attention of the police."

"It also helps to have a deputy police chief on my payroll. I am untouchable."

"I'm still puzzled, though, why you've kidnapped me and brought me to Canada to perish. We've never met, and I've done you no wrong as far as I'm aware."

"Can you be certain that our paths haven't crossed, Burford Simmons? You're quite right. You deserve an explanation. But I'm pre-occupied with a pressing business matter. Satisfying your curious mind isn't my priority."

Another clue, Burford thought. They had encountered each other. But where? There was an aura of vague familiarity about the man he struggled to recall.

"I'm certain that if we met, I dealt with you honorably."

"Honor? A sinner and apostate dares to speak of honor in my presence?" He rolled up the magazine and repeatedly swatted his captive's face, leaving red swelling marks.

Burford winced. "Go ahead, try that stunt with my ropes untied."

"You've forfeited the magazine and your breakfast for tomorrow," his kidnapper said, turning abruptly to exit the room.

A log crackled in the fire as Burford listened for the key inserted into the door at the top of the stairs.

Chapter Twenty-Seven

Pharo's Diary: *I enlisted the assistance of a palm reader to attend the house today with Odette. She traced the lines of my palms and studied the contours of my hand before speaking with authority: "I see a sudden change of good fortune about to enter your life," she proclaimed. "Do you see the way that this line arches upwards?" (I'd never noticed the line before.) "I'll stake my life on it. I'm confident that I'm right." The palm reader left with two dollars and a galloping gait. "She seemed sure, Burford will return," my sister observed. "When?" I asked, and Odette answered. "Be content with the positive news."*

The branch of humor known as sarcasm, with the cutting edge of a carpenter's sharp blade, began (apocryphally) with a recounting in a legal journal of the tale of a criminal lawyer from Cincinnati, Fanner Henein. Fanner's vocation of defending lost souls, with the ferocity of a lion, confounded their next-door neighbor, a pillar of the local business community. At a New Year's party, the neighbor, disinhibited by a few tall glasses of champagne, approached Fanner's wife and asked pointedly: "How do you sleep at night?" Informed of the slight by his aggrieved spouse, Fanner barged into his neighbor's office the next week, interrupted his meeting with the company's chief financial officer, and exclaimed: "For your information, my wife sleeps with an Adonis and hardly ever closes her eyes; your wife, however, sleeps in intermittent bursts beside a blubbering walrus."

*

Clarence Darrow sat in Burford Simmons' former office digesting the files stacked in neat piles on the floor. Simmons had worked in the firm for eight years, and his task had included the review of hundreds of files. Darrow couldn't glide through a hurried review or he risked missing a crucial detail that might be a helpful clue to his friend's kidnapping.

A notable pattern emerged in the legal files. Burford, a meticulous record keeper, had prepared copious notes of the client interviews and witness meetings conducted. The distinctive handwriting of Burford's prized fountain pen included the breadth of the queries and responses, and the lawyer's subjective assessment, including temperament ("the bull's scowl in the ring"), attitude ("breezy affectation") and any detected weaknesses ("eyebrows raised with each mendacious answer" and "sarcastic bombast"). Burford had prepared closing letters to the client for each case, providing a concise summary and a recitation of the outcome. He graded his own courtroom performance and marked himself harshly.

By the lunch hour, Darrow had counted four instances where the highest grade was allotted. He devoted his attention to the files with the lower grades. Two files had been placed in a special pile, each file presenting a potential issue that required further investigation. In the first, the judge had ignored a jointly submitted non-custodial position by the defense lawyer and the prosecutor and imposed a two-year prison sentence. Darrow calculated that the aggrieved client had been released six months earlier, providing ample time to plan the kidnapping.

In the second file, the client had insisted, against Burford's explicit advice, on testifying at his trial. Burford's notes indicated that the client performed ineptly on the witness stand and the jury found him guilty of two counts of robbery after a one-hour deliberation. Mercifully, Burford had been discharged by the client prior to the sentencing.

Alex Proctor peered into the office. "Detective Jacob is on the telephone, asking to speak to you."

Proctor, genuinely concerned about his former partner's plight, had gladly accommodated Clarence Darrow's request to review Burford's client files. "Anything we can do to assist poor Burf," he observed. "Raleigh and I were wary of defending Czolgosz and warned Burford to stray far from the hornet's nest, but he couldn't resist the lure of defending his friend."

"Friend?" Darrow shot back angrily. "That's not remotely accurate. Your attempt at feeble humor is unappreciated. We can't be deterred by the harrowing case or the unpopular client, Mr. Proctor," Darrow reproached him. "The lawyer's allegiance to the client is to ensure that he receives equitable and fair treatment under just law."

Darrow walked down the hall and picked up the telephone receiver. "Is this the kosher baker and French detective who quotes Shakespeare?"

"*Mais oui*, it is me, Clarence! I'll be leaving for court shortly, but I wanted to provide you with an update on the Simmons investigation. A couple of uniformed officers are assembling the front pages of newspapers across the country to compare the typeset. Pharo Simmons has received no contact from the kidnappers. We can dismiss the kidnap for ransom theory. There would certainly be a ransom demand by this time. The police have received no response to the kidnappers' sketches that were widely publicized. Any noteworthy clues in the lawyer's old files?"

"I found a couple of leads. I have a hefty stack of Burford's cases files to review."

"A detective is taking over the Simmons investigation, a Detective Kunstler. I am ordered to dedicate my time and energy to Czolgosz' s murder trial."

"Yes, I understand. I'll be returning to Chicago tomorrow by train. I've arranged for Burford's associate, Mitchell Harris, to keep me updated."

Only a few hours remained for Darrow's case review. Burford Simmons' panoply of former clients included a champion billiards player who pierced his opponent's arm with his pool stick, a steward accused of attempting to drown the ship's captain after hurling him overboard in a dispute, and a fortune-teller caught plundering from her customer's outer garments in her closet. Clarence Darrow saved a bulging file filling a couple of accordion folders for last. The case file name, noted on the cover, read: THE BROWNTON CAP FACTORY FIRE.

He first checked a folder reserved for press coverage

with a front-page story clipped from The New York Times on top. Darrow remembered features of the notorious case and the fact that Burford won the trial. He called him in Chicago during the trial to discuss a tricky evidentiary issue. Darrow perused the police summary of the case:

The Brownton factory manufactured caps for adults and children. The factory occupied the second and third floors of an eight-story building on 414 Niagara Street in Buffalo. On the day of the fire, June twentieth of 1900, eighty-seven employees were working on both floors ranging in age from twenty-four to fifty. The owner of the company, Archibald Solter, had an office on the second floor. There was access to the second and third floor from an elevator and stairway. The stairwell also extended to the roof of the building. An elevator operator, Giuseppe Ruscitto, was working on the day of the fire. At approximately 4:55 in the afternoon, fifteen minutes before the workday ended, a fire started in a scrap bin beside a cutter's table on the third floor where the cloth for the caps was cut. The wooden scrap bin, it had been confirmed, had not been cleaned out for three months and was filled with scraps of discarded cloth. The company's bookkeeper reported that she had dropped two boxes of paper and outdated ledgers into the bin one day earlier.

The narrative included in the file was the product of eyewitness accounts of the surviving workers from the third floor. Cigarettes were not allowed during work, but many employees smuggled them under their aprons and shirts and lit their cigarettes during the foreman's lunch or breaks. On June 20th, a lining stitcher, Sally Jenkins, pulled out a cigarette and match from her pocket, unaware that the foreman had briefly entered the third floor. His voice could be heard shouting an order and Jenkins threw her lit cigarette in the scrap bin. Smoke began to rise from the bin and within a minute, flames were visible in the middle of the floor shooting up to the ceiling. The workers on the third floor began to exit the building through the elevator. Giuseppe Ruscitto successfully made two runs of the elevator down to the ground floor with a total of twenty-eight workers safely inside. On the attempted third run, the elevator stopped working as a result of the elevator rails buckling like a melting candle under the intense heat. Workers on the second floor smelled the smoke and exited the building through the stairway. The door to the stairwell was unlocked. Archibald Solter managed his escape.

Called to the scene of the fire, four fire trucks with steam pumps arrived approximately ten minutes later.

Fifteen workers on the third floor remained after the elevator stopped functioning. The windows were sealed shut. The group was trapped by the flickering fire, unable to get access to the windows to attempt to jump to the ground. The stairway door was locked. The foreman had locked the door at the start of the workday, and he kept the only key. He told the police that it was kept locked to prevent unauthorized cigarette breaks and theft.

After the firemen arrived, they used the water pressure from their hoses to break through the third-floor windows. They poured water into the building until the fire was extinguished. Firemen then entered the third floor and found the fifteen workers on the floor unconscious. Ambulance attendants checked for vital signs and they were pronounced dead at the scene. A coroner's report indicated that the cause of death was smoke inhalation and carbon monoxide poisoning. The fifteen bodies were covered with blankets by the firemen on the third floor and the bodies were transported to the city morgue in body bags.

Charred pieces of the wooden door at the exit to the third floor were among the debris seized by the police. A closed lock attached to one of the pieces of the door was seized as an exhibit.

Archibald Solter and Mowbar, the foreman, were interviewed separately by the police. Mowbar stated that he was instructed by Solter to lock the stairway on the third floor every morning. He confirmed that the instruction was repeated on the day of the fire. In addition to cigarette breaks, Solter informed Mowbar that the stairway needed to be locked because he suspected that caps and tools were being stolen by employees on the third floor. There was a bag check of all employees before they left the building at the end of the workday on the elevator.

Archibald Salter was confronted with Oliver Mowbar's statement and denied giving him instructions to lock the door on the third floor. Salter was observed by witnesses to be acting calmly while waiting outside the building. At no time did he ask about the welfare on any of the workers trapped in the building. Early in his police interview, he requested to speak to his lawyer, Burford Simmons. Salter telephoned his insurance company the next day, to make a ten thousand dollar claim for the loss of property fire caused by the fire. The policy protected Salter from financial loss from fire damage. According to the bookkeeper, the cap factory's business showed losses in the previous two years.

The police arrested Archibald Salter on a charge of first-degree manslaughter and second-degree man-slaughter on June twenty-seven of 1901 at his lawyer's office. Burford Simmons, Salter's lawyer, was notified by the police that arson had been ruled out as the cause of the fire. Salter was co-operative during his arrest.

A list of the deceased followed the summary including dates of birth, address and the names of family members attending the morgue. Darrow recognized none of the names. The file also included Burford's trial brief. The notes for Oliver Mowbar's cross-examination included questions related to a paid interview he'd given to a British tabloid, the *Daily Express*. In the interview, Mowbar described Salter uttering the following statement as they waited for the fire to be put out: "The fire has saved me." Burford recorded the jury's verdict for his client as 'not guilty' after a deliberation of two and a half days.

A typed memo to the file prepared by the lawyer with a date and signature appeared on a separate page. It read:

> As we left the courtroom, Archibald Salter turned to me and said: "Justice was finally served." I agreed with him and advised him to make no statement as we left the courthouse. A carriage was ready to pick him up at the courthouse steps. He put his around my shoulders and stated: "You're a great lawyer, Burford Simmons. You managed to fool those fellows on the jury that I didn't know the door was locked." I then informed Mr. Salter that I would never speak to him again and that I would leave separately. I closed the file when I returned to my law office and prepared my final account.

A press clipping in the file included a description of an uncontrolled and disturbing scene outside the courthouse as Salter descended the steps and approached an awaiting horse drawn carriage. A rowdy crowd surrounded him, with one young man lunging at the owner of the Brownton factory before a friend intervened.

"You're a murderer, you'll pay for this in prison," one shouted. "Rot in hell, Salter," another added, his fists clenched. A stone barely missed Salter's head as he entered the waiting carriage and ricocheted off the side window.

"Ten thousand years together, naked, fasting,
Upon a barren mountain and still winter...
could not move the gods to look that way thou wert"

Before leaving Alex Proctor's law office, Clarence Darrow requested to borrow a typewriter and copied a series of salient passages from a single file from the stack of files he'd carefully reviewed: THE BROWNTON CAP FACTORY FIRE.

Chapter Twenty-Eight

Pharo's Diary: *Bessie cut my hair today. Her fingers rummaged through my hair delicately, as if playing the keys of an organ. She appeared profoundly sad and I insisted that she share the source of her distress. "I can't, ma'am," she replied, but I prodded until she reluctantly agreed. Her story was a hammer blow. A friend of her husband's mourned the grievous loss of his son. The cheerful lad had worked as a bell boy at the Genesee Hotel. He fell in love with a white girl and used his savings to change the color of his skin to gain the approval of the girl he adored. "How did he manage to change his skin color?" I asked. "He tried taking electrical treatments," Bessie said. But the experiment eventually failed, and the dejected bell boy drank carbolic acid. "And he suffered in great agony to his death." The story torments me. I think of the poor child checking his skin color for any sign of change. It's a dreadful shame that race must be a bar to a conjugal relationship.*

The Prime Minister of Canada summoned the members of his cabinet to gather in the parliamentary cabinet room. Laurier took his seat at the head of the dark chestnut table, framed by a panoramic view of the Ottawa River and the thatch-roofed houses and Gothic churches dotting the Quebec valley. Collegial and understated in manner, and unbending on issues of principle, Laurier was the unquestioned leader of the Canadian government. A popular prime minister, recently re-elected, he remained grounded and humble.

Called to order, the cabinet meeting began with a solemn report from the Foreign Affairs Minister, Caron Marshall, on the funeral of William McKinley in Canton, Ohio. Marshall had attended the funeral as the Canadian government's representative in the company of the Governor General, Borden Tupper.

Laurier rose, his head bowed slightly, and spoke. "McKinley was a noble president and a valued and trusted friend to our country. He died under tragic circumstances. I have no doubt that the grave sadness of the American nation is felt by the people of Canada." The prime minister's tribute appeared genuine; not the mere ceremonial words marking the death of a political luminary. Laurier had a keen knowledge of and respect for America's political system.

"Yes, Prime Minister, and that makes two world leaders assassinated in the past year by rogue anarchists," Martin Beliveau said urgently. "Their objective is to eradicate every leader of democratic government. I have witnessed the scourge firsthand. Every precaution must be taken to protect you." The time was ripe for alarmed resistance, he believed, and not to be wasted wallowing in despair.

"My police protection does a splendid job watching over me, Martin. I am not fearful for myself and I will not be cajoled or intimidated by thuggish brutality."

"But the express goal of these anarchists is martyrdom, Prime Minister."

Laurier ignored his friend's admonition. "What do we know about the new American president, Theodore Roosevelt?" he asked. "He seemed a brusque, gruff fellow when we met."

"He's an American war hero." Calloway Lipson, the Minister of Militia, described Roosevelt's gritty charge with the Rough Riders up Kittle Hill in the Spanish-American war.

"I had a promising meeting with Teddy after the funeral," Marshall said. "The president possesses a firm hand to lead his country forward into the new century. Canada will be a priority for his administration, he said, and the door to my home in Washington is open to the Prime Minister. 'Please tell Laurier,' he urged me."

"I trust he has the good sense not to share his predecessor's desire to deliver a crushing blow to free trade and to be an uncompromising champion of protection." Daniel Dubois, the Minister of Agriculture, offered the grim caution. He had been a strident opponent of President McKinley's ruinous tariff policies for Canadian farmers.

The Prime Minister replied, "I believe McKinley's desire for reciprocity between our two countries had been sincere. We had a robust discussion about the effect of tariffs on Canada's economy at the Washington conference. At our first meeting, I will impress upon President Roosevelt the benefit of unstifled trade with its strongest trading partner."

Laurier then introduced the matter tabled for debate in Parliament that morning. "It is necessary to adopt the proposed budget for a sweeping advertising campaign to encourage further immigration to the prairies," he declared. A steady influx of immigrants from European countries including Poland, Germany, Russia and Austria had migrated to Canada and traveled westward on the Canadian Pacific Railway to the spacious plains and the emerging cities of Saskatoon, Calgary and Winnipeg.

"Is more advertising necessary, Mr. Prime Minister?" The pock-faced and stern Minister of Interior, Nelson Mahoney, a persistent opponent of the government's policy of welcoming European immigrants, stared vexedly at Laurier. "Has due consideration been given to the prolific violence and spread of disease likely to be imported to our western provinces? Many of these immigrants are vagrants who will feed from the trough of financial inducements the government offers to settle here."

"Vagrants? Really, Nelson." Laurier responded as a scolding parent. "Our government has been voted into office on a platform of promoting values of diversity and tolerance. Canada will ultimately be the beneficiary of our encouragement to these new immigrants. I refuse to subscribe to jaundiced and unsubstantiated views about foreign Europeans."

Chants of "hear, hear" erupted around the table.

"You are witness, Nelson, to your assessment not being embraced by fellow members of Cabinet."

The decision to select an immigration minister with little aptitude for benevolence, and given to grandiloquent lecturing about the peril of immigrants to Canada, didn't trouble Laurier. He preferred robust and clashing viewpoints from his ministers. Mahoney supported the government's open-door policy at constituents' meetings and in ministerial declarations. He presented as the flexible politician deftly promoting government policy at odds with his personal beliefs.

Mahoney's latest foray was to propose Mortimer Hanus as the new consul general to Scotland, and his stiffest adversary in cabinet was Martin Beliveau. Martin had met Hanus briefly at a Centennial celebration and informed the Prime Minister that a malodorous skunk was better suited for the vacant posting. When pressed by Laurier, he lacked a concrete reason, but he'd heard unsubstantiated stories of Hanus harnessing his bloated wealth to extract political favors and collecting secret files of dubious behavior on members of Cabinet.

The cabinet meeting ended with a broad consensus, Mahoney opposing, to designate a lavish budget for the advertising program for eastern Europe. Mahoney requested, and was granted a private audience with the Prime Minister.

"Have you decided who the consul general to Scotland will be?"

"I haven't confirmed my choice. I will give due consideration to your strong recommendation of Mortimer Hanus."

"Hanus will be a wonderful diplomat. He is a major financial contributor to the Liberal party."

"That's not my criteria for choosing a consul general, Nelson."

"May I ask, Prime Minister, did Isaiah Hayes express his support for Hanus's appointment?"

"I haven't heard from the Minister of Trade, but I did

receive the opinion of another member of cabinet."

Then Laurier's chief of staff interrupted, reminding the Prime Minister of a meeting to finalize the budget committee's report, and Laurier was ushered out by his chief of staff through the halls of the Parliament Building.

Nelson Mahoney checked his watch. He had half an hour before the session of Parliament began. He proceeded to his office, locked the door, and called a telephone number at the Temple Building in Toronto.

"Do you have news regarding my appointment, Nelson?"

"Not yet. Laurier confirmed that you're in the running."

"What about Hayes? Did he put my name forward?"

"I'm hopeful that Isaiah will act soon. Minister Beliveau may pose a problem. He's a close confidante of Laurier and a bitter rival. If he is aware that I'm recommending you, he's likely opposing your appointment."

"I'm not paying you two hundred dollars a month to tell me about obstacles and problems, Nelson. Lobby the rest of your colleagues in Cabinet for my support."

"Understood," Nelson said. It rankled to take orders from Mortimer Hanus. A year earlier, Mortimer Hanus had introduced himself at a Dominion Day celebration. The next day, Hanus sent a cheque for a thousand dollars to his office as a political contribution. Hanus invited Nelson to a dinner party at his home, where the two men were joined by a pair of giggling, scantily dressed women, one of whom dropped into Nelson's lap, looping her fingers through Nelson's curly locks. A photographer appeared and captured the salacious image, and over a bottle of single malt scotch and a vow to keep the photograph in a locked safe, Hanus secured the Minister's agreement to perform a series of minor favors for a monthly stipend.

The first payment came on the fifteenth of the following month --- two hundred-dollar bills slipped under the wrapping of a box of cigars. At the beginning, Hanus requested the minister's presence at a couple of company functions. Then a call then came for government jobs for one of Hanus's associates. Two hundred dollars arrived regularly on the fifteenth of each month. Six months later, Hanus expressed his desire to Nelson to fill an opening as Canada's top official at the consulate in Edinburgh.

Hanus had surprised Nelson with a social visit one evening at his house in Ottawa and invited him for a week as his guest at his beach getaway in Cascais, Portugal. "I have the beach house split into separate quarters. Why don't you invite Isaiah Hayes to join you as my guest?"

At one of their monthly meetings, Nelson had told Hanus that the Minister of Trade was a homosexual. Hanus arranged for Hayes to be set-up by an Ottoman teenage worker and had captured the dalliance on a camera held at an undraped window. A copy of the photograph was left on Isaiah Hayes' pillow. Hayes packed his bags, left the beach house, and delivered a curt message to his host: "The lamb does not track the fox's trail into the dark cave."

Chapter Twenty-Nine

Pharo's Diary: *This morning I took my first brief walk outside since Burf's kidnapping. Sheets of rain overnight had left steep puddles. I heard the splash as I stepped in to one. I envied the people who swirled by me hurrying to get their children ready for school, filling the pantry with baked bread and loading the fridge with milk and cheese. An empathetic neighbor waved from her yard and called out to me as I approached the front door. "We're with you," she shouted. Odette surprised me with a visit in the afternoon accompanied by a woman I greatly admire, Susan B. Anthony. I met Susan at the Suffrage Convention in Geneva, the town where I grew up. I will not rest until women are on the ballot!*

Pharo recalled that on the morning of her husband's disappearance, she had struggled with the task of capturing an unsavory character in her novel and Burford had offered to assist. She vividly recalled their conversation:

"She's an impatient and selfish woman."

"Why not describe her that way?"

"Oh, Burford. My job as a writer is leave subtle clues to arouse the reader."

"Here's a suggestion, then. Have your character skip over reading the obituary of her kindly aunt as she's leaving for the estate lawyer's office for a reading of the aunt's will."

That memory comforted her. "My Burf is a problem solver," she concluded.

*

One afternoon, on a whim, Pharo walked to the nearby ice cream parlor on Earle Street. She sat at a corner table with a strawberry sundae. At the table beside her, a young boy, ten-years-old by Pharo's estimate, appeared on the verge of tears. His mother spoke gently as she stroked his cheek. Pharo overheard the slight, docile child reporting an incident of being picked on by a couple of older students at his school. His mother ordered two cups of hot chocolate with whipped cream. "One day, these brutish boys will look up to you with envy," she assured him. "I'm going to have a talk with your teacher tomorrow. Now let's have some fun!"

Pharo had been picked on after her serious car accident and she had stayed in her locked room and cried for days. She had recently been mocked in a public lavatory by a couple of women because they had to wait for the *gimp* to finish. Who devised such cruel words, she wondered? Is there a man in a stuffy stockroom with cramped legs, his hands dipped in ice water, his belly-aching for food, with a thumping headache, compiling a manual of cruel language?

She'd related the *gimp* incident to Burford. "A couple of jealous shrews," he said, and told her that he loved her more because of her limp.

"Whatever do you mean?" she asked.

Burf reminded her that early in their courtship, they'd been caught on a walk in the woods in a pelting rainstorm. Clothes drenched, water streaming off their faces, they'd raced for shelter at a barn they'd passed. Burford remembered one special moment from that clumsy race in the rain. He'd peered to his side to check on her, and he described the image captured, as if frozen in time: her face clenched in fierce determination, moving in gaping strides, as she had struggled ardently to keep pace. "I knew then that I was madly in love with you," he told her.

It didn't matter if he was fibbing. She was reminded of a passage from her favorite novel, *Tess of the d'Urbervilles*:

"*And it was the touch of the imperfect on the would-be perfect that gave the sweetness, because it was that which gave the humanity.*"

*

Detective Kunstler arrived in the afternoon to present an update on the kidnapping investigation. Pharo greeted him with her father in the parlor.

A question about Eli Jacob's continuing role was deflected by the detective. Fragments of eggshells were strewn around the coffee table. Kunstler apologized for his mess. "I didn't have time for breakfast," he claimed.

The detective's uniform was wrinkled, and he spoke in

a sonorous monotone, which, for a police officer conveying news of her husband's current plight, was disconcert-
ing. The breezy and stolid Kunstler bore no resemblance
to Burford's favorite investigator, Sherlock Holmes. Burf
had read lengthy passages from Arthur Conan Doyle's
books to her in bed and she'd relished correctly guessing
the identity of the dastardly culprit.

Kunstler started by asking an impertinent question
that inspired no confidence in his investigation: "Excuse
me, and I'm sorry to have to bring this up, and I mean no
discourtesy, but can you indicate, if you're able, whether
your husband has a lady friend?"

"That's your theory! That my husband ran off with
some wench and tricked his wife to believe he was kidnapped?"

The detective was unmoved by Pharo's acerbic tone.
"It isn't helpful to our investigation, ma'am, to take telephone calls from strangers. We might miss the kidnapper."

"Detective Kunstler, the stranger who calls daily is a
warm-hearted politician from Canada."

Pharo's father pressed the detective on the status of
his investigation.

"Do you have a single lead that you're following? I
must say, I haven't heard an encouraging word about the
police locating my *kidnapped* son-in-law."

A series of pointed questions elicited the disturbing
fact that the police lacked a single viable lead. Mervin demanded that the detective leave his daughter's house. "Immediately," he added.

Pharo was pleased to have her father's steadfast support. He had stationed himself in a spare bedroom and

attempted to lift her spirits with chipper humor. When a note arrived from John Rockefeller with an offer of assistance from the financial baron, Mervin observed that the card was worth one million dollars in ransom money. "Rockefeller will expect to be repaid with interest," he said.

"What should we do now, father?" Pharo asked now, after Kunstler's abrupt departure.

"We need Detective Jacob in charge of the investigation. Kunstler couldn't solve the mystery of a bleeding nose, if the bloody cloth was resting on the vagabond's shoelace."

"You heard the detective's excuse. Jacob is occupied with the president's killer's trial."

"That is an open-and-shut case. I suspect that there's a wholly unsatisfactory explanation for the change in investigators here. I've concluded that we must contact Clarence Darrow. He appeared to be on good terms with Detective Jacob. Perhaps Darrow can convince him to return to Burford's investigation." He left the room to telephone the lawyer.

That evening, Darrow reached the detective at his home.

"*Bonjour, mon ami*, Clarence. What can I do for you?" Jacob asked.

"Is there any progress in the Burford Simmons' matter?"

"I did check briefly with Detective Kunstler before I left for court today. There are no matches to the newsprint used in the letter."

"And no leads on the identity of the kidnappers either. Am I correct?"

"*C'est vrai.* It is a most perplexing crime."

"Eli, I'm planning on a return visit to Buffalo in a couple of days. I'm grappling with a theory about Burford's kidnapping. Can I enlist your assistance?"

"Of course. I will inform Francoise that we must prepare to host our distinguished guest."

"I can't possibly put you and your wife to trouble again."

"Nonsense, Clarence. It will be our esteemed pleasure. In the words of a wise English playwright, '*Keep thy friend under thy own life's key*'."

*

Willow Hooper reached the address of the box-shaped tenement apartment in Buffalo. She knocked on the front door of a unit on the second floor. "Who is it?" a hoarse voice shouted behind the door.

"My name is Hooper. I'm a reporter with the *Brooklyn Daily Eagle*."

"Leave at once."

Willow Hooper had anticipated the resistance to her overture. Her interview target, Marie Dempster, had been arrested by the police as the publisher of *The Anarchist Wayfarer*. The *Wayfarer* building had exploded into rubble moments after she left with three of her colleagues. Dempster had spent two weeks in locked confinement before the police released the group without charges.

"Look, Marie, I'm interested in telling your side of the story. Please let me in."

The door creaked open a sliver. "My side?"

"You have my word. I promise."

"You have five minutes. We can talk in the stairway."

The gaunt woman's glassy eyes had dark, foreboding rings around them. "I was taking my pills when you arrived. They're for my nerves. I'm hardly sleeping. Leon Czolgosz ruined my life. He's as much an authentic anarchist as you are the Pope. I kept the back issues of the *Anarchist Wayfarer*. I challenge you to find a single sentence in any advocating violent action."

"That's an important story to tell. The American public's opinion is that all anarchists are demons. Give me the opportunity to correct that unbalanced impression. I'll be fair to you, Marie."

"Fair! I am familiar with you, Reporter Hooper. I see through your attempt to flatter me. I read your last investigative article in the *Brooklyn Daily Eagle*. It was my job to check the papers for sham reporting on anarchists."

"Yes, and I exposed neglect in the workplace."

Marie continued: "But you ignored human misery. You blamed an ironworker falling twelve stories on sloppy, neglectful working conditions. Correct --- but who paid the bills for his widow and children after his death? The ironworker's capitalist employer is not interested in compassion and decency. The judges are just as uncaring. The lawsuit by the widow will fail, and the judge will be invited to speak at the Commercial Club banquet as his reward."

"Fascinating," Hooper said. "She had expected to confront the devil incarnate. Marie Dempster instead presented as intelligent, a careful thinker. "Let's go inside and talk about this," she said, nudging her gently from the stairway. "And I'd like to examine those back issues of the *Anarchist Wayfarer*."

Chapter Thirty

Pharo's Diary: *A nun called on me today seeking a donation for the Buffalo Temperance League. She claimed to be affiliated with the Westminster Church. I expressed my supreme surprise that the church supported the cause of sobriety as I had attended several services and not heard a peep about the scourges of alcohol. I pressed for details and the nun reluctantly confessed to being an imposter. The enterprising deception of a reporter by the name of Willow Hooper brought a swift reprise. "Here, take my card," she said, as I swept her out of my home like a dust ball with a broom. "Call me anytime if you'd like to speak about your husband's misfortune." Misfortune? I prefer a more poignant title, like a diabolical crime. The days and nights ticked on and still, no word arrived from Burford's kidnapper.*

"Mr. Bramble, you may proceed with the witnesses' cross-examination."

The lawyer, a black necktie protruding from the top of his vest, approached the lectern and adjusted his spectacles. "Mr. Norman, you were a junior assistant to President McKinley during his visit to Buffalo for the Pan-American Exposition."

"Correct."

"Did you attend at his bedside at Milburn House where the president convalesced after his shooting?" Bramble paused after every question, studying the reaction of the jurors.

"Not all the time, of course. But I did appear every day."

"And would you agree with me that there were days at the beginning of his stay where the president appeared in fine form and well on his way to recovery?"

"I'm not a doctor, sir. I can't speak to his recovery. But I certainly agree that lots of us watching the president were greatly encouraged that he was on the mend. But then his health took a steep decline."

"But at least for several days, President McKinley's heath did improve."

"I'd agree with that, sir."

"Thank you, those are my questions."

Judge Pickett had glass of water on his bench along with a jar of sugar and a spoon. He had developed the practice of gently banging his spoon against the glass as a witness testified. The more credible he found a witness, the louder the chime on the glass rang. On this occasion, the glass registered a sharp clanging sound. "Mr. Bramble," he interjected, the lawyer ending his cross-examination. "Is it your theory that the president had contracted some fatal disease like diphtheria that caused his death?"

"I am not suggesting that the president had diphtheria, Judge."

"Good. I will not permit the jury to be distracted by any far-fetched theories. President McKinley was shot twice by your client at close range and had a bullet stuck in his abdomen. He died eight days later with the bullet still there. That is the uncontested evidence. Two bullets to the president's chest!"

*

Arthur Simon balanced the tray holding a plate of pancakes, syrup and a glass of lemonade. He placed it in front of the prisoner and loosened the rope on his wrists.

"I'll cut a deal with you," the smooth-faced captor told Burford.

"What kind of deal?"

"I'll give you the boss's name, but I need you to promise to get me out of this mess without any criminal charges."

"That's fine. But I'll need to be free to act on my oath."

"Hanus is eventually planning to let you go."

The name was vaguely familiar to Burford. "Hanus is his name?"

"Mortimer Hanus."

"It will be our secret, Arthur. When is Hanus planning to set me free?"

"I have no idea. I told him after we snatched you that I didn't want to be part of any murder and he assured me that he wasn't going to kill you."

"Arthur, I am an honorable lawyer and you have my undertaking to personally speak to the prosecutor handling your case. You'll have your life back. But you must help me escape. Hanus is unscrupulous and misled you.

He plans to kill me. He can't permit a witness to send him to prison for the rest of his life."

"I can't let you go," he said.

"I understand," Burford said. "You're frightened. But will you deliver a letter to my wife?" He began to cut the pancakes as Arthur hovered, his shaking hand brandishing a gun.

Arthur paused before answering. "I'll do it, but only once. I will bring a pen and paper and keep the letter to a couple of sentences. No coded messages. I'll be checking for them."

"The syrup is delicious. Where did you get it?" Burford used his only utensil, a wooden spoon, to cut the pancake into pieces. He dipped them into the dripping syrup.

"The farm here in the village of Sutton is surrounded by a vast forest filled with pine and maple trees. I have a bucket to collect the sap from a sugar maple tree on the farm. I boil the sap."

"Can you show me the maple tree on my next outing outside?" Burford discreetly tipped his plate, allowing the remaining syrup to drip into his cup.

"Hanus left Sutton for a couple of days. He told me that he's taking a trip to Ottawa. He warned me that if you've escaped from the basement when he returns, he'll chop me up with his axe and throw my body parts into the bonfire and watch them burn to ashes. He means every word."

Burford wanted to know more about his kidnapper. "Does Hanus have any family?"

"He's never been married. I'm aware that he had a brother living in Buffalo. The brother died last year."

"Do you know what the brother's cause of death was, Arthur?"

"No, but it shook Hanus up. He smashed a few plates and broke a mop holder. I never saw him that upset."

The intriguing news about a brother living in Buffalo represented another major clue. It marked the first connection to the area of the kidnapping and a closer link to Burford.

"He never spoke about his brother again. I don't even know his name."

Burford noticed Arthur's weapon dropping casually to his side, pointing to the floor. Hanus's temporary absence afforded him an opportunity to implement the next step of his hatched escape plan.

"Arthur," he said. "I'd be grateful if you'd take my boots off and take the rope from my feet while Hanus is gone. I'd like to get the circulation moving in my legs. You can bind my hands if that makes you more comfortable."

"All right, but don't take advantage of my kindness. My gun is loaded, and I'll use it if necessary." He retied the rope around Burford's wrists and removed the bindings from his ankles.

Burford shuffled to the fire and warmed the insoles of his feet. "May I be permitted to ask you a personal question, Arthur?" He deftly pushed a strip of wood between his toes and tucked it under the carpet without Arthur noticing.

"What is it?"

"Were you ever given a once-in-a-lifetime chance to change the course of your life, to improve it dramatically, but turned it down the chance and regretted your rash decision?"

"I can't think of anything," he said.

"Well, you're being given that opportunity now. We

both recognize that once Mortimer Hanus returns, it will be too late to help me. Drive me to the nearest police station and inform the police that you're rescuing a kidnap victim. I'll support your story that you were pressured to be part of Hanus's scheme."

"I wish I could do that. Betty, my girlfriend, agrees with you. But I'm not much good to her with my neck swinging on a noose. I know too much about Hanus's criminal ventures. I know the names of the people he's hurt along the way. The truth is I did nothing to stop Hanus. How do I explain that to the police? Do you really believe that I'll walk out of the police station a free man? Hanus has a crew of henchmen on call ready to handle me if I turn on him. That's the reason he feels comfortable leaving the farm for a couple of days. I'm a dead man if I help you --- I'm probably a dead man if I don't. My chances are better aligning myself with Mortimer Hanus. It's nothing personal against you," he said.

"You can move away from here, Arthur. I have money to help you resettle."

"I'll get the pen and paper now," Arthur said, staunchly ignoring Burford's plea.

After he left the room, Burford surveyed the pile of wood by the fire and selected a few more thin strips and maneuvered them with his feet under the carpet. He heard the footsteps of Arthur coming down the stairway.

"Write your letter," the man said, loosening the rope around Burford's chaffed wrists. Burford began to compose the letter that he'd crafted:

*Dearest Pharo, I'm **s**afe and I **ju**st wanted to le**t** you* *know that I'm being treated properly. 1 will see you soon. Burf*

Arthur took the paper, perused it and tucked it into a shirt pocket.

"I'll make sure your wife gets the letter," he said. "You remember to keep your promise."

*

The ornate ceremonial room at Parliament Hill bustled with orderlies and assistants zig-zagging the room for last-minute preparations for the prime minister's official announcement. The pageantry set in place to commemorate the appointment of a new consul general included careful placement of flags of Scotland and the United Kingdom, florid orchids, a lectern for Prime Minister Laurier's presentation and a cordoned-off area for the Governor General and a couple of international dignitaries. The Scottish prime minister sent a telegram offering his best wishes to the country's incoming consul general, Mortimer Hanus. The interior minister, Nelson Mahoney, had the honour of introducing the new Canadian diplomat to Scotland. Hanus planned to move into the residence at the consulate in Edinburgh at the beginning of November. He had planned a lavish reception after the ceremony at the nearby Elgin Hotel and members of the cabinet, two visiting Scottish government officials and members of the opposition party were invited to attend.

The Minister of Trade had been livid with his cabinet colleague when he learned of Hanus's pending appointment. "You've duped the prime minister," Hayes had said to Nelson, confronting him in his government office. "The man is an extortionist." But Hanus had reminded Hayes of his precarious position. "One word of the truth and your career in government will be finished."

"He has contaminated you with his insipid virus," Hayes had responded angrily.

Nelson refused to permit his buoyant mood be diminished by Hayes' snide insult. Laurier accepted his recommendation for Mortimer Hanus's appointment. He had presented him with a list of stellar references from business, civic and religious organizations in support of the appointment. Hanus promised to bring a box of Cuban cigars to the announcement to express his gratitude to Mahoney.

Chapter Thirty-One

Pharo's Diary: *Early in our marriage, Burford and I brought his rascally nephew to a pantomime performance of Humpty Dumpty at a local theatre. It provided a couple of hours of respite to his beleaguered sister. My most vivid memory of the play occurred when Humpty Dumpty fell off the wall. His valiant and unfailing efforts to climb back up to the wall's perch met with howling laughter from Burf's nephew. The boy's stolid resistance to coming to the performance instantly vanished and for the next half hour I watched as he bounded from his seat at every comedic moment. He thanked us fervently at the end. The lesson I derived from that afternoon is that character can be disguised by the outward shell of the human form. The charmers may be charlatans and the dour studious types may be kind-hearted. Never judge anyone, particularly a mischievous nephew, by a masked cover.*

In the thorny world of criminal law, where losses are heaped on losses, the gracious compliment, embroidered with effusive praise, is frowned upon. Like a poisoned orchid, the disguise foretells disaster for the counsel it lands upon.

"Your lawyer's skilled presentation has kept me awake the entire night," is the predictable quip from the judge forced to devote precious hours to craftily patch a desired guilty verdict. The defense lawyer praising the fine display of integrity and ethical conduct of the opposing counsel is identifying to the jury that the prosecutor mercifully abandoned ship at the trial. The prosecutor informing a judge of a reasoned and ponderous submission by a defense lawyer, is attempting to thwart a later argument of inadequate defense. There is the apocryphal story of an enterprising trial counsel, Frederick Phipps, cited for contempt for remonstrating during a judge's hearty compliment of his final argument. The citation fell squarely between the words "acumen" and "brilliant," as Phipps angrily shook his fist at the offending judge.

*

Judge Pickett excused the jury from the courtroom and leaned forward in the direction of Leon Czolgosz's lead counsel, Titus Bramble.

"Mr. Bramble, I must say, in my thirty-three years of being a lawyer and a judge, that was one of the finest jury addresses I've been privileged to witness."

The thrust of Bramble's jury address involved a modest request to the jurors to consider whether the mere act of shooting President McKinley represented the act of a sane man: "It is shown beyond any peradventure of doubt that it was at the defendant's hand that he was stricken down, and the only question that can be discussed or considered in the case is the question whether that act was that of a sane person. If it was, then the defendant is guilty of murder and must suffer the penalty. If it was the act of an insane man, then he is not guilty of murder but should be acquitted of the charge and would then be confined in a lunatic asylum."

Bramble added that Leon Czolgosz had refused to assist his lawyers and, in virtually every instance, to communicate with them; a defense reduced by exigent circumstances "to do what we can do."

Czolgosz's reluctant defense began at the outset of the trial with his plea before the jury. "Guilty," he declared.

"I'm sorry, what did the prisoner say?" Judge Pickett, with a puckered look of dismay, turned sharply to Titus Bramble. "He said 'guilty.'" The judge rolled his eyes in despair. "The plea is *not* acceptable to this court. He cannot by law plead guilty to murder. Gentlemen of the jury, the prisoner's plea will be recorded as not guilty."

Detective Jacob and Neeru left the courtroom for the prosecutor's office to await the jury's verdict. Neeru monitored the trial from the gallery as an interested observer.

After Burford's kidnapping, Neeru had blamed herself for the lawyer's disappearance and certain death. She'd been warned of the possible danger to him and had relied on Burford to take the necessary precautions. The Attorney General reluctantly granted her wish to be removed as counsel for the trial and replaced her with District Attorney Thomas Penney. Neeru agreed to handle the defense appeal after the jury's verdict.

The trial lasted for two days without disruption. The defendant entered the courtroom handcuffed to an officer on each side and comported himself as neatly as his dress. The abject defense consisted mainly of a cursory cross-examination by defense counsel on McKinley's waning state of health after the shooting and the condition of his body after death. The summing up by Titus Bramble included an emotional valedictory tribute to the president, "a man of finest character."

Defense counsel apologized for defending Leon Czolgosz," Neeru stated scornfully. "Burford would never be reduced to groveling before a jury."

District Attorney Penny adopted Neeru's earlier decision to not call any experts on mental disease at trial, Czolgosz's sanity not being a matter of dispute. The two defense experts who assessed the prisoner's mental state supported a unanimous conclusion that Czolgosz appreciated his act of shooting the president and knew that it was wrong.

Neeru pressed the detective about any breaking development in the Burford Simmons kidnapping investigation. After an extended period of bleak silence, a note had arrived at the law firm of Proctor and Sykes, delivered by the kidnappers. Pharo confirmed that the handwriting was her husband's.

"Well, it's comforting to know that Burford's alive," Neeru said. "And we can be certain that he's being held captive in Sutton. The letters highlighted in bold by Burford spell the location of Sutton. Detective Kunstler shared the note with me."

"Perhaps, but we can't we be sure that it isn't a surname either." The detective flipped to a page in his notebook. "There are five towns and cities with the name of Sutton," he said. "They are in the states of Vermont,

Massachusetts, New Hampshire, Nebraska and West Virginia."

Detective Jacob strenuously appealed to Superintendent Grant to be reinstated as the lead detective for the Simmons investigation after Czolgosz's trial ended.

Grant opposed the request at first: "Kunstler informs me that he's on the verge of cracking the case," he declared. However, with Pharo's and her father's stern intervention, the superintendent agreed. The transition, he'd told the detective, awaited the jury's verdict.

"I don't expect a lengthy jury deliberation," Neeru said confidently. She had managed to drink a few sips of water when an assistant knocked at the door to inform them that the jury had reached a verdict.

"It took them less than a half-an-hour to decide," Detective Jacob remarked.

*

Clarence Darrow arrived at the Jacob residence that afternoon with Francoise Jacob warmly greeting him. "Eli is on his way," she informed him. "The jury just found President McKinley's killer guilty of murder in the first degree."

Eli arrived and checked the guest bedroom, where he discovered Darrow studying the summary of the Brownton Cap Factory Fire. He handed the sheet of paper to the detective to read.

"This occurred before my time as a detective in Buffalo," he said. "But it's undoubtedly worth investigating."

"Do you see the description of the victims' relatives?" Darrow asked. "There's a separate list of family and friends who identified the victims at the morgue. It may be helpful to determine if any of them have criminal records."

"And to determine if they live in Sutton." Eli described the background of the note that Pharo received from Burford, the oblique reference to Sutton and its likely geographical importance.

Darrow seemed relieved to learn that Eli had resumed his former lead investigator role in his friend's kidnapping. He'd heeded Eli's caution to avoid dealing with the bumbling and ineffective Detective Kunstler.

Now Darrow checked the summary for any references to Sutton but drew a blank. "You'll have to check to see if there is a town or city in Canada with the name of Sutton."

"Why is that necessary, Clarence?"

"In one instance, there's a brother recorded identifying one of the victim's bodies. His name is Mortimer Hanus, and his residence is noted as Toronto, Ontario."

"Let me see here." The detective checked the summary. "His niece, Penelope Hanus, twenty-eight-years old, perished in the fire. Her parents have an address in Buffalo."

The next morning, Clarence Darrow joined Detective Jacob on a drive to the address noted for Penelope's parents. They were greeted at the front door by an amiable man in flannel pajamas with overgrown white sideburns, puffy cheeks and smoking a pipe.

"They're both gone. They don't have any connection to this house any longer," he said, after being provided the parents' names.

"Do you know their new address?" Darrow asked.

"I don't think you fellows understood me. They are really gone," he said. "Both parents died in the past year."

"What happened?" the detective inquired.

"I heard a story from a neighbour after I bought this house that their daughter died in a ghastly fire. They couldn't recover from the shock of her loss and both died, one following the other, of broken hearts."

Eli and Clarence returned to the detective's office to review the police file for the Brownton Cap Factory Fire.

"This is a bit unorthodox," the head of the detectives' office told Eli. He'd been informed that the lawyer from Chicago had agreed to assist with the kidnapping investigation, but he frowned on an outlier attending the office.

"Unorthodox, yes, but the contribution vitally important," Eli responded.

The two men sat in the detective's office scrutinizing each document in the police file. "We'll be here for a while," Darrow said, transferring a witness statement to Eli Jacob.

"*Bien sur,*" he replied.

Chapter Thirty-Two

Pharo's Dairy: *Odette stopped by the house with her spaniel and provided me with an article from the Quarterly Journal of Science. The author, Sir William Crooks, conducted an elaborate scientific investigation of the phenomenon of modern spiritualism. Crooks' conclusion, echoed by my sister, is that spiritualism, the ability to connect with the dead with the assistance of a professional medium, is undeniably authentic. Her friend Dottie connected at a seance with her father who drowned five years earlier. "But Burford is alive," I scolded her. "What use is this to me?" She grabbed the article from my hands and huffed: "I'm only trying to help." "You'll help me by keeping the faith," I said harshly. But to be fair to my sister, I struggled to suppress my own rising conviction that Burford is dead. I asked her to give me the article back, with a ghost of a smile.*

The nights passed slowly but steadily, like puddles of raindrops evaporating under a burning sun. Burford Simmons imagined playing spirited games of poker with Clarence Darrow in the smoky drawing room of the law school dormitory. He reveled in flashing three aces to Darrow's lonely pair of kings. Burford wiggled his toes and fingers...*check,* felt the bristles of his moustache with his tongue...*check,* and inhaled the hint of crackling embers wafting from the fireplace...*check.* The next step of Project Dash (the title assigned to his ten-step escape) slotted into place into the accordion file in his mind. He was invigorated, the cresting hill of doubts quelled, Pharo's brimming voice spurring him forward.

Burford hadn't anticipated his early legal training would bring relief to his bleak predicament, but four steps of his plan depended on forensic knowledge he had collected as a weathered attorney. He'd devoted many late hours in his office in the sole company of a lampshade pouring over expert reports and arcane textbooks about subjects as varied and vast as bloodstains, footmarks, bite prints, arson and poison.

In his last murder trial, a chef had poisoned an unruly patron with arsenic in his cabbage soup. He'd read about a renowned pianist named Liddy, who professed devoting hours of practice each week to master the *arpeggio* of A minor. Burford devoted that same obsessive preparation to his client's trial. A man's liberty weighed in the balance.

Burford had made inroads with Arthur, establishing a bond beyond captor and hostage. The day before, his ropes loosened, Arthur had shaved him, cut thick strands of his hair, read to him from the technical engineering books on the shelf, and chatted amiably about his troubled life. Arthur's traits were the scarlet letter worn by the clients of Burford's early years as a lawyer: abusive childhood; poor schooling; a life riddled with poverty, melancholy, and desperation.

Arthur, Burford knew, would fire his gun without balking at the behest of his sinister master. He was mindful of the caution of Sherlock Holmes: emotional qualities are antagonistic to clear reasoning. Burford had attended a lecture by Holmes' creator, Dr. A. Conan Doyle, at a theater hall in Shelton Square. The most rapturous moment was the speaker's introduction as "Canon" Doyle.

The exercise of identifying the schemer of devilry had occupied Burford for days. Focusing on the familiar snarl wedded to his lips a couple of visits earlier, a distant memory snapped sharply into view: an encounter with a stranger, fleeting, but memorable. The elusive quandary was the motive for this diabolical crime; but Professor Sandler, his eccentric criminal law professor, who composed poems to express scholarly principles of law, had disparaged the primacy of motive:

> Some thieve for gluttony and luxury, others to survive
> and cope.
> To require proof of the burglar's reason, of this, there
> is little hope.

Arthur arrived on cue holding a breakfast tray. He loosened the ropes on Burford's wrists and stoked the crackling fire. "Sleep well?" he asked.

"Like a baby at a church sermon."

Arthur cackled. "I brought you a *Globe*, a few days old though."

"I'll put it to good use as an extra blanket."

Humor was a vital part of the lawyer's repertoire, disarming the belligerent witness, diffusing an ornery judge. It was also a handy tool to pry open an abductor's affection.

"I'll return in a few minutes to collect the tray."

Arthur scampered up the stairs, locking the door to the main floor. Burford ignored the food and lifted his cot, placing it squarely against the unused side door. He banged his shoulder against the grey turreted wall, the cot buffering the impact like a muffled drum. After a few attempts, the door frame budged and pried ajar. A welcome draft whipped past his face.

"Well done, Counsellor," he congratulated himself.

Pondering his next step, he took a few moments to gulp down his porridge and crackers.

He couldn't rely on the police finding him. His kidnapper was shrewd; the scalawag had hoisted him from Buffalo to an Ontario farmhouse without a glitch. Pharo must be his foil, outwit him and be even cleverer.

As a boy of twelve, Burford's father had asked him to carry a suitcase down the stairs. It was packed to the brim and Burford couldn't budge it. Dejected, he'd told his father he'd been assigned an impossible task. "That's because you're approaching it only one way. Now go back, keep trying something different." Burford returned to the bedroom, and after some thought pushed the suitcase to the floor, kicked it to the staircase, and allowed it to fall as he controlled it along the steps, gliding the suitcase to the front door as his father appeared.

"Every invention starts with failure," his father sagely said.

The thumping of footsteps on the stairway portended danger. Burford counted three people.

Hanus entered the room first.

Burford surveyed his jailer.

"Late night for you. I'm sorry the affair with your lady friend wasn't consummated. Sipping too much wine?"

"What are you talking about, Simmons? You're mad!"

"Hardly...your jacket is wrinkled; it was in pristine condition on your last visit. You must have slept in it. There is a lipstick mark in the middle of your sternum, an irregular spot. A woman --- wearing burnished red lipstick --- placed her head there as she slept, her mouth falling to your shirt during the night. The effects of too many bottles of wine led both of you to slumber rather than lust."

Hanus gave Burford the cold stare of a witness impregnably trapped.

"I envy you. French Bordeaux 1900, an excellent vintage."

"How did you know that?"

"You left the empty wooden container under a table --- I recognize you." Burford continued. "You attended the Brownton Cap Factory trial. You sat in the front row of the courtroom on the far-left side. Your bowler tipped over the rail and I retrieved it for you. You were most ungracious."

"Do you recall the couple seated beside me?" Hanus brandished his pistol. "My brother and his wife, both deceased. Do you know why they were in court?"

"You are about to inform me."

"Your client killed their only child, Penelope. And because of your bag of lawyerly tricks, he walked free from the courtroom."

"I regret your niece is dead, Hanus, but it was a tragic accident. The jury found my client not guilty and it's your sticky problem if you're unable to accept the verdict."

Burford studied his captor's reaction.

"So you remember the name. It wasn't a tragic accident," he said, his voice rising, "it was murder. Salter deliberately locked the stairway that prevented Penelope's escape. Murder!"

"You'll forgive me if I don't quibble about the crime of murder when the jury absolved my client."

"The artful dodge of a courtroom artisan. Bravo, Simmons. But how do you account for your *innocent* client's haste to claim the pot of money from the insurance company?"

Hanus was now engaging in battle on Burford's surefooted terrain and the lawyer moved for the score. "If he'd waited a couple of months, you'd accuse Salter of deliberately staking his claim to the insurance money after the tragedy's shadow had faded."

"He shouldn't have claimed the blood money."

"Blood money is claiming a life insurance policy on the wife you murdered. Your circle of acquaintances, right Hanus?"

The man lurking behind Hanus lunged forward, fist clenched.

"No Charlie," Hanus ordered. "His time will come."

Burford continued, undeterred. "Why was your niece working in a cap factory, Hanus? Couldn't *you* provide her with gainful employment? Or did you not dare risk her discovering that you operated a sophisticated criminal enterprise? She might have exposed you. It's your burden that Penelope was engulfed by the smoke. Uncle Mortimer amassed his riches while his niece labored in a cap factory."

"Oh, shut up, Simmons. I've had enough of your bafflegab."

"Allow me to go free and your albatross will vanish."

"You've reminded me of the reason for my visit. I have an update on your former client, Czolgosz. The trial is over, and the judge set a date for the execution. It's an important date for you as well. You'll be stamped upon like a cockroach on the same day."

"You're a sick man, Hanus. A vile, cold-blooded killer."

Hanus checked the rope bindings on Burford's wrists and ankles. "Charlie," he said. "Teach Arthur how to tie a tight knot."

"Is revenge for my defense of Archibald Slater the purpose of my kidnapping?" Burford asked.

"If I was searching for revenge, Simmons, you'd be a dead man already."

The answer baffled him. "Then what is the reason, Hanus? Tell me... what is this about?"

"We're finished talking, Simmons. I'm taking a trip overseas. Arthur and Charlie will be in charge. They're instructed to kill you if you try to escape."

Hanus motioned to Charlie and the two men bounded up the stairs.

Arthur said admiringly. "You're a brave man to stand up to Mortimer Hanus."

This introduction of a third party put an unwelcome wrinkle in Burford's planned escape. He recognized Charlie Tarte as the second kidnapper in Buffalo, responsible for placing the cloth soaked in chloroform against his face. His entire body appeared chiseled with muscle, accentuated by his tight-fitting clothing. Arthur explained that Tarte acted as Hanus's enforcer, called on to handle a delinquent payment or a reneging customer. A quick session in a back room with Charlie Tarte and perhaps a few broken bones, led to a *fair* settlement of Hanus's outstanding accounts. Burford determined to be vigilant with the brute.

To his good fortune, Hanus's underlings rotated days of supervision. Charlie attended to his employer's collections. This permitted Burford, on alternate days, to bathe, sleep with a pillow and move freely in the basement without ropes. Burford convinced Arthur to bring him copies of the *Telegram* and the *Globe* that Hanus kept on the kitchen table. There was also an edition of the *New York Herald*. The *Globe* included an interview with an anarchist publisher, quoted as saying "anarchists don't condone murder or kidnapping."

The *Herald* contained a feature article about Burford's kidnapping, and he scoured the article like a castaway discovering a bottle floating ashore, a rolled note inside.

The lead investigator in his case, Detective Eli Jacob, described the frenetic pace of the investigation. Burford reread the detective's quote several times. "I will not rest until I find Mr. Simmons and apprehend his kidnappers." The French detective described the kidnapping of Czolgosz's lawyer as *le grand mystere*. ("That's not encouraging," Burford thought.) Jacob refused to confirm the rumors that anarchists held the lawyer hostage.

The *Herald* also included an exclusive interview with Caleb, citing his claim to be the kidnap victim's closest friend. Burford guffawed as he read that. Caleb the Crab boasted of monitoring the missing lawyer's caseload in his absence. "I certainly hope that's untrue...for the clients' sake," Burford exclaimed.

A separate section of the newspaper detailed the

pending execution of Leon Czolgosz for October 29th. "Ten more days," Burford calculated in a whisper, checking a calendar pinned to the wall, Hanus's threat looming.

"Did you send the letter to my wife?" he asked Arthur.

"Delivered as I promised."

"Thank heavens," Burford thought, relieved. "At least my poor wife knows I'm alive."

Pharo would certainly have deciphered the letter's coded message --- he hoped she'd employed Sherlock Holmes' method of scientific deduction to pinpoint his location. He imagined it in this way:

Well, Dr. Watson, Sutton must be highlighted in the letter because it refers to a name or place. Unfortunately,' Sutton' is equally well suited for both purposes.

First, we must check Burford Simmons's history of contacts for any person named Sutton. It may be a surname or a first name. If that fails, consider the possible methods of Simmons learning the kidnapper's name if he is a stranger.

"*He wouldn't likely introduce himself as a gentleman might. Perhaps it's the name of the steamer he's on.*"

"*Yes, on its way to the tropical island of Tahiti! Your problem, Watson, is that you have a fatal habit of looking at everything as a fanciful story rather than a scientific exercise. How would Burford Simmons send the note from a ship?*"

"*Not easily.*"

"*Correct, Dr. Watson, which leads us to Sutton as a likely location to examine. A surname leads to an overflowing catalogue of possibilities. Simmons desired to narrow our selection. Study the sentence in the letter carefully: '1 will see you soon.' The number one replaces the letter I, a*" *cypher message for a numerical address."*

"You're right, Holmes."

"Sutton refers to a place. We need to check all villages, towns and cities described as Sutton and match them with Simmons's previous travels. Is there a courthouse in any of the Suttons? We must also check the distance of locations matching Sutton from Buffalo and investigate each in order of closest to furthest. Determine if there are signs at the various entry points identifying Sutton. Simmons would be conscious and bound by rope by the time of his arrival. He wouldn't need to be blindfolded. There has been no ransom demand. The kidnapper plans to kill him."

"Would the ideal detective consider Canada?" he wondered.

On his brief outdoor outings with Arthur, Burford surveyed the countryside with scrupulous care, ignoring its rustic charm. He observed every detail with the narrow, beady watch of a Sherlock Holmes. Passing the open door of the cottage, he stopped and peeked into Arthur's tight quarters: a bundle of keys attached to a nail over the center of the bed, an overcoat dangling on a hook, a pair of galoshes, a crimson umbrella with an ivory handle.

Burford gained a view of the dirt road beyond the perimeter of the property which reminded him strangely of the fairy tale of Jack and the Beanstalk. Hulking stalks of overgrown weeds and long grass filled the road's boundaries. He searched for impenetrable barbed wire but discovered only a rusty and dilapidated wire fence. A stone driveway led to a wooden barn, a ladder at the side. At the intersection of the road and the driveway stood an arched wooden gateway with a lock. Arthur opened it with a key. Burford had to devise some ruse to guarantee that Arthur keep the door open from the basement to the main floor. He listened every night as the lock latched shut with a key.

Arthur took Burford to the tapped sugar maple tree with the tap to extract the sap embedded in the tree. Burford had two cups to collect the sap, which he boiled by the fire to convert it to syrup.

"Why do you need all this syrup?" Arthur asked.

Burford explained the syrup boosted his energy. He continued to gather strips of wood in front of the basement fireplace. They needed to be sufficiently thin to be spread and stored under a corner of the carpet without drawing attention.

His confrontation with Hanus had impressed Arthur, and on their casual outdoor outings, Burford continued to befriend Arthur.

"Can you believe he's an ambassador?"

"What are you talking about, Arthur?"

"Canadian ambassador to Scotland. That's what he told me. He's on his way to Edinburgh now to set up his residence. I'm amazed how he fools so many smart people," Arthur added. "Mark my word, the first day Hanus gets to Edinburgh, he'll plan some crooked scheme."

"Has he informed you of the date he's returning to Canada?" Burford asked.

"Charlie will have a better idea, cause he's Hanus's lackey. Charlie told me that Hanus ordered a desk and furniture for the embassy. I expect he'll return after setting up the place."

"Yes, to watch me die. It will be your death sentence too."

"What do you mean?" he asked.

"Arthur, you read the newspaper article. The police

will not halt their investigation. They will find you and arrest you for murder. Czolgosz will serve as a helpful practice run for the electric chair. You'll be fastened by the warden to the same chair and the electrical current will charge through your body until you're declared dead. You won't be given a chance to say goodbye to Betty. There won't be a funeral either."

"I'm warning you, Simmons, for the last time," Arthur said, anguished, "I can't allow you to escape."

Chapter Thirty-Three

Pharo's Diary: *The headline in this morning's paper is that Annie Edson Taylor will be toppling over Niagara Falls in a barrel on the 24th. Below that, a story that Leon Czolgosz has been sentenced to death. The judge asked him if he wished to make a statement before pronouncing sentence and Czolgosz's reply was that he had nothing to say about that. The paper described the president's killer as not trembling and his muscles not quivering as he was sentenced. He reclined in his seat in the same indifferent manner that he exhibited during the trial. The officers shackled him and took him to the jail. Indifferent? I am indifferent to my breakfast egg being hard-boiled or soft. I get shivers and palpitations contemplating that my husband's life may be extinguished for defending this dastard assassin.*

A stooped, stocky porter, bronze medallion buttons lining his velveteen uniform, led Clarence Darrow to an empty compartment in the last passenger car on the train.

"You can stretch your legs here, Mr. Darrow. Get some

reading done before the train gets to Buffalo."

"Thank you, Nat. Any suggestions for a good cigar shop in Buffalo?"

"Paddy's on Wilburn Street has the best Cuban stogies. Can't say I tried any. My lungs *ain't* too good. But if you're looking for the finest fried chicken and wheat biscuit, head over to Molly's Kitchen by the river. You tell Molly Nat the porter sent you and she'll slip an extra chicken wing onto your plate."

"Walking through the train, I noticed a lot of empty seats."

"Yes sir. We *was* packed every day during the Pan-American Exposition until poor Mr. McKinley got shot. God rest his soul. People traveling from all over the country. Darn shame that fool anarchist had to go and kill our president. I had him on the train too. Wish I *knowed* he was planning to shoot President McKinley. I'd a rounded up the porters on the train and tied him to his seat. Wait for the coppers to take him away."

"Did you speak to this fellow on the train?"

"Speak to him? I guess you can call it that. Smooth face, blue eyes, thin as a rose-leaf, and crazier than a wounded possum. He told me he didn't believe in no marital relations or going to church because they talked nonsense. He says he's just like me, a worker, and we needed to bring down the government. You *ain't* like me son, I told him. I've been riding these here trains for thirty birthdays. I don't own no place. This train is my home. Last night, I ate supper at my friend Ebenezer's, and I heard a trumpet player on his phonograph. First time I heard music on a machine. Made me think about leaving the train. My joints hurt and I have trouble with these heavy bags people carrying around. Regular folks like you, Mr. Darrow, I see coming back to the train, keep me moving."

The door to the cabin opened and a voice bellowed. "Five minutes till the train leaves the station. Five minutes."

"Hello Roger."

"Hello, Mr. Darrow. Sorry I shouted. Didn't know you were alone in the cabin."

"Hey, what about me?"

"I don't count no porters."

Nat laughed heartily. "I'll join you in a minute," he said. "Tell me this, Mr. Darrow. You can sit anywhere in the train, but you always sit in the back. This the colored car for the train when we goes to Biloxi and Nashville. Why do you ask to sit in the colored car?"

Darrow pointed to a window. "Do you see that mighty willow tree by the rail fence?"

"*Yessir.*"

"What if Roger snapped a branch off and started smacking you and me on our arms?"

"It sure would hurt. We'd both be howling like a hungry wolf under the moon."

"The same hurt for both of us?"

"*Yessir.*"

"Well, Nat, the day we stop feeling the same pain will be the day I stop riding the Jim Crow car."

"I sees that. You're a smart man, Mr. Darrow. I best be going."

Darrow placed a couple of dollars in his palm.

"What's this for?"

"You take care of your joints, Nat. And I'll do fine carrying my bag off the train."

*

Pharo Simmons invited Mitchell to accompany her to the opera, abandoning any pretense of waiting by the telephone. The kidnapper had no intention of calling.

Mitchell arrived with six members of his youth group from the Michigan Street Baptist Church.

"What can I do for you boys?" Pharo asked, after introductions were made.

Amos, the oldest in the group, answered. "We're offering our youth group's support to you, Mrs. Simmons. We have a couple of rifles and we can guard your house day and night. We're here if you need us to stock your groceries or run to the butcher shop. Pastor Hutch preached at church that the Simmons name must be spoken of with reverence and respect by members of the church. He suggested after the service that we stop by and visit."

"That is very kind of the pastor and you boys," Pharo said. "But the police are doing the guarding, and Mitchell's mother has been an angel with kitchen errands and cooking. Mitchell and I are leaving in a few minutes for the opera house, but you boys must be my guests for dinner. I'll ask Bessie to make one of her scrumptious apple pies. I picked the apples myself."

"Excuse me, ma'am. Do you have lemonade?"

Pharo surveyed the sweet boy's dimples and joyful bounce. He was the shortest in the group.

"You're Booker?"

"That's right ma'am."

"I'll be sure to ask Bessie to pour you a glass of fresh lemonade, Booker. All of the rest of you boys too."

*

The manager of the downtown concert hall, a former client of Burford's, provided Pharo with a private box on the balcony. A few patrons shot scornful looks in her direction as they sat down.

She imagined the whispers: *"Hussy! Jaunting merrily to an evening performance of Puccini's* Tosca *with a colored boy while her husband is stranded, struggling to stay alive --- or worse, dead!"*

A night at the opera with a dashing young colored man, with her husband in captivity, breached every social norm and convention. Suspicion for her husband's kidnapping might even be drawn to her. Oh, the horrid scandal! Pharo would resolutely ignore these locusts of gossip.

She vividly recalled the day she'd met Burford. She'd been walking alone on Delaware Avenue, admiring the mansions lining the sides of the boulevard. Streaks of gleaming sunshine obscured a lamppost directly in front of her and she strode straight into it, face first. She was knocked to the ground and struggled to get up, barely conscious.

She had a vague recollection of being lifted, but her next clear memory was of a hospital bed and being tended to by a nurse. "You got quite a lump on your forehead," the nurse told her.

A concerned stranger stood beside the nurse.

"Who is this?" Pharo asked.

"This is the kind gentleman who picked you up from the ground, carried you and brought you to the hospital. He happened to be driving by when you fell. He's paid your hospital bill too."

The man doffed his hat and said: "I'll be on my way now. I'm pleased that you've recovered, Miss."

"What's your name?" she asked.

"Burford Simmons."

Even in her discombobulated, weakened state, Pharo had tried to repay the man's generosity, but he adamantly refused. An arrangement was reached to meet at a café to share a plate of patisserie after her release from the hospital. The relationship soared like an eagle pointed to the sky after the first bite of the croissant. Burford proposed marriage to her one month later.

*

Pharo had asked Mitchell Harris to handle all of Burford's criminal files. She gave him the use of Burford's study, access to his shelves of law books and a cheque to cover his sundry expenses. "Burford had complete confidence in your skill, and I do too," she told him.

Bessie acted as office manager and coordinated Mitchell's client meetings. Most of the clients insisted on adjourning their trials until Burford returned. The judges in the Buffalo courthouse were extremely accommodating; the senior lawyer's absence was handled like an extended period of convalescence for a lingering illness. It was tacitly accepted that no-one would dare speak of Burford Simmons as the fatal casualty of a brazen kidnapping. The police would foil his kidnappers, the lint from the suit in his closet would be brushed away, and he'd return in glory to Buffalo to his venerable position at the Bar.

Mitchell's first criminal trial involved the defense of a

client, Nathan Sprague, with a long record for committing robbery. Nathan's current charge related to the robbery of a milliner's shop. The police apprehended him hovering in the area of the shop within minutes of the robbery. The owner of the shop positively identified the client as the man holding a gun while pilfering his cash drawer, claiming that he saw the robber take off a mask outside and had a clear view of his face through the shop window.

"So --- the robber wore a mask, but conveniently removed it in time to afford you a clear view of his face. Correct?"

"Yes, that's right."

Mitchell had discovered a note in the arresting officer's report describing two stacks of untrimmed hats with ostrich plumes and quill feathers and large hats of black mohair straw in front of the shop's window.

"Are these the type of hats you had stacked in your window the day of the robbery?" Mitchell had purchased a replica of the hats noted by the policeman and spread them across the counsel table.

"I think so."

"You know so!"

"Yes."

"Stand up, Nathan," Mitchell directed his client in the prisoner's box.

"Quite a short fellow, wouldn't you agree. About five feet tall?"

"Yes, that seems right."

"If this five-foot-tall man was standing in front of your shop window with hats stacked, you could not see his face, could you?"

"Well, I *think* I could," the shop owner stammered.

"No further questions." Mitchell dropped to his chair. Burford had instilled in him the danger of asking one extra question that could sink his case quicker than a torpedoed submarine.

*

Going through files, Mitchell learned that Burford Simmons had been contacted about a fraud trial shortly before his sudden disappearance. Burford recorded that the prospective client, Lord Halsham, a bumptious member of the British House of Lords, with stately homes in England and America, had delivered his retainer to the house in a cloth sack containing a wrapped bundle of cash.

Halsham insisted on proceeding with dispatch to trial, demanding that Mitchell Harris mount his defense.

"I'm being framed," Halsham told the young lawyer, "and my entire business depends on exposing this unfathomable decision of the police to charge me."

A major part of his business was Halsham Lumber, the largest lumber company in the northeastern United States. The company owned a steamboat dock at the bustling Buffalo port on Lake Erie. His company also operated a second profitable business shipping evergreen trees in the autumn around the Great Lakes traversing parts of the United States and Canada. The chances were high that a Halsham Christmas tree decorated the houses in all of the cities and towns dotting the Great Lakes, such as Milwaukee or Chicago.

Lord Halsham sat in Burford's study, his arms crossed below a monogrammed silk shirt with a vieux rose cravat. In a chagrined tone, he related the events leading to his legal conundrum.

On September 5th, the day before President McKinley's shooting, a paddle steamer set out from a Halsham dock carrying a shipment of evergreen trees for Toledo. The steamer never arrived --- it stalled in the middle of Lake Erie. A thorough investigation revealed the cause: a paddle box had been shattered with a sledgehammer and the stern wheel badly damaged. The crew of seven were picked up hours later by a passing steamboat after sending out a distress signal. The men were fortunate, as a gale picked up in Lake Erie followed by a fierce hailstorm that night. Halsham's boat, along with a thousand dollars' worth of evergreen trees, sank to the bottom of the lake.

"Did anyone witness the paddle steamer sinking?"

"No witnesses, Mitchell. You've captured the nub of the problem. After it was reported that the steamer failed to arrive in Toledo, word spread quickly that it had sunk. J. Moore Stanks, a former company bookkeeper who I'd fired for his glaring incompetence, accused me of bragging to him that I'd arranged to have the paddle steamer sink deliberately in order to defraud the insurance company. It's true that I contacted my insurance claim company about a claim on the same day that I learned that the steamer sank. Stanks brought his fabricated account to the police and here I am, arrested and charged. The police claim that I had a member of the crew conspiring with me."

"But I don't understand," Mitchell said. Even to the eyes of a discerning novice, the charge seemed as fragile as a piece of birch bark. "It doesn't strike me as much of a case."

"I'm doomed if a jury believes that I confessed to Stanks.

The ship sank, didn't it? I have a couple of well-heeled private investors who funded half of my shipping business. One of them threatened to bring a lawsuit against me after hearing about the police investigation. The insurance company refused to pay the outstanding claim. I indicated that I'd already contacted a Buffalo lawyer and sent the nasty investor Burford Simmons' business card. Before he was kidnapped, he planned to interview the entire steamship's crew."

"And now you're charged with attempting to defraud the insurance company?"

"Correct. Stanks contacted the *Daily Mail* to ensure that the story received prominent coverage in England. A member of the House of Lords and the owner of a British steam-boat company being charged with a serious crime is salacious news. *Harper's Weekly* picked up the story in America. J. Moore Stanks is quoted as calling me 'a charlatan and a rank thief.' I'm ruined."

Mitchell paused to reflect. The scurrilous accusation published in *Harper's Weekly* expanded the client's legal remedies.

"I think we'll need a lawyer specializing in calumny," he said.

"Bring in any lawyer of your choice," Lord Halsham brusquely replied. "My priority is to restore my business and repair my good name as soon as possible."

Chapter Thirty-Four

Pharo's Diary: *I am obsessed with death every waking moment. I fuss over every detail of Leon Czolgosz's planned execution. His ruthless crime against the leader of my Republic deserves the most severe punishment. Hundreds of requests from all over the country have been submitted to witness the execution. An official electrician shall oversee the switch to shoot his body full of electrical current. I wonder how one is chosen for the task. When Burford's kidnapper is caught, I shall volunteer to be the electrician, turning on the death switch with glee. I shall unreservedly relish the moment.*

Twenty-four hours...

Clarence Darrow had a one-day window to remain in Buffalo to assist the police to locate his good friend. His partners in Chicago managed his law practice in his absence, but he had an upcoming criminal conspiracy trial in Oshkosh, Wisconsin, for a union leader who had been jailed during a woodworkers' strike.

He told Jacob that his client had been stifled by the owner of the factory when he tried to introduce collective bargaining. The meagre pay and the conditions of the factory, like Oliver Twist in the almshouse, led his client to call a workers' strike. The owner expended considerable effort to break the strike and solicited the assistance of the local police force.

Detective Eli Jacob shared a cup of stewed tea with Darrow in a secluded corner of the police cafeteria. They had checked every document in the police file for the Brownton Cap Factory Fire. Photographs and witness accounts depicted the harrowing account of the fire and its aftermath. After going through the files, Darrow suggested the break.

Jacob sensed that his time with the great lawyer was nearing its end.

"*Dis-moi*, tell me, Clarence, when you look back at your life, what legacy do you wish to leave?"

"That I made a measurable difference in the lives of the unfavored and disdained, that I broke through barriers of oppression and ignorance, and that in my defense of the downtrodden, on their choppy road of misery, the alter of innocence was attained. And what of you, Detective Jacob?"

"*Moi*? I'm a police officer, forgive me if I choose to emphasize convicting the truly guilty. I hope that I leave this world with a modest inheritance for my children; a reputation as an honorable and respected detective and the Jacob name recalled fondly. A good name, to borrow from Othello, perhaps most:

"Who steals my purse steals trash.
'Tis something, nothing:
Twas mine, 'tis his, and has been slave to thousands.
But he that filches from me my good name
Robs me of that which not enriches him
And makes me poor indeed."

He looked at Darrow who appeared downcast and distracted.

"You're worried that we're too late to save your friend. Permit me to share a story with you, Clarence. At the end of Alfred Dreyfus's court-martial, the French military ordered him confined to an island in the Atlantic Ocean known as Devil's Island. His conditions were treacherous; he had to live under constant guard in a prison hut the size of a cupboard, in sweltering heat, with his legs clamped with chains through the night. At his court-martial Dreyfus appeared sickly, his skin white as snow, his body feeble. He'd just spent three hard months in prison. Many of my fellow detectives didn't believe he would survive the dreadful voyage to the remote island. *Pouvez-vous deviner le résultat?* Can you guess the result?"

"Dreyfus survived the trip and years of harsh captivity before being vindicated."

"Ah, *oui*, but do you know what sustained him? The prisoner exchanged letters with his wife, Lucie. The letters were monitored and many of Dreyfus's letters never reached his wife. He didn't know that. The Ministry of War decided to bring a Jewish police officer to assist --- a gullible general thought it might be prudent to have a Jew on the lookout for any type of religious coding. *I* was the officer chosen to read those letters. I felt shame and revulsion for being assigned to such an unworthy task. But I discovered in those letters profound expressions of love from Dreyfus towards his wife and children. Lucie's abiding commitment of support and belief in his innocence helped sustain him through the ordeal. Her faith nourished the prisoner with hope. The unrelenting capacity for a human being to cling to life should not be underestimated, Clarence."

A uniformed policeman presented himself at their cafeteria table.

"I apologize for interrupting, sir," he said to the detective. But I urgently needed to locate you. I collected the information you requested. I found three towns and villages of Sutton in Canada: one in Ontario, one in Quebec, and a third one in Saskatchewan.

"Where is Sutton, Ontario located?" Darrow asked.

The policeman examined his handwritten notes. "Here it is. It's about fifty miles northeast of Toronto. The village listed as having a population of eight hundred residents."

Detective Jacob thanked the officer and turned to the lawyer. "Mortimer Hanus's home address is in Toronto."

"It's the closest link we have in the Brownton Cap Factory file to Sutton. I was interested to read that Penelope Hanus worked as an assistant to Archibald Salter until a week before the fire when she moved to the third floor."

"And a grieving parent or uncle listening to that evidence would hold Salter responsible for the move. If she had stayed on the second floor, she would have escaped."

"It may be helpful for you to place a call to a detective with the Toronto Major Crimes Squad. Let's find out if there is any useful information to be shared about

Mortimer Hanus. It may provide the police with a lead to a suspect."

"It will be our only lead, Clarence. *D'accord.* I'll make the call now."

Clarence Darrow withheld the content of Burford's confidential memo, but asked, "Did you obtain any information about the whereabouts of Archibald Salter?"

"Yes, I obtained a coroner's report. He drowned last summer at a beach on Lake Erie. He swam out too far and got caught in a current. An initial concern by the police of suspicious circumstances was discounted by the coroner. The victims' families were certainly not shedding any tears for his passing."

"And if they're angry enough, that only leaves Salter's lawyer at his trial to target."

The detective left and returned to the cafeteria a few minutes later. "Our fellow, Mortimer Hanus, has quite the reputation."

Darrow straightened up.

"But not what we hoped for. The officer at the Major Crimes squad recognized the name. He is a successful businessman and a Canadian diplomat. He's on very friendly terms with the Deputy Chief of Police."

"Was the officer aware whether Hanus owns a home in Sutton?"

"He hung up the telephone after I mentioned that Hanus is being investigated in connection with a kidnapping investigation."

"You'll have to do the police legwork on your own, Detective Jacob."

*

Mortimer Hanus paced anxiously along the edge of Pier Six at Halifax harbor, waiting for the captain's call to board the gangway to the steamship H.H.S. *Ophir* to Glasgow. The boarding had been delayed, without explanation, by over an hour. Hanus expressed his disappointment at the ticket counter that no city or government officials had arrived to bid him farewell. He thrived on being referred to by the title: Mister Ambassador. The ticket agent duly obliged after being tipped a nickel. The fictitious title, an improvement on the drab Consul General, suited Hanus's opinion of his own stature. He inscribed a written direction that he planned to leave at the stewards' desk that the ship's staff and the captain officially address him by his government title. He had forged ahead with his plans for Scotland. A lavish opening reception at the consulate and briefings with the Scottish prime minister awaited him.

But he must return to Canada at the first opportunity. Simmons had become an irritant and intrusion, and he needed to be permanently expunged. From the newspaper reports he'd read, the Buffalo police doubted that anarchists were responsible for the kidnapping. He needed to act quickly.

An olive-skinned woman in a pearl gray velvet turban with pheasant plume, an emerald green shawl draping her shoulders, and her hands bejeweled with diamonds, approached Hanus's direction. She carried a piece of embroidered hand baggage. She passed close enough to exude her redolent perfume. A long strand of white pearls circled her neck, a medallion announcing her wealth and stature. He checked for an escort, but the woman walked alone. He gathered her age to be in her early forties --- likely a rich widow traveling overseas. Perhaps she could be enticed for a walking tour of the Scottish Highlands.

A chance for an informal chat presented itself as she circled back. Hanus stepped into the woman's direct path to intercept her with a benevolent request that she join a lonely stranger at dinner.

The quest was stalled as a groggy voice from the deck of the ship crackled over a noisy megaphone:

"I regret to inform everyone boarding that the boat's departure to Glasgow will be delayed until tomorrow morning at the earliest. You will be permitted to spend the time waiting on the ship in your quarters and a meal will be served after boarding. The band will be playing dinner music on the deck."

"At least our evening's plans need not be disrupted," Hanus said.

The woman introduced herself as Gwendolyn Hastings. He complimented her on her exquisite taste in jewelry.

"I was trained to acquire my developed style and tastes," she said matter-of-factly. She explained that for a couple of years during her early thirties, she had helped plan Queen Victoria's extravagant entertainment at Buckingham Palace. "Quite a contrast to this boisterous new king," she added.

Gwendolyn told Hanus her itinerary before landing in Halifax, starting in New York with a rolling endless tour of museums, theater and fine dining. She had been a guest of the president's family at his house on Twentieth Street and Park Avenue. "Tell me about your own adventures," she said, curling her arm into his. Her coat was trimmed with two rows of tiny silver buttons.

Hanus regaled her with adventures he conjured of an African safari and a camel ride in the scalding heat of the Sahara Desert, and then described the purpose of his current overseas trip.

"The Canadian ambassador to Scotland, I'm impressed," she said.

Hanus examined the strand of pearls of this Cleopatra model close-up. It suggested a treasure trove of jewelry stashed in her luggage. After being transported aboard to her room, he'd need less than five minutes of solitude to pilfer a few precious items. "You must come to Edinburgh as my guest at the embassy," he said.

"Impossible," she replied. "I'm only in Glasgow for a day to see my aunt. I'm informed that she is in the final throes of life, and I want to be certain that I secure my inheritance. I'm her closest and dearest relative. The steamships to Glasgow from New York were filled to the brim."

A couple of teenage boys with matching sailor caps rolled up the bunting extending below a large welcome banner.

"Any reason for the delay?" he asked them.

"Fierce storm out there, sir," one of the boys replied. "The captain said the ocean is mighty rough. He doesn't want to take any chances of taking water on board the ship."

Gwendolyn spoke. "We wouldn't last two minutes in the freezing water if the ship flipped over."

Hanus listened intently. A splendid idea presented itself.

"Come, dear Gwendolyn," Hanus said with aplomb. "Let's get settled on board and order a bottle of Pommery champagne." He clasped her arm inside his and walked up the carpeted gangway to the steamship. "I want to know everything about you, my dear," he said, mustering a glimmer of charm.

*

Step number seven.

The plot arched forward.

Burford's neighbor in Buffalo, a professional mime by the name of Paul-Erik Wick, occasionally dropped by the Simmons house to demonstrate a pantomime he'd been practicing. On one visit, Burford asked which sentiments, on the roulette table of human emotions, were the easiest and hardest to perform.

"Solemnity and earnestness are the simplest," Paul-Erik said. "Drooping eyes, pursed lips and shrugged shoulders. The most challenging is surprise. The eyes always betray the visage."

*

"What is happening?" Arthur asked, scurrying to the basement with a hand-lamp. "I heard a banging sound."

"I'll be honest with you, Arthur. I've been hitting my head against the wall."

"There are drops of blood dripping down your forehead."

The cot had been removed from the door and restored to its original place on the floor. "I'm going stir crazy down here. I know that I only have a few days left to live. I've reconciled myself to my fate. And I really do thank you for helping me deliver my letter. Can you see fit to grant a dying man's final wish?"

"I'm not permitting your escape, if that's your request."

"No, nothing like that, of course. A good lawyer knows when the argument's lost. My wish is modest. I'd like to be able to take a walk in the clear night air for a few minutes."

"That's all?"

"It's not as if I can go anywhere with the gate locked and these ropes around my wrists."

"I'm not making any promises. I will think about it. You can't let Charlie know."

"Is it possible for you to leave the door to the stairway open at night?"

"And if I agree, no more headbanging?"

"I promise. It stops now."

Burford listened as Arthur bounded up the stairs in his carpet slippers to the main floor. The door shut but he didn't hear the distinct sound of the door's clamped lock. Two major strokes of progress in a matter of minutes. The aged oak side door in the basement finally twisted ajar. Burford narrowly missed plunging through the door to the outside ground on his last heave. One further push with his shoulder ensured access to the outdoors.

The plotted flight moved steadily forward.

Chapter Thirty-Five

Pharo's Diary: *I bade welcome to three girls from the neighborhood, aged twelve by my approximation, who presented me with a bowed sandal-wood box. The girls resemble young Tess Durbeyfield at this time of their lives, vessels of emotion untinctured by experience. I opened the box to find a magnificent Barbotine vase, with the raised decoration of a turtle. "Whatever is this for?" The tallest of the girls, curtsied, and explained that the girls knew of my anguish and resolved, at a tree-house meeting, that the sweet smell of a bevy of roses might bring me cheer. "And now you'll have a vase to place them." I had long ago considered my tear duct drained, but the tiny vessel surprised me, and a gush of tears burst forth. "This is the loveliest gift I have ever received," I told them, with real gratitude. "I shall cherish it forever." The vicissitudes of life continue to astonish me. And on that melodic note, my publisher delivered in person a dollop of good tidings today. My novel will be published in the fall. A muffled cheer of "hurray" is all I can muster.*

Neeru scheduled a late-night meeting with Detective Jacob at her office for a wrap-up session on the Czolgosz case. The team had disbanded temporarily while the detective immersed himself in the murder trial. As he picked at a jar of artichoke hearts --- his dinner, he apologized --- she updated the detective with the news that the lawyers for Czolgosz had confirmed that their client had no interest in appealing the jury's verdict.

"He would only have appealed a not guilty verdict," the detective noted wryly.

The execution date was circled on a date in the third week of October on a mounted calendar Neeru displayed. Three physicians planned to attend the electrocution chamber to complete an autopsy after the prisoner was pronounced dead. The anatomical structure of the killer's brain would be examined for any clues to the assassin's deviant and violent behavior.

"*Bon chance.* I studied the prisoner's simper of odious pride during the trial. He was calm and unflappable. For all my years in police work, he is by far the strangest creature I've confronted. I am invited to attend his execution, but I passed. I take little pleasure in seeing a man's life ended."

Neeru pressed the detective for the latest progress on Burford's kidnapping investigation.

"We're pursuing a lead to Sutton, Ontario," he said, referencing the coded letter received by Pharo Simmons. I have requested authorization to send one of my officers across the border. The delay is an unfortunate setback."

"Are you focused on a particular suspect in Canada?" she asked.

The detective hesitated. Disclosing that information, even to the trusted Neeru, might jeopardize the ongoing investigation. He measured his words cautiously, like treading on a pathway of slippery ice.

"Neeru, I will tell you, because I know that you despair about your colleague's fate, but you must give me your word that it can go no further."

"I promise," she assured him.

Jacob described Burford's role as the attorney in the Brownton Cap Factory Fire trial. When the detective identified the Canadian suspect as Mortimer Hanus, Neeru appeared stunned, her eyes circling like moths to a light.

"Is there a problem? Are you feeling well?" the detective asked.

"Mortimer Hanus!" she exclaimed. "I'm retained by Mitchell Harris to investigate a potential defamation claim for one of his clients. Mitchell took over the case from Burford."

"Tell me," the detective said, his interest aroused.

"The client is charged with an insurance embezzlement. And the former business partner pushing the case is Mortimer Hanus. I recall Mitchell telling me that he lived in Toronto."

"*Le meme personne*! We have stumbled on an important clue, *je pense*. Two separate cases where Burford Simmons is the lawyer and Hanus has a stake in the outcome."

The detective mulled the perplexing link and then pressed Neeru for the details of Halsham's criminal case. His brow twitched upward as each item was recited. At last he asked,

"Why would a financial mogul like Lord Halsham

concoct such a rank, amateurish crime? It's preposterous."

"Mitchell and I echo your opinion. But how can we fail to link the case to Burford's kidnapping?"

Detective Jacob conceded that he had no suitable answer. If Mortimer Hanus lived in Buffalo, he'd bring him to the police station *tout suite* and pose the question directly. But he was in Canada, buffered by the unwillingness of the local police to investigate a notable citizen. Jacob was mired in unchartered waters.

Clarence Darrow had warned Jacob that he'd need a substantial piece of incriminating evidence to break the logjam. The lawyer had departed to Chicago earlier that day. Jacob embraced his friend before Darrow boarded the train.

"You'd make a fine police detective, Clarence," Jacob told him.

"The line of clients waiting at my law office to be rescued might be chagrined," Darrow responded.

Turning on the step, he offered the detective one piece of parting advice. "Eli, check the newsprint from the Toronto newspapers for a possible match to the kidnapper's note."

*

Hanus waited for the blaring *"All ashore that's gone ashore!"* horn to signal that the ship was finally setting its course from the Halifax harbor. He glanced at the freckles on the back of the woman lying next to him in bed. He'd gleaned a lot of useful information from Gwendolyn Hastings over the evening. At dinner she had recounted, between glasses of bubbly champagne, the woes of her first marriage to an entrepreneur from New Jersey currently serving a lengthy prison sentence for manipulating a stock's price to attract investors on the stock market. She had visited him in prison after the imposition of sentence and extracted his signature on a document giving her legal authority to handle his finances. In turn, she had tearfully promised to patiently wait for him. Her patience had apparently waned after three months and the divorce was a huge scandal. She boasted to Hanus about her daily jaunts to the best shops in New York, purchasing the finest ornate jewels, silk bedding, lace handkerchiefs and a glamorous hat collection. The shop clerks in Bloomingdales routinely invited her to the store on Lexington Avenue for a private perusal of the latest dresses and gowns from Paris.

Gwendolyn's second husband, Max, was a childhood friend of President Teddy Roosevelt. Max owned a large gun factory in a village in New Hampshire, but never stayed at their New England mansion more than a few days before leaving for another gun show. Max encouraged his wife to travel and she had booked this overseas trip at his urging. Budapest, Prague, Hamburg and Vienna were on her itinerary.

"A lonely, solitary traveler," Hanus thought, disguising his smirk.

After dinner, they retired to Hanus's room where they sat on his bed and he planted soft kisses on Gwendolyn's neck, whispering that he was swept away by the siren's enthralling beauty. He invited her to undress and join him under the covers to make love. He waited during the night for her to fall asleep. Hanus located the cabin key from her handbag, and sauntered down the floor's hallway, checking to see if he was followed. She had mentioned at dinner that her cabin number was forty-eight. He put the key into the door, wiggled it, and it opened.

"It appears that we're neighbors on the ship."

Hanus peered across the hall at the grey-haired man with a cane who had spoken --- and recognized the man who had sat alone at dinner, across from their table.

"My name's Major, old chap" he declared, pointing the cane. "I was a major in the army which made my war career terribly confusing. Major Major." His chest heaved at the stale joke. "Do you fancy a game of billiards tomorrow? I rubbed my thumb along the felt table. It's first-class."

"A splendid idea," Hanus said curtly. "Until tomorrow then."

"Lovely woman, your wife. In my day as a dilettante, we called her a stunner."

"I'm sorry, I'm late," Hanus said. "Billiards tomorrow, I look forward to handily beating you."

Hanus studied the room like a cat at a robin's nest, a portable lamp guiding his view. The strand of pearls worn by Gwendolyn Hastings lay on the dresser next to a thick pile of British pounds. Burford counted fifty pounds from the pile and tucked the bills into his pocket. "Those wouldn't be missed." He spotted a painted jewelry box with a dancing figurine in the center in the corner of an open trunk. Hanus opened the box and surveyed an array of neatly packed gold and silver rings, bracelets and earrings. One of the bracelets was encrusted with sparkling diamonds along the edge. "That was for the last day of the voyage," he cautioned himself. Gwendolyn would surely blame the ship's staff for pilfering her dazzling jewels if they went missing now.

Hanus slunk back to his cabin undetected.

"Where were you?" Gwendolyn asked, yawning. She sat upright and appeared perturbed. "I'm not accustomed to being abandoned by my courtiers," she said.

"I needed some fresh air on the deck," Hanus replied in a guileless tone. He waited for Gwendolyn to turn back to bed before slipping the door key back into her bag.

"The purser's knock at the door woke me up. There's a telegraph waiting at the ship's telegraph office."

Hanus hurried to retrieve the telegraph wired by Charlie. He looked around before reading it:

---- ARTHUR SAYS BS PLANNING ESCAPE STOP --- DON'T TRUST ARTHUR --- STOP SEND INSTRUCTIONS C

Hanus slid the telegram into a pocket and dispatched a coded wire to the Beaverton Street Post-Office:

DISPOSE OF GARBAGE ON NEXT VISIT MH

As he exited the telegraph office, the ship's captain greeted him cheerily, saying,

"Why, good afternoon, Mr. Planter!"

Chapter Thirty-Six

In the trolley-car of cases spanning Burford Simmons' luminous career, one case emerged from the bunch; the murder trial of Thomas E. Pendleton. Pendleton had been charged with the murder of his business partner, Quincy Rutherford Minden. The two men operated a blacksmith shop on Michigan Avenue in Buffalo. Pendleton suspected his partner of looting the cash drawer as sales were measurably lower on the days Minden managed the shop. Pendleton hired a Pinkerton investigator to trail his business partner and received a report that Minden was observed through a side window surreptitiously drawing cash from the day's proceeds into his waistcoat pocket. Burford's client chose to avenge his grievance by foul play. He found an abandoned sewer cover, and one summer evening under the cover of darkness, carried it up a ladder to the roof of Minden's house and covered the chimney. Minden was discovered the next day dead in his bed, asphyxiated by smoke. Pendleton was interviewed by the police but had collaborated with his wife on a secure alibi. He expressed regret that his partner was dead and informed the police that he planned to pay the funeral expenses. "What a manner of departing this earth," he expressed to the interviewing detective. "A sewer cover over a chimney --- who'd want to kill Quincy like that?"

The problem for Pendleton was that the police hadn't released the detail of the sewer cover to the papers. Only the police and the killer knew that fact. Pendleton was arrested and charged with murder.

Burford defended the case valiantly but was unable to overcome his client's slip. The jury deliberated for a day before finding him guilty. Pendleton was sentenced to die, and Burford was present when he was fastened into the electric chair and his breath extinguished. It was Burford's first and last losing death penalty case.

*

"The kidnapper *must* be Mortimer Hanus," Pharo declared, after Detective Jacob updated them on his investigation. "And he has been appointed consul general to Scotland? What an utter disgrace. Shame on Canada. Shame!"

"We have no proof yet. But if it is Hanus, he is living a double identity, Mrs. Simmons. He is adroit in his chicanery. *C'est dommage que l'intelligence soit utilisée pour le mal.*"

"I attended the Cap Factory Fire trial. My hankie was drenched by the end of each day."

"*C'est une grande tragedie.*"

"May I pose a question, Detective?"

"*Bien sur*, but of course."

"Do you have a photograph of Mortimer Hanus?"

The detective rummaged through the file he brought. "He may be in this snapshot of the victims' families confronting Salter after the verdict."

Pharo studied the photograph, bringing the picture close to her face. "That's him," she said, pointing. "I'm sure of it."

"To whom are you referring, *madame*?"

"During the trial I would often chat with my husband during courtroom recess. I made no secret of our connection. I passed the victims' families frequently, respecting their privacy, and they never bothered me. With one notable exception. Him!" She jabbed at the man in the photograph, captured in a frothing pose in front of Archibald Salter.

"I left hastily on the morning of the verdict. The courtroom had erupted in pandemonium after the jury uttered the words 'not guilty' --- Burford had to meet privately with his client and urged me to scurry home."

"Continue..."

"I had just walked past the orchards of Dewberry Gardens when the man in the picture blocked my path. I knew him from the victims' section in the courtroom."

"You're certain it was the man in the newspaper photograph?"

"Yes, Detective Jacob. I insisted he move, but he resisted my overture and scowled. I served him a memorable lesson not to impede my path."

"What kind of lesson, *madame*?"

"I kicked him hard on his shin, and he toppled to the ground like a spinning top. He stood up and raised his fists, leaving his face exposed like a rank amateur. I'd been to boxing matches with Burf; we had watched Terry Mc-

Govern knock down Joe Gans. I faked with my right hand and hit him a solid McGovern uppercut with my left. Blood flooded down and he complained that I'd broken his nose. A few boys watching at the side of the road cheered me on."

"What did the boys say?" the detective asked.

"Bop him another one, Miss." Pharo gesticulated with a clenched left fist. "The man was in a daze, cursing. I remember his crooked nose and beet-red bulbous cheeks matching the blood on his chin. He drove off on a bicycle that he had parked by the shrubbery."

"Did the fellow mention why he tried to block your path?"

"I never did ask. I assumed he'd intended to badger me since Burf wasn't available."

"Did you inform Burford of this incident?"

"No, he'd have been livid, so I banished it from my mind." She sheepishly turned to her father. "I did tell a priest at Confession."

"My only query is, why hasn't Mortimer Hanus been arrested yet?" Mervin said.

"It is difficult," the detective responded. "I don't have any jurisdiction or authority to investigate and arrest a suspect in Canada. I require the cooperation of the detective's bureau in Toronto. *C'est la différence.*"

"Well, then stop the dilly-dallying and get their authority," Mervin ordered.

"*Nous travaillons.* We're trying. But we're encountering resistance from the Canadian police. They refuse to accept that Mortimer Hanus is a criminal."

"Or they simply choose not to care because the victim defended McKinley's murderer."

"That is not correct, *monsieur*."

Pharo stood and marched towards the front door, her gait stiff as a mannequin. "My husband's life is in grave danger, if he's still alive. Don't these detectives grasp this elementary fact? I'll be on the next train to Toronto. Let them tell me directly that my husband's life is trivial."

Mervin nodded in approval. "I'll join you," he said. "I'll make inquiries about the train schedule."

"I don't think berating the Canadian police will have the desired effect." Detective Jacob spoke sympathetically, but with finality. "I will confirm the identity of the man in the papers. I have another lead that I'm actively pursuing."

"Will you give me Hanus's address in Sutton if you locate it?"

The detective shook his head. "*Mais non*, madame. It's strictly police business."

"You'll forgive me, but I've lost confidence in the police," Pharo said. "I'll locate the address on my own."

"I assure you my police investigation is focused on bringing your husband home safely."

"Thank you, Detective Jacob. Please don't take umbrage. We appreciate everything *you're* doing to find Burford."

She escorted the detective to the front door and went to find Bessie in the kitchen. "Is Mitchell at court?" she asked.

"He's in the office working."

Pharo went straight to the office and pulled up a chair. "I wanted to ask you about the group of boys from the church youth group who showed up at the house yesterday. Was the offer to assist me sincere?"

"Of course. I've heard my mother tell the story of

Burford's mother saving her family from the slave catchers many times. She still wakes up nights thinking about how close they all were to going back to the plantation."

"I have a favor to ask. Can you select four of the boys and invite them to the house? I have a project for them."

Mitchell readily agreed.

The four boys, dressed for a Sunday church service in white shirts and bowties, arrived within the hour and met Pharo and her father.

Pharo asked Booker to pass around a tray with four cups of hot cocoa. "What are your names boys?" she asked the others.

"Amos, William and Shank."

Pharo inquired about the boys' ages. They ranged from seventeen to Booker, the youngest, at fourteen. She brought out a letter sealed with wax.

"I have a letter that I need delivered in Canada. I'll arrange for the tickets for two of you on the overnight train to Toronto and provide you enough money to cover your trip. Your ultimate destination is the Parliament building in the city of Ottawa. I'd like this letter delivered to a Mr. Martin Beliveau." She handed it to William. "His address is on the envelope. He is a cabinet minister in the Canadian government. I want you to be sure to deposit the letter right in his hand." In her telephone calls with Martin since the kidnapping, he had offered to help, and Pharo intended to hold Minister Beliveau to his word.

"The second assignment is likely to be quite dangerous and I want you boys to think carefully before volunteering. I'll bear no ill-will if you decide not to join my adventure, but I'll brook no cowardice in my company either. All four of you boys will travel with me to Toronto. We'll split into two groups there. While the others proceed to Ottawa, the two boys joining me will take a carriage to a village north of the city called Sutton. Be back here at 4 pm. Wear warm clothing, but you won't need any food or money. Bring a blanket and book to read on the train. Do you boys have any questions?"

"No, ma'am," Amos declared for them all.

Mervin bounded out of his chair as soon as they left. "What's this all about, Pharo?" he asked. "You're not traveling to Canada without me."

"I'm sorry father, but my mind is made up. I'm not prepared to lose the two people in my life who mean the most. You'll mind the house with Bessie and Mitchell. Mark my words. I'll be returning home with Burf."

Mervin realized that changing his daughter's mind was as likely as shifting the Rock of Gibraltar.

*

The boys appeared five minutes before the appointed time. Booker and Shanks stepped forward.

"We'll be joining you in Sutton, Mrs. Simmons."

The two youngest boys had volunteered for the dangerous assignment.

"Can I ask why you boys volunteered?"

"Cause we're the best shots, ma'am," Shank stated. He opened their sack to reveal two Colt revolvers.

"You can't go there with guns," Mervin said, his consternation evident. "We must put our trust in Detective Jacob."

"I'm sorry, Father. I've given the police every opportunity to crack this case. But I've been sitting here like a half-baked log long enough. I'm taking matters into my own hands and I will not be thwarted. I'm bringing my husband home."

Pharo retrieved John Garcy's note with his telephone number from her bedroom dresser. There was an address in Sutton she needed to acquire from an obliging detective in Greenpoint seeking redemption.

Chapter Thirty-Seven

Juliet heard the wailing echo calling the people for Friday morning prayers. She looked through the haze at the nearby royal mosque and its pointy minaret. The muezzin appeared like a black dot on the balcony. Pelting rain beat against the apartment wall like a steady drumbeat and the wooden shutters on the windows shook slightly. She watched raindrops bounce off the reflective pool in front of the palace. The courtyard remained empty as the sultan and his waddling cortege of palace officials delayed their advance to the prayer hall.

The ripe moment had arrived for Juliet to implement her escape plan. She perched on the opened windowsill of the apartment's second-floor window. The closed door of the barren dressing room buffered the constant noise of the beating rain from the women sleeping inside. Her dangling legs were soaked, and raindrops splashed playfully into her face. Beneath lay a garden lined with fruit trees, clay-potted plants and a bed of soft, muddy ground that would serve as her landing pod. A puddle had formed there.

The drop was at least fifteen feet. She held a strip of curtain tied to a sturdy rock that she wedged underneath a protruding corner of the window. She found the heavy rock on the edge of a garden and she'd struggled mightily to carry up the staircase. The rock and piece of curtain had been stored in empty hat boxes with her name inscribed on the top. She hurled the line of curtain out of the window, glancing at the rock. It held securely in place.

On a typical morning, the sight of a dangling curtain would likely draw the attention of a passing palace guard. The apartment complex abutted Sultan Hakan's palace.

The steady beat of the rain intensified. Still no sign of the sultan's guards. Several seconds passed, followed by silence.

"Stay calm," Juliet told herself as she looked skyward to check the clouds.

This first step, the most perilous, relied on the tightly tied knot circling the rock holding as she slid down the sheaf of curtain that extended halfway to the ground. From the curtain's end, she'd plummet to the soft splashing pod, knees bent, and hands outstretched to protect her on landing. She'd be soaked, her clothing drenched in wet mud. But Juliet preferred a speedy death to confinement in the harem, although Sultan Hakan rarely used her for sexual pleasure. Each time he called her from the harem she prepared a basin with scented water to place at the sultan's feet and give him a vigorous massage of each foot in turn.

But she dreaded the visits of Robert Planter. She despised the Canadian businessman and even bathing in sweetly scented oil could not purge her of his decadent sweat and odor. She had learned that he was in the palace in the past weeks but had left in a rush --- to her good fortune. As a frequent exalted guest of the Sultan, Planter had been given her in the harem. Planter derived sexual pleasure measured by the degree of pain he inflicted. If she had a dagger, she'd strike it through his unmerciful heart.

Other girls had earlier shared similar ghastly experiences with Planter and were exultant that he now insisted on Juliet. At the end of his session, ignoring the bruises he'd inflicted, he would inquire if he had pleasured her. "Very much," she would answer, keenly aware that any objection would be conveyed to the sultan and bring down his considerable wrath.

The loquacious Planter enjoyed the sound of his own voice, and Juliet pretended to be his enthralled audience. Conversation diverted Planter from inflicting more pain. He'd linger on the bed, engaging in endless and unguarded boasting. He mentioned that he was from Toronto. "We're bonded by the same language and culture," he added.

Juliet cloaked her questions with pretended interest and pried out every sordid detail of his illicit business schemes. She learned that he conducted an export-import business to cover the clandestine sale of arms and weapons. Sultan Hakan was his best customer. He described the vast treasure of currency he'd amassed, deposited in banks in Athens and Cyprus. Planter's international connections included governors of banks, ministers of government, presidents and prime ministers.

Planter churned out intimate details of his background; he even disclosed that Robert Planter was an alias, and that his true identity was Mortimer Hanus. He studied Juliet's face as he told her, but she evinced no reaction. But it seemed to her that it was dangerous to know this.

She made one final check of the knot --- if it failed, she would plunge to the ground, likely breaking several bones. She'd be immobilized, waiting for inevitable capture by palace guards.

"Here I go," she whispered, and dropped out of the window. The sense of escape felt exhilarating. She felt none of the panic she had feared might overwhelm her. The stark alternative, to spending more years of her life in an Ottoman palace, overcame the risk.

She scraped a knee during the fall, but suffered no serious injury. The rain began to subside, and the minutes passed, but no garbage wagon appeared. She had watched as it passed by the window of her apartment every morning shortly after sunrise --- why would it be late today?

Hearing a scraping sound from above, she looked up to see the curtain strip being drawn back through the window. The smiling face of her best friend in the harem, Derya, emerged from the window. Derya waved energetically at her, a fond farewell. She had urged Derya to join her.

"Where would I go?" she asked.

Her entire family had disappeared from her Ottoman village after it was pilloried by a rampaging band of thieves. She accepted that they were dead. Derya had been taken captive and dropped at the palace door as a gift for the sultan. Years had since passed. Derya measured the passage of time by counting the seasons. Four summers had passed at the harem. She had been promised her release after serving nine years.

Juliet owed a huge debt to her friend, who had saved her life. During the first difficult days adjusting to life in the palace harem, Derya had adopted her as a sister and educated her in the ways of the harem, teaching her the dances that entertained the sultan and helping her with her ornate head ornament and silk gown. They had shared cups of Turkish coffee under the harem's flowered porcelain ceiling in gay laughter and whispering jokes. Derya had stroked her hair with a brush as she bathed in the harem pools and protected her from jealous barbs and fighting in the harem. She had comforted her on the frequent occasions that Juliet's mood spiraled into despair --- and she had encouraged the escape. "You have a family and a beloved waiting for you in Australia," she told her. "You must return home to them."

At last, the plodding garbage wagon approached, and Juliet climbed into the back compartment. The garbage had been packed into sacks and Juliet found a secure spot between them. As the wagon passed beyond the iron courtyard gates of the Sultan's palace, Juliet began to dream of reuniting with her family in Brisbane and taking long walks with Harry on the white sandy beach of the Gold Coast. He'd proposed to her on the last walk. She had told him he was silly. They were both students without an income. Marriage was unrealistic, she'd chided him. She was less certain now.

The baroque facades of the historical buildings of Istanbul passed in a panorama as the wagon continued its journey to the dump. A building appeared with three bulging arches on the roof and three overdrawn arches on the front --- the spice bazaar. She had visited it a couple of times on her journey through the historic city and purchased saffron and corekutu spices and jasmine fruit tea to bring back to Brisbane.

Juliet bounded from the back of the wagon and walked the cobbled stones to the entrance. Her damp clothing clung to her body and she reeked of garbage. Inside the bazaar, shoppers scurrying from one stand to the next were too preoccupied to notice her.

She stopped, startling a stooped, elderly man restocking his piles of spices.

"Can you please help me?" she pleaded.

The old man gently took her hand. He noticed the silver locket glazed with small diamonds. "Have you come from the Sultan's palace?" he asked.

Juliet began to sob.

"Do you have family?" he asked.

"Yes, my parents and sister are in Australia."

"Quick, come with me. Ottoman police patrol the bazaar." He motioned for her to step behind a draped partition. "Please, please, dry yourself off and put the robe on." He pointed to a chair. "It will cover you to your ankles. Leave your wet clothes on the floor."

Juliet noticed a pile of newspapers. On the top she observed a bold headline in English from the *Paris Herald* describing the shooting of President McKinley. "Can I have this?" she asked.

"Of course," the man replied. "I collect old newspapers to use to wrap the spices."

Juliet checked for the name of the journalist listed in the story. "Willow Hooper --- *Brooklyn Daily Eagle.*"

"Here, please take this," the man said after she emerged from the partition.

She took the *keffiyeh* and tucked her hair underneath it.

"Follow me," the man told her. He gave her a wheelbarrow with bags of spices to push.

"Where are we going?"

"Ahmet has a telephone, a gift from a prosperous uncle. You will be able to call your parents. Ahmet will shelter you until you're rescued."

Juliet appeared baffled.

"Don't worry," he told her. "We are all brothers in the spice bazaar. You have nothing to fear."

"You are so kind," Juliet said, pulling the wheelbarrow and shielding herself behind the man. "How can I ever repay you?"

"I am the one who owes you a debt of gratitude. My prayers to Allah will be received today like a bouquet of sweetly scented orchids."

The wheel barrel reached Abdul's stall and the old man whispered a few words in his ear before bidding Juliet farewell. She slipped the locket into his vest pocket. Abdul ushered her to a telephone in a private corner. She held the *Paris Herald* tucked under her arm as she anxiously dialed the number. Her mother's soothing voice greeted her.

Chapter Thirty-Eight

"Minister, this arrived for you, marked PERSONAL AND CONFIDENTIAL."

Nelson Mahoney locked the door to his office and opened the package: a box of cigars. At the bottom of the box were three one-hundred-dollar bills and a hand-written note. Nelson opened the note reluctantly.

"My old friend! I'm raising your monthly allowance to three hundred dollars. You've earned the extra stipend. I'm considering a run in the next election for political office. I'm not interested in spending the rest of my days in Scotland. I'll become prime minister one day and you will serve as the senior minister in my cabinet. I'm scheduling a trip to Ottawa at the end of October --- have a strategic plan prepared."

MH

"*Prime Minister Hanus*!" Nelson could stomach a corrupt businessman clamoring for an overseas diplomatic posting. But to invest him with the responsibility of governing the country? That smacked of tomfoolery. He had his disagreements with Laurier, but his strength and capacity to lead Canada into the new century was impressive.

But Hanus's capacity for ruthless ambition was insatiable. What could Nelson possibly draft as a strategic plan to satisfy him? He slipped the note into a jacket pocket and hurled the cigar box with the bills into the waste-paper basket. *My old friend.* He was ten years the consul general's junior! He'd finished doing dirty business for Mortimer Hanus.

*

Superintendent Grant cancelled a meeting with one of his deputies, a breakfast with the mayor and an appearance at the ceremony for graduating police cadets. The message relayed from Detective Jacob that Pharo Simmons had departed by train to Canada to locate her husband's kidnapper had set off the equivalent of a five-alarm fire. "Get to my office now!" the superintendent instructed Jacob.

Grant met him as he walked up the stairs and led him into the office.

"I just finished a frantic telephone call from Pharo's father. He's understandably concerned with his daughter's crazy trip. He demanded that the Buffalo police halt her journey, and I agreed to return his call after our meeting concludes."

"I don't understand what Pharo expects to achieve," Jacob said. "Brave, yes, but foolish also. She can't march into the kidnapper's house and leave with Simmons. She places herself in the line of fire."

"Exactly right. And we can't have the victim's wife on a lark doing police work." The superintendent paced nervously as he spoke. "If anything happens, who will shoulder the blame? It won't be you, Detective, and it won't be law enforcement in Canada either. It's my watch as the head of the Buffalo police. Do you understand?"

"I understand, Superintendent Grant. But I lack the authority to stop Pharo Simmons from taking the trip. I contacted the detective's bureau in Toronto and insisted on speaking to the captain. I briefed him and he's agreed to assign a couple of constables to greet Mrs. Simmons at the train station. But she'll demand a plan of action."

"Well, you're going to have to provide the grounds to arrest the kidnapper. There's no alternative. Tell me where you currently stand with your investigation."

Detective Jacob briefed him fully.

"What's your opinion of the photograph from the Brownton Cap Factory case?"

"I'm convinced it's Mortimer Hanus. I asked the captain for a physical description and it matches the photograph. Pharo is certain that it was the man who angrily confronted her on her walk from the courthouse."

"So, what's your theory of motive, Detective Jacob?"

"It's about avenging a grotesque insult after the unsettling verdict in his niece's tragic death. When he learned that Burford Simmons represented Leon Czolgosz, Hanus had discovered his opportunity to extract vengeance. The letter was sent to the Buffalo police to shift the investigation to anarchists. And then Hanus waited, secure in the knowledge that as each day passed with no word of her husband's fate, Pharo Simmons's misery heightened. Our kidnapper, *je pense*, is a cruel man."

"And what's his end game?"

"Hanus plans to kill the witness to his kidnapping scheme --- and the beloved of his tormentor. His goal from the outset had been to murder Burford Simmons. He is as much an assassin as Leon Czolgosz."

"And the police must spoil the assassin's plan. But we need to act quickly. Did you get a response from Canada about the composition of the *Globe's* newsprint?"

"I've sent Officer Jennings to Toronto."

"You should have checked with me. I want an immediate update from Jennings when it's available. I will call the Toronto police chief and involve him in the investigation. I admire the tenacity of Pharo Simmons, but she's walking into a death trap. And those boys with her as well. I'll hold you personally responsible if any of them is harmed. Am I clear, Detective Jacob?"

"Perfectly."

"That was exceptional work on the Czolgosz trial. The killer's execution will take place in a few days --- and one more thing." The superintendent's tone softened. "You were right, Detective Jacob, and I owe you a sincere apology. Czolgosz did act without confederates. The police have released the anarchists being held in jail, even that heretic, Emma Goldman. I expect the lot of them will receive a frosty welcome back home."

Chapter Thirty-Nine

Mortimer Hanus approached the captain's table at dinner.

"My name is not Robert Planter. May I ask Captain, where you obtained that name?"

"It was pointed out to me by one of my assistants as you left the telegraph room that you're a Canadian ambassador. I checked the telegraph log and found your name there."

"Thank you for clearing that up, Captain. The name of Robert Planter is on my mind lately. You see, it's the name of my dear cousin in Toronto, bedridden now with the late stages of a bout of cancer. Sadly, he only has a few days left. You'll forgive me, of course, for my mistake."

"Of course, Mr....."

"Hanus, Mortimer Hanus." He shook the captain's hand, tipped his hat and returned to his table.

He was dining alone. His paramour on the ship, Gwendolyn Hastings, had abruptly frozen him out of her life. She ignored him as they passed on the ship's deck --- she evidently suspected that he'd pilfered the cash from her cabin. 'But there were other fish swimming in the sea.' The more bothersome issue was his sloppiness in using the Planter name in the log. The mistake could never be repeated.

The ship was finally scheduled to leave port the next morning. He'd quickly put the journey across the ocean and his aborted dalliance behind him. Like a fresh gust of wind, an austere new life in Scotland awaited. He repeated the title over and over in his mind. '*Canadian Consul General to Scotland*'. He smirked as he imagined the Sultan's reaction to his diplomatic status. Of course, the Sultan must never know.

*

The telephone rang twice on Superintendent Grant's wall.

"Superintendent, we have a match. The newsprint in the note was from the Toronto *Globe*."

"Good work, Detective Jacob. I'll contact the Toronto police chief."

*

Two boys arrived at the parliament building in Ottawa and asked to see Martin Beliveau.

"What do you need to see the Minister about?" the administrator inquired politely.

"We have a note for him, and we won't leave until we present it."

A security guard approached the counter, but the administrator signaled him to leave.

She smiled benevolently and spoke. "You must understand, boys. I can't bother the Minister with everyone who shows up and wants to see him."

"With respect, ma'am," Amos pleaded. "Minister Beliveau gave his word to the person who wrote this letter to help."

"Who is the letter from, boys?"

"Pharo Simmons," one of the boys declared.

"Give me a moment. I'll check with the Minister's clerk. But I expect you'll leave here disappointed."

Martin Beliveau arrived at the counter several minutes later. "Yes, boys. Please show me the note from Pharo."

The note contained a brief message. Martin reread its jarring content three times.

Dearest Martin,

My husband's kidnapper is a Canadian diplomat, Mortimer Hanus. He must be arrested and brought to justice. I have met with a Buffalo detective in charge of the kidnapping case and have the proof. I'm sure that Hanus is the one responsible. I implore you to believe me. Please instruct the Canadian police to act immediately.

I'm on my way to bring Burford home!

Pharo Simmons

Knowing he must update the prime minister urgently,

Martin barged into his office unannounced. But Laurier shuffled the note aside after reading it.

"I sympathize with the woman. She has suffered a terrible ordeal. But Martin, she has no evidence to support her allegation against Hanus. Do we know if she's contacted the police?"

"I don't have that information, Prime Minister. But Pharo Simmons has expended a great deal of effort to bring this matter to the government's attention."

"What are you proposing that I do about it?"

"Order him to return to Ottawa. It will be a major political scandal if you ignore the warning about Hanus and take no remedial action. We'll suffer a blow if we cut our losses now, but recoverable."

Laurier mulled the suggested strategy from his friend and trusted minister. "I agree. You have my authority to issue the order for Mortimer Hanus to return immediately."

*

A rushed meeting at the Buffalo prosecutor's office to discuss Lord Halsham's case had been called for two o'clock. Mitchell requested Neeru to attend.

"What's it about?" she asked.

"I haven't any idea."

Neeru recognized that it wasn't the normal practice for prosecutors to summon defense counsel to an urgent afternoon meeting.

The prosecutor plunged into the purpose of the meeting as soon as he greeted them. "I'm dismissing your client's charges," he said matter-of-factly.

"Why?" Mitchell asked.

"You haven't read today's edition of the *Brooklyn Daily Eagle*, have you?"

For the next several minutes Mitchell and Neeru sat listening intently as they learned about the criminal exploits of Mortimer Hanus. The reporter, Willow Hooper, had been contacted by a young Australian woman who had been absconded and taken to the palace of the sultan for the Ottoman empire. The woman, her identity protected, met Hanus in the palace harem. He confessed to her over the course of many trips a list of his crimes and misdeeds.

In one paragraph of the four-page salacious expose, Hooper referred to Hanus bragging to the woman about swindling a blowhard British lord by setting up a phony insurance fraud scheme involving a sunken frigate. The frigate never sank, and after being towed to port, it became part of the convoy of boats Hanus had amassed in his private harbor. He had paid some of the ship's crew and a disgruntled former bookkeeper to make a bogus complaint to the police about Lord Halsham's complicity in sinking the ship in order to make a false insurance claim. Hanus's expressed desire was to gain control of the business empire of the disgraced and ruined Lord Halsham.

"Your client is innocent, Mitchell."

Neeru left the prosecutor's office and went straight to the police station to inquire after Detective Jacob, but was told that he had left for the train station. "Where is he headed?" she asked his partner.

"Toronto," he replied.

Neeru felt relieved.

*

Two loud knocks on his door awoke Mortimer Hanus in his cabin. He checked his watch. The ship's departure time for Glasgow, Scotland was scheduled to occur in less than an hour. The foghorn sounded and Hanus peeked out of the window to see the ship's plank being lowered.

He opened the door, and two familiar assistants of the captain shouldered in menacingly.

"We've been instructed to inform you that you're being recalled to Ottawa," the larger said. "You will be disembarking the ship. You'll not be a passenger on this ship when it leaves."

"If this is someone's attempt at humor, it's missed the mark. I'm not amused."

"Do not attempt to leave the ship. You'll be halted. That's all."

The captain's assistants stayed outside the cabin, standing guard.

Hanus checked his silver pocket watch for the time, but the pocket was empty.

"Gwendolyn!"

His former paramour had accurately pegged the unsavory scoundrel from the start.

*

Arthur Simon returned to the basement to retrieve the dirty plates of the kidnapped lawyer and to throw sticks of wood into the roaring fire.

"Bad news," he said. "Charlie just called me. He received a message from Hanus that he needs to dispose of you."

"Why? What has happened?"

"You've become too much of a liability to Hanus, I guess. Charlie will be returning from Toronto early tomorrow morning. I convinced him to make it painless. A single shot to the back of your head."

"That's comforting," Burford said. "Will my wife be told?"

"I'll make sure she knows. I wish that there was another way to end this."

"I'm sure you do, Arthur."

"I'm going to loosen your bindings today. It's your last night. No more letters though."

Burford stared bewilderedly at his callow captor. "Tell me, Arthur. Why did Hanus choose you to kidnap me?"

"Simple reason. Last man available."

"A farewell glass of bourbon?" Burford asked.

"All right. I'll share a shot with you at the kitchen table. Meet me there in a few minutes."

Burford's bindings were loosed. He had a few hours left to implement his plan before the executioner arrived. He pulled a thin slat of wood from under the rug and placed it under his pant leg, tucked into a sock. Standing in the kitchen while the drink was poured, he memorized the route from the front door to Arthur's bedroom.

"I had a bloody nose today," he said, "May I have a wet cloth?"

Arthur immersed a washcloth in a pail of water and handed it to Burford. Phase two completed, he thought. He placed the compress over his nose, careful to retain the water in his cloth.

"I think I'll call it a night," Burford said, after finishing his shot. "Thank you, Arthur. You've made these last few weeks manageable. Are you planning to stay for my final act?"

Arthur drank his shot and refilled his cup another two times. "I'm going to pass."

Burford knew these would be the last spoken words between them.

The lawyer retired to the basement, but not before he wedged the strip of wood in the doorway. He decided that he couldn't rely on Arthur leaving the door unlocked. He briefly gathered his thoughts in the basement, but he couldn't tarry. Burford placed his wrists over the fire until it burned through the rope. The scalding flames tinged his skin and he bit his lip to keep from screaming. With his wrists free from the bindings, he uncovered the rug, found the two cups of maple syrup he had hidden in a corner, and began the next phase of his plotted escape.

He dipped the wooden strips into the maple syrup and bonded them into a square board. He squeezed, taking care not to exert too much pressure causing the strips to collapse. Burford took his pillowcase and gingerly slipped the board inside. The pieces collapsed in a heap. There was no time to abort the plan. Burford scurried around the basement until he found a sturdy board under the empty wine case and held it in front of the fire to measure its size.

Burford then used the second cup of maple syrup to bond the outer edges of his cot. He listened for any sounds upstairs. Arthur needed to be asleep for the next phase of his plan. He leaned his shoulder to the basement door, and it fell to the ground. He carried the pillowcase and cot outside, bundled in a blanket. Burford pressed hard against the padded cot covering the outside door frame. The maple syrup held it securely in place.

He then moved the old ladder he'd seen at the side of the house against the brick wall and carefully climbed to the roof, blanket around his shoulders, the board in one hand. Grey smoke curled from the chimney.

Memories of childhood flooded back; his father delicately balanced on peaked and angled rooftops. He used to watch in wonder from the ground as his father carried the long-handled brush to the chimney to begin the filthy task of sweeping the chimney clean.

Safely positioned on the jaded roof, Burford executed the final phase of his orchestrated plan. He lifted the square piece of wooden board and placed it over the chimney top, blocking the draught for the chimney. It covered the open space.

For a long time, Burford lay prone at the flat ridge of the hipped roof, the blanket keeping him warm, and gazed into the endless sky. The dark night sky teamed with gleaming stars. He recalled his conversation with Sammy the shoe-shine boy. He devoted the rest of the night counting the stars. The tally ended with a number in the thousands.

At the first sign of daybreak, Burford went down the ladder. He removed the cot, and smoke flowed out of the basement in a thick haze. He waited, then pulled the damp cloth from his pocket and covered his face. He had estimated that getting in and out of the house would take thirty to forty-five seconds. Even with the cloth, the short trip was a risk. Smoke-laden sooty air now filled the interior of the house and he'd be unable to breathe. Recalling his father's lesson about there being more oxygen available closer to the ground, he folded his body into a crouch and held the damp cloth over his face. "Go!" he shouted, immersed in a ghostly grey fog.

He tracked the route mapped out by memory. Smoke overwhelmed him as he groped in the darkness, and he held his breath. One breath he knew, and he'd be wheezing for air. In Arthur's room, he grabbed the overcoat and keys hanging on the nail, then hurried to the front door. He coughed, inhaled clear air and took several deep breaths, wiping the black soot from his face with the cloth. Dazed and barely conscious from the effects of the smoke, he walked awkwardly on the graveled driveway to the gated fence and fumbled with the keys until he found one that fit.

The gate opened and he stumbled down the road.

"Hey, where do you think you're going?" a voice shouted.

Burford looked back in fright. Charlie running towards him holding a gun. He must have arrived early and slept in the barn. Burford mustered his remaining energy and ran down the road in a weaving pattern to avoid gunshots.

Up ahead --- what was this? He caught sight of Pharo, running towards him. Two young boys ran at her side brandishing revolvers.

"Burford," she cried excitedly.

The boys stopped and pointed their guns. "Fire," one shouted, and two pistol-shots rang through the still night air.

The pounding steps chasing him halted and he looked back to see Charlie on the ground, a twisting trail of blood seeping into the gulley of the road.

Burford collapsed to his knees, his face touching the ground. Pharo fell to the pavement too, embracing him. A stream of police cars careened down the path in their direction.

For a moment all was peaceful, the road surrounded by a kaleidoscope of autumn foliage and robins chirping from brittle ledges.

"Burf, this is like Tess Durbeyfield's lesson of the serpent hissing where the sweet birds sing."

Booker approached grinning, his eyes eloquent, harboring a tale of grand adventure.

Chapter Forty

Members of Parliament had been called to attend a special session. The arrest of Mortimer Hanus upon disembarking a ship in Halifax created a political frenzy. The nation's consul general to Scotland, the birthplace of Canada's first prime minister, had been implicated in grievous, diabolical crimes, including the violent kidnapping of a Buffalo lawyer. The opposition party in the House called for a motion of non-confidence to topple the government of Wilfred Laurier and force him to resign. Ominous rumblings led by Isaiah Hayes, suggested Liberal renegade parliamentarians supported the motion.

Martin Beliveau asked the prime minister for permission to address Parliament.

"Permission granted," came the reply.

The speaker of the House called on the Railways Minister.

"I thank the prime minister for this opportunity," Martin began. "I accept full responsibility for the folly of Mortimer Hanus's appointment. The prime minister approached me first about the impending appointment and I heartily endorsed his selection. His ruthless villainy was masked from us and we were duped, but that is no excuse. It is fortuitous that Hanus never stepped on Scottish soil and perpetrated any harm to our glorious nation. But the reputation of Canada has been diminished and the burden of this travesty is mine alone to bear. Therefore, I have determined that if a single member of this esteemed House calls for my resignation from Cabinet, it shall be tendered immediately. However, I would like to first read a letter from Pharo Simmons, the wife of the kidnapped lawyer, that landed on my desk this morning. Mr. Speaker, may I be permitted to read the letter onto the record?"

"Proceed, Minister."

"Dear Martin,

It is a couple of days since Burford was rescued and the whirlwind of events that followed have truly exhausted me. I would be remiss if I didn't write a heartfelt note of gratitude to my Canadian friend. I know that Mortimer Hanus fooled you. He fooled a legion of people. He was a clever assassin --- though not as clever as me, I might add.

In the many weeks when my faith in my husband's rescue dimmed, the columns of support who kept me upright were few. You were one. We met only fleetingly, and lived in different countries, yet you gave me unwavering strength. My unbridled loyalty to you led me to deliver the dire warning about Hanus. Your help meant so much to me.

Thank you again, my dear Canadian friend."

Martin placed the letter on the lectern. "Who seeks my resignation?" he asked.

The House remained silent.

"So be it," Martin said. "Let us get back to the honorable task of governing this great nation."

He sat, to a thundering ovation from the fellow members of his party and a smattering of the opposition.

"You've saved the government," Laurier whispered in his ear.

"Prime Minister, I'm not a hero."

"Shush, Martin. I know everything --- I am more astute than you give me credit for."

"You're not cross with me, are you Wilfred?"

"Certainly not, *meilleur de mes ami*s. Nation first, Martin. Nation first."

Chapter Forty-One

The postponed reception to raise funds for the modernized manual training school, hosted by Pharo Simmons, at last, took place at her stately home. The party overflowed with guests prepared to donate. Clarence Darrow, Detective Eli Jacob, Neeru, Bessie, and Mitchell were feted as honored guests.

Burford had sought out Sammy, and at Pharo's behest, Booker, and invited them to attend the manual training school. He promised to pay for their university education if they qualified.

The room hummed an excited pitch. "They came to see you, Burf," Pharo told him. "You're a celebrity."

"If it helps raise heaps of money for this worthy cause, then I'm all for it."

"Over a thousand dollars!"

"I passed Mervyn and John Rockefeller in the hall --- they were enlisting Darrow's assistance to acquire tickets to see Sarah Bernhardt in *Cyrano de Bergerac*."

"We must make the trip to Chicago," Pharo said.

"Sarah is a wonder."

"I'm concerned that Clarence may have overindulged in the stock of Sancerre we carried over from Paris. He's organized a midnight swim in the nude for every willing man. Wilson was the first to agree."

"Edwina will scold you, Burford. Are you taking the plunge?"

"I volunteered to be the official photographer."

"Oh, my publisher is excited about the prospects all this acclaim will bring to the sales of my novel."

"I'll deliver Mortimer Hanus an autographed copy to his prison cell."

"You must do that, Burf," Pharo said, with a glint of mischief.

Fig Golem interrupted their genial chat in the kitchen. "I'm sorry," he said. "I went to retrieve a hanky from my coat, and there is a fellow at the door insisting on speaking to Mr. Simmons."

"I'll see about that," Pharo said, marching to the front door, where a worried man stood waiting.

"Can I help you?"

"Yes, ma'am. My name is Horace Quilty. I'm a client of Mr. Simmons --- I must be in court tomorrow to schedule the date for my trial."

"Quilty, the flying trapeze artist?" Pharo asked incredulously.

The man nodded.

Pharo weighed conflicting options. She could stop the client from interrupting her charitable event and keep his call hidden from her husband. But Burford was alive, every day a blessing, her romance novel was soon to be published and her life flourished with gaiety and exuberance. In the end, a preferred maxim decided the matter: "Don't fret over a trifle."

"Come in, Mr. Quilty. I'll get Mr. Simmons for you."

As she turned, the front door opened and a portly, puff-faced stranger appeared.

"Excuse me, but I am a distinguished guest of Mr. and Mrs. Simmons at this gala."

"Well sir," she said indignantly, "I am the hostess of this charity event and I haven't the foggiest notion who you are. What is your name?"

The stranger paused, elevated his double chin and spoke in the octave pitch of a piccolo trumpet. "Caleb, and I know you well, ma'am."

A memory flashed into Pharo's mind.

"Caleb the crab!" she shrieked.

Acknowledgments

I benefitted from reading the following excellent books in researching the historical setting for the novel: Margaret Creighton, *The Electrifying Fall of Rainbow City*, W.W. Norton, 2016; David W. Blight, *Frederick Douglass Prophet of Freedom*, Simon & Schuster, 2018; W.E.B Du Bois, *The Souls of Black Folk*, Amazon Classics 1903; John A. Farrell, *Clarence Darrow Attorney for the Damned*, Vintage Books 2012; Robert W. Merry, *President McKinley Architect of the American Century*, Simon & Schuster, 2017; George Ade, *Stories of Chicago*, University of Illinois Press, 2013; Phillip Blom, *The Vertigo Years Change And Culture In The West 1900-1914*, McClelland & Stewart, 2008; Chaim M. Rosenberg, *America At The Fair Chicago's 1893 World's Columbian Exposition*, Arcadia Publishing 2008; Robert Harris, *An Officer And A Spy*, Arrow Books, 2013; Desmond Morton, *A Short History of Canada*, McClelland & Stewart, 2017; Leigh Benin, Rob Linne, Adrienne Sosin, Joel Sosinsky with Workers United and HBO Documentary Films, *The New York City Triangle Factory Fire*, Arcadia Publishing, 2011; W.E.B. Du Bois, *Black Lives At The Paris Exposition 1900*, Redstone Press, 2019; Ünver Rüstem, *Ottoman Baroque The Architectural Refashioning Of Eighteenth-Century Istanbul*, Princeton University Press, 2019; André Pratte, *Wilfrid Laurier*, Penguin Canada, 2013; Winston Spencer Churchill, *Savrola*, 1900, Longman, Green, And Co. I also utilized the archives of the Globe and Mail.

The cover design is a photograph of a painting by the Canadian artist, Jennifer Ross.

I am fortunate to have the following distinguished writers as teachers and mentors: Martin Amis, Marina

Endicott and Joe Kertes. I thank Bill Gallagher, a criminal defense attorney in Cincinnati, Dr. Val Rachlis, Miguel Singer, Ian Colford, Montana Beth Skurka and Jordana Sierra Skurka for their valued assistance.

About Atmosphere Press

Atmosphere Press is an independent, full-service publisher for excellent books in all genres and for all audiences. Learn more about what we do at atmospherepress.com.

We encourage you to check out some of Atmosphere's latest releases, which are available at Amazon.com and via order from your local bookstore:

Comfrey, Wyoming: Birds of a Feather, a novel by Daphne Birkmyer
Relatively Painless, short stories by Dylan Brody
Nate's New Age, a novel by Michael Hanson
The Size of the Moon, a novel by E.J. Michaels
The Red Castle, a novel by Noah Verhoeff
American Genes, a novel by Kirby Nielsen
Newer Testaments, a novel by Philip Brunetti
All Things in Time, a novel by Sue Buyer
Hobson's Mischief, a novel by Caitlin Decatur
The Black-Marketer's Daughter, a novel by Suman Mallick
The Farthing Quest, a novel by Casey Bruce
This Side of Babylon, a novel by James Stoia
Within the Gray, a novel by Jenna Ashlyn
Where No Man Pursueth, a novel by Micheal E. Jimerson
Here's Waldo, a novel by Nick Olson
Tales of Little Egypt, a historical novel by James Gilbert
For a Better Life, a novel by Julia Reid Galosy
The Hidden Life, a novel by Robert Castle

About the Author

Steve Skurka is a highly respected criminal defense lawyer in Toronto. He defended the landmark racial profiling case in Canada of R. v. Brown involving a former player on the Toronto Raptors. In other precedent-setting cases, he led evidence of marijuana-induced psychosis to mitigate his client's sentence and relied on the battered child syndrome in a homicide case. Steve taught at Osgoode Hall Law School, acted as the legal analyst for CTV, and wrote a book about the sensational case of media baron Conrad Black. *Pharo and the Clever Assassin* is his first novel.

CPSIA information can be obtained
at www.ICGtesting.com
Printed in the USA
BVHW031411050521
606414BV00011B/870

9 781637 529409